Chris Malone has been a teacher, headteacher, and an Ofsted inspector, as well as setting up and managing pre-schools, and leading a further education centre. She has worked in county councils, most recently as Assistant Director for Education in Warwickshire, previously occupying leadership roles in Gloucestershire and Oxfordshire.

To Ken.

Chris Malone

ZADE

AUSTIN MACAULEY PUBLISHERS™
LONDON • CAMBRIDGE • NEW YORK • SHARJAH

Copyright © Chris Malone (2020)

The right of Chris Malone to be identified as author of this work has been asserted by her in accordance with section 77 and 78 of the Copyright, Designs and Patents Act 1988.

All rights reserved. No part of this publication may be reproduced, stored in a retrieval system, or transmitted in any form or by any means, electronic, mechanical, photocopying, recording, or otherwise, without the prior permission of the publishers.

Any person who commits any unauthorised act in relation to this publication may be liable to criminal prosecution and civil claims for damages.

Austin Macauley is committed to publishing works of quality and integrity. In that spirit, we are proud to offer this book to our readers; however, the story, the experiences, and the words are the author's alone and portrayed to the best of their recollection. In some cases, names and details have been changed to protect the privacy of the people involved.

A CIP catalogue record for this title is available from the British Library.

ISBN 9781786930415 (Paperback)
ISBN 9781786931078 (ePub e-book)

www.austinmacauley.com

First Published (2020)
Austin Macauley Publishers Ltd
25 Canada Square
Canary Wharf
London
E14 5LQ

Special thanks to my husband, Ken Malone, for going the extra mile. *Zade* would not have been possible without his unstinting support. Ken, I thank you for all your encouragement, criticism reality-checks, and for the many hours spent reading and re-reading, sometimes in tricky circumstances.

Thank you, too, to Liz Van Santen for invaluable enthusiasm and proof-reading during thunderstorms in French forests.

Finally, I thank the hundreds of now unidentifiable adults, who spent time with me as children, in my many classrooms and nurseries. I learnt from you. Thank you, especially, to one called Zade.

Part 1

Chapter 1

I am going to jot my thoughts down in my notebook because, in future years, they may make sense to someone. I fear for my future; it is not safe for me here, and there are only a few people who I can trust.

My name is Zade. I know that it is my real name, given to me by my parents before they disappeared, but I have no surname. I used the surnames of a string of foster families so that I would blend in better; firstly Marriott, then Wilkinson, then Better-Smith, but I didn't blend in. I was always different. I am pretty confident that my birthday is 21st of December, and I am 15 years old. I stopped attending school last year when my most recent foster family departed for the Periphery, and I have stayed in their small flat, which is conveniently tucked away out of sight, off the street. I expect a representative of the Landlord's Association to appear and evict me any day, but have survived here for nearly a year now. There is no power, which means that I live by daylight and sleep when it is dark, in a circadian rhythm. Although the water is turned off, there is, mercifully, still a trickle of water from one tap. I use a system of glass water bottles, circulating them to keep it fresh.

If you saw me, you would think I was under-fed, which is true, but I am strong; strong of body and stronger of mind. Even when I have been well-cared-for, I have always checked over my shoulder for what lurks behind me, as well as constantly asking questions to find out what motivates people. There are few people who I trust. This has helped me to survive, but has not always endeared me to adults.

When I wash myself, clean my jeans and jumper, and brush my hair, I still look unkempt; there is a wildness about me which I wish I understood. But most striking are my eyes. My year-group was the first to experience scintillation. People take it for granted now, but when I was born, it was new. I don't know why, but my eyes are amazing; they sparkle and glitter much more strongly than other children's. Adults love this, pet over me and take photographs. Children gather round, seeking my ideas, my plans, which may be why I have ended up in trouble over the years, leading minor rebellions. It was quite nice to have special status among my peers, because of my eyes, but now I am older, they draw attention to me in an unwelcome way.

Most children's eyes start to fade at my age, in fact, by sixteen they all have plain adult eyes. I wish mine would start fading. There are expensive products sold by the Prophet Corporation, but I don't think that they really work, they simply make you feel that you are doing something about it. I prefer to wear a hat to shade my face, with dark glasses, and I move quickly, before they see my eyes too clearly.

There is something odd about scintillation which I am determined to understand. Firstly, the displacement of families is inhuman. Over the years, it has become accepted by society, but why is it always the poorer families in the Central Area whose children's eyes fail to scintillate? Is it due to poor nutrition, if so, why doesn't it occur in the Periphery? Who decided to prosecute the parents who home-educate their children out of desperation to stay put? Who manages the Education Enforcement Officers? How is the ethos of the Central Area of grammar academies growing such momentum at the expense of the victimised Periphery?

I have so many questions and very few answers. Meanwhile, I feel driven to find out and to record the evidence. That is what we were taught in science, and in history lessons; to pose the question, to collect the evidence and to come to a conclusion. We were taught other things which I refused to adopt; to obey without question, that profit trumps moral imperative, and that material wealth precedes intellectual wealth. What rubbish.

To start my investigation, I tried to find out about the Area School Commissioners. My cover story is that I am writing an essay for school about the history of education. It is true I suppose, just not for school. I use the Biblio, which is short for the Bibliotheque Commerciale; the public commercial resource centre, where I can sit in comfort, and two hours on a static Prexia doesn't cost. I found out that the big chief is Michael Morgan. He is the High Commissioner for Future Success, which is the national High Council role in charge of education. He has a team of five School Commissioners; someone called Alexandra Essex in the Central Area. This is the area that I live in, where all schools are grammar academies for children with scintillation, from age four through to sixteen. Sean Price is the Commissioner in the West, Manya Gray in the East, Peter Edwards in the South West, and there is a new Commissioner in the North called Sue Sutton. Last year the north and the central seem to have merged. In the North, there is currently a mix of grammar academies for scintillated children and ordinary schools for the others, but headteachers have mounted an ongoing protest about the changes. Sue Sutton seems to have been put there to sort this out.

The West (Wales), East and South West, are all called "The Periphery". They only offer old-style schools, educating all the children without scintillation. In the Periphery, schools are filled with children already living there, plus all unscintillated children from the Central Area, who are forced to migrate. Their eyes are plain like those of adults, blue, brown, a few green or grey, but without any sparkle; no "designer-eyes" as some call it. At first, parents of unscintillated children tried tricking the system by giving them sparkling contact lenses, but the Education Enforcement Officers soon became wise to this.

Living alone, when I am not legally independent, is a challenge. Fortunately, my foster carer, Lyn, still manages to collect my allowance, getting it to me whenever she can, and this funds my food, bus tickets, essential items, but not much more.

Last year, I travelled to Wales to visit Lyn who had moved there because her own daughter, Kira, did not develop scintillation and was therefore banished from the Central Area. I learnt a lot on the trip. Travelling out across the policed Marches' border with the hoard of migrating families was easy, but getting back into the Central Area would have been tricky had I not flashed my eyes in the direction of the guards at one of the terrifying gates, and then at the bus drivers. There's a lot of suspicion out in the borderlands.

While I was there, I accompanied Lyn when she took Kira to school. Kira is just five years old, and failed the Four Plus last year. She is a happy-go-lucky character. Compared with grammar academies in the Central Area, the school was chaotic and massively overcrowded. New children seemed to arrive every day, and there was no space in the classes. The atmosphere was free and easy, one teacher struggling to keep track of over fifty children, but there was a quality that I cannot put my finger on; a huge amount of care for the children, not like in the central grammars that I knew. I hung around, and no one minded. The children all settled on the carpet and took turns to talk about their weekend. I warmed to the teacher as she smiled encouragingly, giving each child time and organising talk in pairs and small groups. The chattering noise was excessive, but she regained control with dignity. In the grammars, from my own experience, pupils are repressed. Not so in Kira's colourful, chaotic and yet nurturing school. When I returned to collect her at home-time, she was buzzing with anecdotes from her day.

I asked Lyn how it was living in the Periphery, and she was happy enough. She said that you felt less supervised, less controlled out there. There were more work opportunities than she had imagined, with all the factories in the valley that provided the Prophet Meals for the population of the Central Area. However, the unreliable cyberspace, the frequent power cuts and failure of water supplies frustrated her, used as she was to more efficient services in London. She was still really angry that she and Kira had been forced to relocate away from the area where she had grown up as a child, but in her optimistic way, she had made the best of it, and Kira was obviously thriving. It crossed my mind that those of us blessed with scintillation might not, after all, have the best deal.

Chapter 2

Meanwhile, in Grammar Academy CXIX in central England, Lucas Patel clutched his treasure map and climbed the walls of the imaginary castle one-handed, jumping on to the top platform with supreme confidence. His two friends followed, and they huddled together studying the colourful scribbles of the map. They were surveying the playground below, agreeing that the treasure might be under the wooden crates in the far corner, when a bell rang and the playground emptied. The scurrying children formed lines and obediently filed back inside in silence, their ten minutes of freedom over for the morning. The treasure could wait for the lunchbreak.

The three boys were last in, and Lucas planted himself keenly at the front on the large colourful number mat. It was always maths after play, and he loved maths. The teacher flicked up a hundred square on the low screen, and started asking questions. Lucas put his concentrating face on, and his hand kept shooting up. He knew all the answers. He collected the small personal digiboard and pen from his drawer and focused on forming the numbers correctly. After a few minutes, and with great enthusiasm, he thrust the result at the teacher, a slightly wobbly 0 to 20. He was first to finish, all numbers facing the right way. The teacher automatically handed him a sticky silver star, with a sparkling eye in the centre, which he placed proudly on his sweatshirt to show his parents later.

Unusually, his dad looked sad when he showed him the sparkling silver star at home-time. He hurried Lucas into the driverless, strapping him in next to his younger brother, Noah, and they travelled home in silence. His mum was at home when they arrived, which was again unusual. He sensed that his parents were putting on an act; looking as if nothing was wrong when actually something was. He remained respectfully quiet through supper and was not surprised when his dad said, 'Lucas, come with me, there is something we need to talk about.'

Lucas put on his serious face, climbed up on to the high stool in his father's study, and sat level with him. The worried father put all his energy into explaining to a five-year-old why the family might have to break up, and why it was going to hit the national press. 'Lucas,' he started, pulling a small shaving mirror from his desk drawer, 'look at your eyes.' Lucas tried to help him out; he had heard his parents talking about this.

'Daddy, Noah's eyes aren't going sparkly like mine, are they?' he suggested. His father sighed, impressed by his son's perception.

'That's right, so he will not pass the Four Plus, and cannot go to school with you.' Lucas looked sadly at his father who continued, 'Mummy might have to take Noah away for a while, but don't you worry because I will stay here to look after you while they are gone.'

'Okay, Daddy,' said Lucas woefully, understanding the dilemma.

Sensing that his father had more to say, he waited encouragingly for him to continue. 'Mummy and I are doing all we can…we have contacted a news reporter who is writing about this…and we have contacted a lawyer; someone who can help us. They might want to speak to you too.' Lucas nodded. He remembered how a little girl called Sparkle had started school in his class, how her eyes didn't really shine properly, and after a few days two men in suits – perhaps they were lawyers – were led into the classroom by the headteacher, and they took her away. She screamed, bit their hands, and never returned. He didn't want that for Noah.

'Daddy, it is not fair,' he said quietly.

***

Early the next morning, while still in bed, Alexandra Essex, Central Area School Commissioner, and head of the CenSA Grammar Academy Trust, reached out for her Prexia and flicked it awake to see the news headlines. A very well-dressed family was looking sadly into the camera. Large red letters announced: "It is not fair", says Lucas, aged five, with the sub-heading: "Scintillated Child Displaced to Periphery".

'Shit,' she said, getting up quickly, adding to herself, 'How did this happen?'

Chapter 3

I am walking past the highly acclaimed Grammar Academy XXX. Its pupils wear immaculate uniform emblazoned with the celebrated three Xs. I step cautiously along the pavement, on my way to buy bread, my scintillating eyes obscured by my soft black peaked hat. I watch the blank-faced teenage automatons who stride and smile, eagerly looking forward to another day of brainwashing.

The grammar academies that I attended were very similar to XXX, and I can feel my heart beating unpleasantly fast. My shoulders slump, as I remember the mental torture. I became exhausted from resisting, my head filled with conflict, while I presented a willing outer face, and secretly nurtured my opposition to the whole regime.

As I moved from one foster carer to another, I developed the skill of scanning a room full of unfamiliar pupils, pinpointing the covert rebels. Early in the morning, at registration, their scintillating eyes flitted around, revealing their unease, and they made eye-contact with me, the new girl, testing me out. I hoped that I had at last found kindred spirits, but after morning break, when, along with their friends, they had devoured their frothing sherbet soda, they were won over by the regime, totally compliant for the remainder of the day.

Even when I was in primary school, I corralled groups of rebels to follow my example and quietly pour away the brightly coloured sherbet drink. I was punished each time I was caught. But the drink is addictive. Once they had drunk gallons of the fizzing stuff, over weeks, they were hooked. It took a great deal of bribery to turn their minds, and even then, they were only half-hearted in their rebellion.

In one academy, there was a row of tasteful indoor plants running along the side of the dining hall. At break-time, if I sat alone, on the edge of the room, I could surreptitiously pour my soda into the plant trough. I had to be careful not to be spotted by the surveillance cameras which circulated across 180 degrees. After I had attended that academy for a few months, the plants in the middle troughs started wilting, and only I knew why.

I was moved to a different foster carer, and a new school across the city, where there were no ornamental plants, and I had to think quickly. I was thin, and my uniform hung loosely over my body. It was easy to secrete a spare empty soda bottle under my clothes, and to swap the bottles when no one was looking. I placed the empty bottle back on the tray and tipped the soda down the toilet at the next available opportunity. It disappeared, fizzing angrily, overcome by the flushing water.

Pausing on the pavement, I pretend to reply to a message on my phone, and I watch. These pupils look as if original thought no longer passes through their minds. Grammar Academy XXX is the pinnacle of the system. Many parents sell up and move house into the blocks of apartments surrounding the low-rise academy buildings, in order to secure a place for their darlings. Sam, at the advice bureau, tells me that the waiting list is huge. I pity them; the misguided parents, and the young victims of the system. Valuing my independence so highly, I congratulate myself on having successfully escaped the system, but right now I can see an Education Enforcement Driverless drawing up at the school gate and parking in a reserved space.

I dice with fate, my heart beating fast, and remain on the pavement, under my hat, pretending to focus on the screen of my phone. I can see three Education Enforcement Officers, safely cocooned in their protective armour and helmets, festooned with stun-sprays and shrill-alarms. They emerge from the vehicle, joking, laughing, and saunter into Grammar Academy XXX. My instincts serve me well, and I notice one boy in the crowd of children arriving, obviously spooked by their presence. He slips behind the trunk of a tree, one of the ancient plane trees that border the streets around here, and he stands silent and still. No one notices him, except me, from across the busy street. He waits while the other pupils stream past, and while the Enforcement Officers disappear into the security of the building.

The leaves of the plane tree rustle in the breeze, and he continues to stand still behind the majestic trunk. I hear the ubiquitous warning bells summon the final few pupils, but he doesn't move. As the distant chime of nine o'clock announces the start of the academy day, he flits, and disappears, not into the school gates, but back down the street and into the park. I cheer silently, and continue on my way. I must remember that, even though it might seem that it is me against the world, I am not alone in my fight after all.

***

Alexandra Essex was not looking forward to chairing the contentious regional meeting on behalf of her boss, Michael Morgan, because she was nervous about his instruction to obscure any refences to the latest case in the newsfeed of Noah Patel. She wanted an hour's quiet preparation before the start-time. She hadn't taken a work driverless from London out towards the West today because she was nervous of hold-ups on the approach to the Marches, but the train had been irritatingly noisy, even in business class, and she still felt unprepared for the challenges that the Board members would inevitably throw at her. She had swept into a gaudy independent café, under the viaduct. close to the station, and was sitting in a corner tapping furiously on her Prexia. Messages constantly flashed across her screen and she focused intently on successful multi-tasking.

A young mother, in a silver Lycrene fabric from head to toe, was watching, her baby asleep in an elaborate buggy festooned with characters from The

Earlies. The mother glanced at Alexandra's pristine black creaseless trouser-suit, and at her sharp heels with burnished shoe straps matching her shoulder bag. Then she gazed lovingly at her baby daughter, who was oblivious through sleep. She sighed with relief as she detected the faintly glowing eyelids, now confident that her child was a chosen one, and would benefit from the highest-class education on offer. Maybe one day her daughter would be a successful executive in a creaseless trouser suit too.

Alexandra was skim-reading a Department document entitled "The Four Plus; Ensuring Success, 2080 Edition" to find the paragraph about aberrations. She skimmed across the familiar words: 'It is clear which children hold the intellectual capacity to succeed in the higher-class educational establishments of the Central Area. Once infants are nine months old, Eye Scintillation will always be evident. The Four Plus assessment confirms this by individual, and schooling is allocated six months before the child begins attending a grammar academy, in the academic year in which they are five years old...' She flipped the virtual pages over and over, finding the section that she was looking for: 'Classified: evidence shows that there is a one in a hundred thousand chance of the eyes of a child in the advantaged classes NOT developing scintillation, and therefore not giving early proof of intellectual potential. In such cases medical intervention may be necessary in order to avoid parental disaffection.' The document cross-referenced an outdated Department of Wellbeing publication from 2078 that was said to have looked into scintillation aberrations. *Two years ago*, she thought, grunting and raising her carefully defined eyebrows. Much had changed since then.

She secretly acknowledged to herself that the Four Plus now simply fulfilled a bureaucratic exercise to formally allocate schooling. The historical assessment had become meaningless in that, these days, it was scintillation itself that proved eligibility to a grammar education, but the Four Plus was an important ritual, and she believed that it demonstrated to the populace Michael Morgan's clear vision for the operation of his Department, achieving transparency.

More parents were arriving in the café, and the initially quiet haven was turning into a chattering crèche. Despite her irritation at the noise, she noted with satisfaction that all the little boys, girls and neutrals, had already scintillated. They were each destined for greatness, would be schooled with precise attention to detail, maximising their academic potential, and being prepared for their adult lives as planners, programmers and professionals.

A perfectly polished woman strutted into the café, and all the parents turned to look at her. Alexandra was reminded of pictures of air hostesses in the previous century. The woman wore a bright red costume, and her face could have been made from plastic it was so smooth. 'Welcome today to the Prophet Corporation's Eye Shower for...er...Melissa,' she drawled, checking her Prexia for the child's name. The keen parents and their glowing children trouped off behind the air hostess look-alike into a back room, carrying their sparkly wrapped gifts for Melissa. They closed the partition and the café settled into its previous calm.

Alexandra tried to return to her reading. She was overjoyed that so many parents all across the Central Area, even out here near the Periphery, were now celebrating scintillation, with parties and gifts. A glimmer of pride flicked into her consciousness as she was playing such a significant part in the programme. She pushed away the nagging doubt that the Prophet Corporation had devised yet another opportunity to squeeze sterling from hard-pressed parents.

As if by chance, an advertisement flashed up on her Prexia: "Eye Showers for your princess". They didn't come cheap, with optional extras like sparkling helium balloons and gift tokens for guests, all adding to the price. The gender stereotyping didn't seem to bother her, the traditional pinks and blues, and now green for the celebrated neutral children, a triumph for genetic engineering, giving a spectrum of non-binary gender-choice later in their lives. She was, however, relieved that her daughter was born before the scintillation and gender-neutral programmes had started. She thought of her daughter with uncharacteristic emotion. She didn't talk about her time as a teenage parent; it was a past life, irrelevant to her current ambitions.

Unsettled by her memories, she gathered her belongings, and under the gaze of the security cameras, swiped her fob to exit. Security had to be even more rigorous out near the Periphery.

It had started to rain and a family with two young children was sheltering under the café awning. The baby and the toddler did not have glittering eyes, and they were already wet from the rain. The parents were having a disagreement. The father was seething, 'Forget the eye showers, it's too late…' and the mother was saying, 'But…'

The father insisted under his breath, 'We have to cross the Marches; it's the only way…'

On seeing Alexandra, they stopped talking and stood stock still, blending into the dim world under the viaduct. As she walked on, Alexandra made the mistake of glancing back, by accident looking into the eyes of the older child, deep blue-grey eyes as beautiful as the sea on a calm day, simply majestic even without the sparkle. In return, the mute child looked into Alexandra's eyes with innocent accusation.

Chapter 4

Alexandra's meeting was taking place at The Morton Hotel, a short walk towards the City Centre, close to the border of the Periphery, but still in the Central Area. An android scanned and body-checked her, and once she had swiped in, she relaxed, relieved to see familiar colleagues. Sean Price, the Western Area School Commissioner, greeted her with enthusiasm. His area was called WalSA, because it was originally the Wales School Area, but as the Marches border shifted, in response to various skirmishes involving local vigilantes protesting against the encroachment of the Central Area, it had been officially renamed the West. Sean was responsible for schools in the West, bordering on Alexandra's much larger Central Area. 'We can completely reorganise schooling in the country, but we cannot stop the rain,' he joked, noticing her damp shoulders.

'Haha, yes, thank goodness for self-drying fabric,' was her response.

Board members had already arrived and were standing awkwardly around the small boardroom, drinking coffee and indulging in idle conversation. As Alexandra swept into the room, they took their places wearily around the table, anticipating the usual tortuous and tightly managed bureaucratic discussion.

She thanked the local intern who had been allocated to monitor the auto-record, and to service the needs of attendees, took the chair, and called the meeting to order. In her characteristically crisp and authoritarian voice, she reminded attendees that their dialogue was now on auto-record. She led the niceties of the introductions, explaining that she was covering the role of chair for Michael Morgan. Having endured more of Sean's cutting jokes, and checked that all attendees had copies of the e-papers, she talked them through the business for the afternoon.

'Colleagues, you will see that we have eight lengthy papers to consider today. The High Council has asked that we focus particularly on officially approving the recommendations at the end of paper one.' She noticed that the bottles of drinking water on the boardroom table were sponsored by the Prophet Corporation, and thought again of the Eye Showers. 'Today we are empowered to bring the Western borderland up to the same standard as borders in the East and the South West. Paper one outlines the case to strengthen the border checks through a digitisation programme, so that we know more precisely who is leaving the Central Area and when, therefore confirming how many school places will be needed in the CenSA grammar academies, as well as assisting the Education Enforcement Officers in locating criminal parents who attempt to home-educate rather than relocating.' Sean asked provocatively if this procedure would also inform him of how many school places were needed in his Peripheral Area, but she reminded him that Peripheral Areas organise their own schooling locally, outside the control of the Department for Future Success. He also asked about the current situation on the northern borders. She thought that this was out of order. He knew very well how resistant the northern headteachers were to recent changes and was stirring trouble. 'Let's focus on the West,' she said.

The meeting droned on as the officials worked their way through a virtual mound of e-paperwork. After an hour, Alexandra, as Chair, decided to end the pointless discussion. She tapped the table with her manicured nails to attract the attention of the verbose attendees, and continued purposefully: 'Colleagues, I am drawing us back to consider paper one, which, as you know, is intended to assist us in planning ahead and in clamping down on illegal home education. It will also enable us to check more thoroughly for errors in the scintillation programme; unusual, but costly when they do occur. We have been asked by Michael to look at this today because of the recent high-profile case out here.'

Last year, four-year-old twins had appeared in a Welsh school. One child was scintillated and the other was not. The furious parents had created a huge story in the newsfeed detailing their experience of being banished from the Central Area and claiming that their scintillated child had been denied the education that he was due. Sean had not handled the incident well. It had hit the national press and was even debated in the New Parliament before Alexandra or Michael Morgan were aware of the case. The parent representative on the Board wanted to discuss this example in detail, but Alexandra hurried on, anxious that no one should raise the latest case of Noah Patel which she had seen in today's newsfeed. She glibly referred Board members to the useful appendix in paper one so that they could find the information they sought.

The officials had now been sitting around the table talking for nearly two hours. Alexandra decided to wind up the meeting with a warning on publicity, as requested by Michael. 'Finally,' she said with relief, 'I must draw your attention to the current heightened risk of negative newsfeed. We believe this is a direct result of action by the education underground, and emanates from the Marches. Amateur filming is appearing on the public newsfeed at such a rate that the High Council Communications Department is running behind in taking down the offensive content.' The communications representative attending today's meeting, a serious-looking bespectacled young man nodded in agreement.

She moved to the vote, which usually completed proceedings. Personal views were, in a sense anonymous, as the audio-record didn't identify individuals. Despite a clear majority voting to strengthen and digitise all border-checks into the West, Sean visibly abstained. She would message Michael from the train to alert him to Sean's rumbling insubordination. Was he working in league with the education underground? she wondered.

With relief, after a long and largely uneventful meeting, she swiped out of the hotel, and strode purposefully through the puddles to the station. She regretted her decision to take the train, as at dusk there would be a steady flow of families heading for the Marches crossings. Why did they travel at dusk?

She noticed how the two station platforms visibly represented current divisions in society. The down-platform was packed with migrating families, carrying heavy bundles and pushing loaded trolleys. She was immune to the emotional draw of their tense faces, and the pathos of the subdued children clutching at a few treasured possessions. Directly opposite, the up-platform was busy with executives on their homeward commute, dressed well and averting their eyes from the travelling crowds across the rails.

She had seen photographs of the railway before the protection fences were installed, and before the migrations. Now, on both sides, the platforms and the tracks were not only separated with a wire mesh to prevent accidents and suicides, but benefitted from 100% camera coverage. Her train drew in and she selected a seat, secretly relieved to escape the incessant reminder of the impact of the policies for which she was partially responsible. Flipping open her Prexia, she tried to lose her vaguely troubled conscience in the welter of messages which had flown in, but she was distracted by her memory of the deep blue-green eyes of the child sheltering from the rain outside the Eye Shower. Alexandra had schooled herself into the mind-set of a successful twenty-first-century business executive, but her innate ethical core could not always be held down.

As the train screeched through the suburbs, she remembered to message Michael. She selected the classified messaging service, checked the security of the connection and opted for brevity: 'Michael, Western Peripheral Board approved increased security on outward migration. SP abstained. Alex.'

Michael Morgan was waiting for this message to arrive; he urgently needed the security agreement in place and was relying on Alexandra to deliver it today.

He had joined the High Council in the 2060s, running down a successful legal career as his governmental seniority increased. His childhood had prepared him well for the role, with his tycoon father grooming him for greatness. Alexandra was his protégé. He remembered her interview for the position a couple of years ago, how she left the other candidates standing, with her drive, her perception and her strength of belief in Future Success. He respected her concern about Sean's disruptive activity and would increase surveillance. They couldn't risk the West turning into the North.

Meanwhile, Zade only allowed herself shallow sleep, staying dressed in case she needed to flee quickly. She clasped her torch, her hand hiding under the cushion she used as a pillow.

Chapter 5

The papers for the monthly management meeting of England's Area School Commissioners had been circulated through the secure messaging service. It was July, and the end of the 2079/2080 academic year. Alexandra swiped through the welter of documents, pausing on the inspection spreadsheet which showed all 9,970 grammar academies in her area hitting the 4.5-star expectation, compared with the two- and three-star averages in the Peripheral areas. The North was even lower than last quarter at barely two stars. What was Sue Sutton doing there? She found the e-paper which she sought: "Summary of Current Challenges in CenSA, A. Essex July 2080" and opened it.

She was anxious about this paper because she had been uncharacteristically honest, and although she had run the content by Michael Morgan, she didn't think that he had been listening at the time. As she opened the document, she caught the sub-title "Summary of Current Strengths in CenSA". That was odd, had she said "strengths"? She double-checked. Had someone changed her paper? Time was not on her side as she was being ushered into her next meeting by a keen young Intern. Closing the document and turning on her automatic smile to greet her visitors, she checked the figure on a message from Michael which had just appeared on her Prexia for her imminent meeting: 'Must settle Patel case today – do not exceed £1.5m.'

Alexandra knew that Michael had to present an account of all individual items of expenditure over £1.5 million to the New Parliament. Whereas the High Council operated as the decision-making board attended by senior employed officials in the civil service, the New Parliament comprised elected members from across both the Central Area and the Periphery, although those from the Central Area dominated these days. Michael liked to keep as much education business as possible off the record of the New Parliament.

She had been allocated a Senior from the High Council Legal Team, an older lawyer called Ed Sergeant, so Michael must be worried about this case. The High Council Communications Director, who was uninvited, also joined them, flustered at the last-minute instruction, her hair blown by the wind as she had run the two hundred metres from Whitehall. She was panting and busily untangling her silver scarf.

Mr and Mrs Patel, the impeccably presented parents of Lucas and Noah, had travelled to the capital especially for the next 30 minutes, and were accompanied by their lawyer. After the formal introductions, Alexandra took control. 'We have all read your case files,' she lied, 'but perhaps you could summarise for us?'

The parents were nervous and angry. Ed Sergeant, the High Council lawyer, appeared disinterested, which visibly irritated the Patel's young lawyer. Alexandra let the parents talk for five minutes, knowing that she must then move on to negotiate the agreement. 'There are two options available to us in this very unusual circumstance,' she continued and passed over to Ed Sergeant to outline the choices. Firstly, cosmetic eye surgery could be offered to little Noah but they could not guarantee its success, and there would be a heightened risk of blindness or visual impairment. Alternatively, the High Council could provide a one-off Relocation Grant. The lawyer explained that such grants were discretionary. They were only made available to parents of scintillated children who very unusually also bore an unscintillated child, who did not pass the Four Plus and could not therefore legally be schooled in the Central Area. He emphasised that the offer of the discretionary grant could be withdrawn at any point before the parents signed the agreement, and he stressed the word "discretionary", spitting it out through his prominent teeth.

Mr and Mrs Patel had already discussed the two options at length and their lawyer explained that they would proceed with the second. They would relocate.

At this point Alexandra resumed by explaining: 'If you accept the High Council offer now, in front of witnesses, then the matter will be closed and the agreements can be signed this morning.' She started low at £500,000, claiming that £1 million was the ceiling. The parents appeared slightly overawed by the situation, and were patently desperate to do the best for both of their beloved boys. Their lawyer tried to push the figure upwards above the million, but Alexandra was adamant. She was more concerned about returning to check her papers for the management meeting. 'How about we settle at the million, which is more than we would expect to offer in such a case, but also pay your expenses for today from our Courtesy Fund?' To her amazement, they agreed, *Out of fear of losing the grant entirely*, she thought. The parents did not realise how unusual such cases were, or how determined the Department was to silence them.

Alexandra sent Mr and Mrs Patel, and their lawyer, off with Ed Sergeant to sign the previously drawn-up agreements, briefly exchanging a triumphant look with the Communications Manager as there was a gagging order carefully buried in the small print of the document. Relieved that these situations were extremely rare, she swept out to return to the privacy of her office upstairs, on the way asking the Intern to grab her a coffee. She messaged Michael, saying, 'Patels settle @ £1 million,' added a smiley face, reflected, and deleted it before sending, deciding to remain formal.

Chapter 6

At this time of year, I am up with the sun around five o'clock, having slept in my clothes in case of disturbances. I prefer bright weather, because on days like today, when the sky is heavy, the polluted London air hangs in the courtyard, and I cannot see well enough indoors, Lyn's electricity having been switched off. I am nervous to open any curtains, so use my large wind-up torch sparingly to see, to freshen up, and to write in my journal.

Lyn's curtains were once a plush synthetic velvet, but now it is hard to determine their colour, and the pile is flat. Dust has settled on the folds for lack of the usual rhythm of opening and closing, and I leave it trembling there to add to the impression that the flat is uninhabited, should an Education Enforcement Officer track down the address. Although there is scant footfall on the paving outside, occasionally labourers come and go. Sometimes young people older than me, educated before scintillation was initiated, creep by, looking for empty properties where they can smoke and drink out of the eyes of the enforcement system. I lie low, ready to exit at the back of the flat, through the small yard. They are armed, generally with knives, and my best option would be to leave rather than face them, or, of course to join them. The protection of a group could be handy.

Yesterday, I suffered a setback; when I returned from the local Biblio, a crisp white envelope had been forced through my letterbox. The letterbox was taped up when Lyn left, so this letter was important. As I dreaded, it was from The Landlord's Association announcing imminent repossession of Lyn's flat due to unpaid rent. It had taken them long enough! I know why there are delays; so many properties are left empty as families flee to the Periphery to escape the Education Enforcement Officers, and as a result landlords and Councils are overwhelmed. Generally, families whose children do not scintillate live in rented places, but there is a growing problem with mortgage default too. Some families wait until the Four Plus before they finally accept that they must flee. Others plan ahead, and once their baby reaches a year old, if there is no sign of scintillation, they know that they need to go. I am friendly with Sam, the volunteer at my local Advice Bureau, who hears all this. I just keep asking why is it necessary at all? Scintillation seems unnatural to me.

The letter is signed by the Chair of the Landlords Association. It is a Final Warning for repossession any day following July 20th. I don't understand how it can be "final" as I haven't received any previous warnings. There are only three days to prepare.

Peering through the gap between the curtains, I focus on the small patch of sky which shines down on my flat through the rooftops. The sky is brightening, and I know that, as a priority, I must pack, just in case. I have a sturdy rucksack and a few possessions. My most treasured item is a delicate silver cross on a short, fine chain. I was told that it was round my neck when they found me, a small baby, not more than a few days old. I had been placed on the doorstep of the St Thomas Maternity Wing in a wicker shopping basket. I was dressed in a soft white nightdress and wrapped in an expensive cashmere shawl. The nurses remembered this because it was unusual for abandoned babies to be so beautifully bundled up. I wore the cross when I was younger, but the chain is too short now, and I am not really a Christian, so I keep it safe in a tiny black box. Of everything, I would be most sad if I lost my cross because it is the only solid link I have with my parents, whoever they were, and it has travelled with me everywhere.

Next to be packed is my Prexia; my invaluable Prophet Corporation personal communication and information tool, my journals, including the latest, where I am writing all that I find about scintillation, and then my pencil case which is crammed with pens and small useful items; paper clips, scissors, sewing needles, thread and matches. I have a few good strong clothes, bought with my allowance, spare shoes and washing kit including an unusually large wooden hairbrush. It seems to be the only one that can force its way through my thick black hair without breaking under the effort.

I add a toilet roll, bottles of water, emergency Prophet Nutrition Bars, my wind-up torch and a small solar radio which Lyn left behind. The rucksack is full to bursting. I walk round the flat, checking whether I have forgotten anything. My school uniform is hanging sadly in the wardrobe; the badge looking ridiculously antiquated with scrolls encircling the proud words "Grammar Academy". I certainly will not be needing that.

Passing through Kira's small box room, abandoned toys turn their beady eyes on me. At first, the room smelled of Kira, fresh and pink, but not now. I wonder how many children's bedrooms across the Central Area are looking like this, with the toys and books and little clothes which parents had chosen for their darlings, all preserved in aspic, like a museum to childhood, awaiting the inevitable Landlord's Association house clearance. I know it isn't the fault of the landlords; the root cause is something to do with scintillation. And at the same time, all the chosen children, the privileged ones, the plump ones, are allowed to stay, to enjoy their many advantages, far too many expensive e-games, toys and knick-knacks, and the unlimited love and care of doting parents, like all of my friends at the Grammar Academy.

I glance into the bathroom, which with no water it is of little use to me, except for occasional use of the toilet. I keep the cistern filled with rainwater from the downpipe in the yard at the back, and the flush works well when needed, but is noisy. In preference I use facilities in the coffee houses, in the biblios, or in the Civic Hall. As I leave the bathroom, I spot Lyn's first aid kit, dusty on the top of the mirrored cabinet. It is in a smart green cardboard box, too big for my rucksack, but I tip out the contents and squeeze painkillers, antiseptic sachets, plasters and cream into the side pockets, returning the half-empty box to its original place.

Finally, I need to secure my ancient mobile phone and wireless charge-boost, key fob and my few documents, on my person. Since the microchipping health scare, most Central Area residents have reverted to standalone haptic devices, but they outstrip my budget. One of the reasons I favour jeans and my heavy canvas coat is for the pockets. I have no birth certificate, but do have a letter from St Thomas's, explaining that I was admitted to the maternity unit before being transferred to foster care, which I occasionally use to prove my identity in addition to my passport. I fold it, carefully zipping it into my jeans; I am less likely to be separated from jeans than from a coat. I take my passport from the drawer; I look so young in the photo even though it is only a couple of years old, but it is definitely recognisable as me, due to my hair, and my eyes. Even the photograph shows the intense sparkle of my eyes. I reflect on my date of birth. If you don't look too carefully it seems to say 2064; 21.1. rather than 21.12. That would make me 16 already, rather than five months off that significant milestone. This could be helpful I reflect, trying to scuff out the remains of the final "2" with my thumb. Once sixteen, I can legally live by myself, which will make things a lot easier. I have no desire to be captured and placed with yet another foster family at this late stage in my childhood.

It is already eight o'clock, and I plan to visit the Advice Bureau this morning. I trust Sam and want to show him the letter from the Landlord's Association. My carefully packed rucksack is ready in case I have to leave in a hurry, and I hide it in the back wardrobe under some blankets, zipping the Landlord's letter in my pocket. I check that the coast is clear, double-locking the door with my fob as I leave. As a scintillated over-fourteen, I also have higher-level public access included on my key fob. This allows me to enter the better-class coffee establishments, biblios and community buildings. I am a living dichotomy; I have the privileges of the advantaged classes but the lifestyle of the displaced.

Having honed my exit down to a fine art, I cross the courtyard quickly and confidently, emerging into the street with the air of someone who had just come out of the shower and has a nice air-conditioned home to return to. I am heading for the Westminster Chateau-Privee this morning. Chateau-Privee restaurants are only available to the advantaged classes and their scintillated progeny. I like to go there because it is frequented by Westminster bureaucrats and I sometimes overhear useful conversations. Also, the bathroom is palatial unlike in the Prophet Cafés or public buildings.

As I cross Lambeth Bridge, the sun breaks the clouds and the glass panes of high-rise London shimmer across the grey water of the Thames. I think of the painter Whistler, I think of William Blake, and recite to myself, over and over, to the rhythm of my feet, 'I wander through each chartered street, where the chartered Thames does flow.' I dredge my memory, recalling that "flow" rhymed with "woe" and that there were "mind-forged manacles" like now, like scintillation.

I look forward to walking through the park in the mornings, avoiding the muddled gaze of street-sleepers who sit blearily on benches waiting for the surge of commuters so they can start begging. There was a time, in my younger days, when I could still hear birds singing in the London parks. I even saw a squirrel once. Now there are occasional magpies and the genetically modified black seagulls overhead compete with flocks of drones, aerial freight and private aircraft. The pigeon flu epidemic happened before I was born.

Reaching the Chateau-Privee, I stand tall, swipe in, and head for the bathroom, emerging smelling of orange and bergamot. Having collected my coffee and bagel, always secretly relieved when my payment is successful, I settle in a corner where I know I can charge my phone easily, hooking up wirelessly to the power ring. Well-dressed take-away customers are flowing through at speed in a blur of silver and gold jackets and coiffured hair. I scan the restaurant; not much of interest today; the usual suited bureaucrats; a stand-out woman in a pristine black creaseless trouser-suit, her shoe straps and sharp heels matching her shoulder bag, totally absorbed in something on her Prexia.

I glance at my phone to check the state of the charge; it had been totally empty. I left the scanning app on by mistake last night and it drained all remaining power. As I look at the old misted screen, an icon in the shape of an eye flashes up, and immediately disappears, which is strange, and has not happened before. I think no more of it and look up. The standout woman has left, no doubt for her first meeting of the day at 9am. It is time for me to head to the Advice Bureau.

Chapter 7

Alexandra was concerned that her paper for Michael Morgan's imminent management meeting had been doctored. There were just twenty minutes for her to check it. Closing the door of her office, she illuminated the engaged display indicator. She was right to be worried; her carefully authored paper summarising current challenges seemed to have been skilfully rewritten. Who had checked the papers? Who had done this without letting her know?

The coffee arrived and she now had eight minutes to decide upon her course of action. Reflecting carefully, she told herself to act cool today, and listen, rather than blow up about it. She could investigate the issues with her paper after the meeting. Taking on a professional and dignified demeanour, she left her office looking resolute, carrying her coffee, and made her way up to the High Council boardroom.

Michael Morgan was in the Chair, and she knew from the open way in which he greeted her, that he had not sanitised her paper. Sean Price was already sitting beside him, head down in his messages. Manya Gray had come to London for the meeting, from Cambridge, representing the East. She was often an ally for Alexandra, who took the seat beside her. Sue Sutton was generally late to meetings, and had not yet arrived. Where was Peter Edwards, from Cornwall? As if reading her mind, Michael told the assembled Commissioners that Peter would join them on the screen. At that moment the screen flickered into action and Peter's grizzled face appeared, fumbling with his Prexia, swigging his coffee, unaware that the digital feed was already switched on. Lance Richardson, Michael's executive assistant, arrived noisily, and smiled warmly at Alexandra; he had not changed the paper either, she could tell.

This group of senior officials represented the pinnacle of national educational intelligence, led by Michael Morgan, the lawyer and businessman. Alexandra was the youngest, a teaching professional, promoted from a Central Area Grammar Academy headship. Sean and Peter were both historically qualified and experienced teachers, with a reputation for defending out-dated practices. Manya was a lawyer, and Sue Sutton seemed to be a career bureaucrat, like Lance. Alexandra often thought that her colleagues from the Periphery failed to understand the Department's focus on success, championed so strongly by Michael. This high-level board of people formed the operational decision-making body for the Department for Future Success, which reported directly to the High Council itself.

There were historical tensions between the High Council and the New Parliament, which had, for years, been papered over. The High Council took the lead on all matters relating to national education, and as long as the current dominant political party in the elected Parliament retained its large majority, this situation would continue. There had consequently been a lack of independent challenge to education policy for many years. Michael ran management meetings in his characteristic style. Having formed his opinion on the matters on the agenda, he expected his team of senior managers to fall in line with his recommendations.

The meeting progressed from one paper to another, following the corporate ritual. Sue arrived half an hour into the meeting, trailing scarves and bags, apologising excessively. Michael accelerated over Alexandra's paper saying, 'And we have a useful paper from Alexandra; a Summary of Current Strengths in CenSA, which I commend to you…there is not time to discuss this paper now.' She smiled inanely and the meeting continued.

Later that evening, in the privacy of her tiny flat off the Vauxhall Bridge Road, sitting in her expensive polka-dot onesie with a large glass of red wine, she re-read the original version of her paper. It dawned upon her that someone had actually done her a favour. The paper was too honest, even superficial, and far too long. She would go back to Michael when he was less busy, and would tackle the challenges with him behind closed doors, before committing her thoughts to black and white.

Chapter 8

On weekdays in the summer, Alexandra rose with the sun around 5am. She liked to have caught up with all messages before arriving at the office as early as the security systems allowed, which was 6am. Despite nagging concerns about her challenges paper, she had been tired and slept well. The air-conditioning was a blessing in July. A woman of precise grooming, habit and routine, she needed 45 minutes to prepare herself for the day and could then walk to her office in Great Smith Street in 15 minutes. She always carried a personal alarm, directly linked to the office 24-hour security, and so if she happened to be recognised and attacked, drone assistance would be immediate. She had only needed to use it on a couple of occasions, once when an inebriated street-sleeper had tried to wrench her bag off her shoulder, and last year, when an angry parent had drawn a knife and threatened her outside the Department buildings. On both occasions drone security had shot the offenders with tranquiliser darts, within seconds and the culprits were imprisoned. The anonymised stories were used in the public newsfeed to deter other would-be street antagonists.

It was a grey, oppressive start to the day. She emerged from the front security doors of the apartments into a dull, damp street and headed for Rochester Row. Her route was hard-wired into her brain and she no longer noticed the hands at the upper windows, drawing their blinds, or the caretakers raising grills in coffee houses ready for the early shift. She didn't even glance at the school on her route, its entry barrier proudly announcing that it was a member of the CenSA Grammar Academy Trust, of which she was the Director. She simply focused on the day ahead; what was needed. Today she was concerned about the questions she would pose when she met her boss, Michael Morgan. The rhythm of her clicking feet accompanied her thoughts. She was battling to achieve the greatest possible success for her schools. For a reason, which she didn't understand, she remembered some stray lines from a long-distant poem: 'I will not cease from mental fight, nor shall my sword sleep in my hand…' She repeated the lines as she walked.

Alexandra had left her job as a highly successful secondary Grammar Academy headteacher, and had started working in this senior role a couple of years ago. It had lived up to her expectations. She was treated with respect, enjoyed privileges and could access the highest-level Civil Servants, although Michael still tended to cover liaison with members of the New Parliament. She put in long hours, leading her Central Area Department with skill, to keep the show on the road despite the current challenges. *Ah, the challenges*, her thoughts returned to the paper and her imminent conversation with Michael.

Two years ago, on her walk into work, she had seen occasional sparrows and pied wagtails pecking crumbs on the pavements outside the many cafés, but even if her eyes had been open to them, she would not have seen them today; the smaller birds had either died out or had forsaken the city centres. She strutted quickly, balancing on her heels with poise and purpose, combating any nervousness on the streets with an automatic and well-practised bravado, her hand clutching the alarm in her pristine jacket pocket.

She ignored the daily drone freight deliveries, which sailed over her head, delivering the materials from the Periphery factories to the successful city before the day began. Food, ready-meals, medications, items of clothing and household goods were flown in each day, and distributed to the affluent homes, and the cafés. There were no shops here. The Periphery provided the workforce for all manufacturing, leaving a diminishing residue of low-paid service-workers in the Central Area. The scintillation programme, combined with rapid digitisation, was intended to gradually drive all lower manual workers out to the Periphery.

As she arrived at the imposing frontage on Great Smith Street, she waved her fob across the first security scanner and was admitted into the vestibule. It was too early for the reception staff and so, each day, she used the internal back stairway, pausing at every doorway to scan her fob, finally entering the sixteen-digit code which had been messaged to her for the day. Her manicured fingertips darted across the keypad and the laser-proof doors opened.

The office was generally empty at this time, but she could see that the latest Intern had been the first to arrive and was looking out for her. He was hovering outside her office looking guilty, anxious, even frightened. 'Sorry to pounce on you so early,' he said, 'but I need to talk to you urgently.' This was both irritating and unprecedented; interns usually came and went, made coffee, copied and archived, and did their best to disappear into the blur of the Department.

'Come straight in,' she said, without any encouragement in her tone, hanging her pristine, latest-fashion, small-check jacket on the coat stand. The Intern burst out;

'I didn't sleep at all last night. You know the papers for yesterday's management meeting? Well I mistakenly submitted an old CenSA paper instead of yours. I have checked and it had a very similar descriptor. I am so sorry. It was my fault.' He looked at the floor, at her high heels slightly splashed from the damp pavements, and up at her face. 'It was my mistake,' he added. To prevent the Intern from trailing on further she put him out of his misery;

'Actually, it needed re-writing anyway; please can you delete it from the system, oh, and book me an hour with Michael this week, to discuss it. I won't mention your error.' She winked at him. The Intern looked greatly relieved and scuttled off to his desk downstairs, to do just that.

At eight twenty she had a short break between meetings. As she needed coffee and breakfast, she took the glass lift down to street level. Her delicately outlined eyes scanned across the street before she emerged. She gulped the air, which was far from fresh, hurried along the busy pavement and dived into the Chateau-Privee at the end of the street. Messages were buzzing on her Prexia; she swiped the extraneous ones straight into the trash without reading them. Hovering over a message from Ed Sergeant she saw that the parents of Lucas and Noah had signed all the papers and were preparing to leave for the Periphery. 'Good,' she said to herself, relieved and proud that she had successfully averted a major embarrassment for the Department.

She hardly gave herself time to enjoy her trendy yogurt and oat compote, consuming it automatically, drinking the coffee as if it were medicine, while she poured over her Prexia. She checked the time, scanned the restaurant before rising, in case she had overlooked a colleague. She noticed a teenager on her way to school, dressed in black, with the most amazing scintillation, charging her phone from the ring. What eyes the girl had. Feeling proud at the success of the programme, she swiped out of the Chateau Privee and returned to her day of meetings.

It was not until later in the afternoon that she found time to pause and reflect. There was no point in targeting Michael today as she had heard from the Intern that he had travelled up north to an emergency situation with Sue Sutton, anyway, she wasn't ready to face him until she had reconsidered her paper. She checked that the Intern had removed it from the system, and he had, so she pulled up a confidential copy on her Prexia and started reading, editing furiously.

'Summary of Current Challenges in CenSA, A. Essex July 2080,' sounded far too pompous. She deleted the title, deleted the introduction and removed the corporate background paragraphs so that she could focus on summarising the issues.

The resulting text provided clarity, saying, 'Between the ages of six and nine months the irises in the eyes of infants mature. At this stage, academic selection for future schooling begins. Approximately 75% of infants in the Central Area gain scintillation by the age of nine months. Scholarly literature quotes the research by S. Herbert, Oxford, 2048, which proves that excess inherent intelligence leads to scintillation. The potential for children to succeed academically therefore causes the iris to sparkle. A quarter of the infant population not suited to academic study does not scintillate.' She paused, sighed, and continued working on the text.

'The legal age to start schooling is the academic year in which a child reaches their fifth birthday. The Four Plus assessment in the Central School Area (CenSA) consists of the matching of scintillated children to grammar places, and the allocation of unscintillated children to Peripheral schools. This maximises educational achievement of pupils in Central grammar academies and improves productivity of the national powerhouse in the longer term.' She nodded, pleased with her summary of the current situation, and continued.

'Central Area grammar academies started working together thirty years ago. They all joined the ground-breaking CenSA Academy Trust during the reorganisation of 2050. The Central Area education system is therefore both innovative and educationally mature, unlike the Periphery, where schooling is historically based and consequently less advanced.' She wanted to add a detail about scintillation diminishing between the ages of fourteen, and sixteen, and paused, remembering that there is currently an issue with unscintillated children returning illegally to the Central grammars for the final two years of compulsory schooling. Knowing that she should be doing more to prevent this, she added it to her digi-list of challenges.

She wondered whether the much-quoted research by Herbert had been peer-reviewed at the time, or whether it had been reviewed for relevance in the 2080s? It occurred to her that she had never seen this research and should obtain a copy so that she could understand the scintillation process better. Her brain ran on, ahead of her reading; what about the Periphery? Firstly, why don't any infants in Peripheral areas scintillate? Secondly, why do parents settle for the sub-standard education in the Periphery for their children? Does the removal of Central Area families to the Periphery create trauma for the children? Has anyone studied this? Are there infants with academic potential being born in the Periphery, who are unnoticed, who fail to be stretched to their potential? Why doesn't the scintillation process happen there? What about the Northern Area? Until recently the North had operated like the Periphery but there were already just over a hundred grammar academies run by CenSA in the North, and the few instances of scintillation there, along with overflow from the Central Midlands, had ensured that those grammars were fully utilised. The northern association of headteachers was locked in dispute with Michael Morgan himself.

She was starting to feel overwhelmed by such a welter of thorny issues, when she was disturbed by a tapping noise outside her office. It was Manya Gray, her equivalent in the Eastern Area, EaSA. Manya was still in London after yesterday's management meeting, and she was gently drumming her manicured fingernails on the glass. Alexandra genuinely liked Manya, with her calm, well-informed approach, and beckoned to her. Manya peeped in, 'I am leaving for Cambridge shortly and wondered if you would like a catch up before I go?' Alexandra invited her in, and called a nearby Intern to make tea. Manya liked tea. The two young women embraced; it was expected at their level, and their perfumes mixed into a heady scent.

They discussed operational matters; the disruptions on the Isle of Ely, where overnight queues of families at the gates, at this time of year, could be excessive, the new Commissioner in the North, Sue Sutton; what was she actually doing asked Alexandra rhetorically. Unexpectedly Manya gave her a frank answer,

'Between you and me, she is the partner of one of Michael's old buddies on his Future Success Committee. She has been planted in the North for two reasons, firstly they needed somewhere to put her because she creates muddle wherever she goes, but is too young to be signed off, and secondly if the mess in the North continues for a while, it will help your takeover of NSA by CenSA. Keep that to yourself,' she said with a smile.

The Intern arrived bearing a pot of fragrant tea with cups and saucers, and they enjoyed the ceremony, sipping in mutual pleasure. Alexandra told her colleague and friend about the latest case of scintillation aberration involving

Noah Patel. She found it helpful to offload her frustrations when with Manya, and also told her about the child under the viaduct. She was still disturbed by those beautiful unscintillated eyes, and the parents arguing about crossing the Marches. 'What happened to your "challenges" paper?' asked Manya, with a quizzical look. Alexandra told her the story, how she suspected sabotage, but it was the intern's error. Manya simply raised her beautifully accentuated eyebrows. 'If it would help to run your paper by me before you approach Michael, just ask,' she invited with an endearing smile, adding, 'Why don't you come to the East for a visit sometime? But now I must dash; see you Alex!'

Chapter 9

As I arrive at the Advice Bureau, I look for Sam. I am keen to discuss the letter from the Landlord's Association with him, but he is busy, and there is a long queue of dishevelled older people outside his door. I flash my eyes at the volunteer receptionist, and ask if he can add me to Sam's morning schedule, which he does willingly, fitting me in at 10.30. He says that Sam has something to give me; I wonder what it might be?

Not long to wait, I make for the bookshop on the top floor, in the old converted attics. The Advice Bureau, like many others across the country, is a self-help charity staffed by volunteers. There is no requirement to swipe in, and as a result, people from a wide spectrum of society come and go. The volunteers often undertake day jobs as well. Sam, I know, works in the Prophet Café nearby. He sometimes brings surplus cakes across at the end of the day. These are pounced upon by the rag tag of debtors and addicts still in the building near closing time. There is a volunteer café in the basement, a stark contrast to the Chateau-Privee where I started my day, and ancient toilet facilities which are always blocking up. On the first floor there are meeting rooms which charities rent for a peppercorn, and where I sometimes see High Council officials make guest appearances at public meetings. On the second floor, various enterprises have set up, including a second-hand bookshop. Books are niche these days and the shop attracts older local residents as well as trendy alternatives, tattooed and pierced, looking for poetry or novels from past centuries, still in book format. As ever, I don't really fit in because of my eyes. During the daytime all scintillated children have to be in school. But the Bureau is a place where misfits congregate, and I always receive a warm welcome there.

The bookshop smells of a past life, with musty paper volumes piled up chaotically on the sagging shelving. This room, I know, holds many keys to the universe. You only have to scan the spines to spot the grandees of a once-literate time; Tolstoy, Dickens, Austen, Bronte, and mythical wordsmiths like Milton, Hopkins and Eliot, banished from the grammar academy curriculum where 21st century digital literature dominates. The pinnacle of current abomination is the sanitised compendium version of Shakespeare, presenting action plots and stereotypical characters to teenagers writing final assessments. I remember being dragooned to complete the Macbeth Colouring Book in the infant class, and having to write the obscenity of reworded quotations in handwriting exercises: 'All that glitters is gold,' and, 'Profit is the best policy. If I lose profit, I lose myself.' When I faced the teacher with the correct versions of the quotations, I was told that my versions were outdated and that we must study a curriculum fit for the 21st century. I have learnt more in biblios and bookshops than in grammar academies.

I stoop to look at the lowest shelf of free-to-a-good-home books, seeing the usual garish pamphlets with curling corners, a few children's stories and deteriorating ex-biblio books. Nothing of interest to me today, and as it is nearly time for my appointment with Sam, I return downstairs. Even here, I am allowed to step through the long queue thanks to my eyes.

'Hi Zade, how's things?' he greets me with his usual enthusiasm. I explain about the letter from the Landlord's Association, taking it out of my pocket and showing him. He can tell that I am anxious, and I am surprised by his relaxed response. 'Ah, I see loads of these,' he says, adding, 'To be honest, the Landlord's Association is really behind with the follow-ups. Of the thirty, even forty people who have come to me with letters like this in the last few months, no one has come back to say the bailiffs have called. It's because of the increased Four Plus migrations at this time. They simply don't have the staff, and the automated system keeps sending the letters out. Are you ready if they do call? It is unlikely but possible.' I nod. 'Anyway,' he adds, 'Your situation is different. They couldn't simply turf you out on to the streets, could they?' I naively ask why on earth not. 'Zade,' he said emphatically, 'You would only have to look at them. They wouldn't touch someone with eyes like yours. Remind me, when are you sixteen?' I show him my passport, with the unclear date, but he is not convinced, commenting that my biggest worry should be that the bailiffs would report me to the Education Authorities and they would get me on the re-fostering list, and back into school. His overriding message for me is to keep under the radar and hope luck is on my side. If the worst happens, try to charm my way out of it, and with a good wind, their disorganised systems will not get to me until after I am sixteen. It means continuing to live on a knife-edge, but I am used to that.

I thank Sam, saying that I am one of many people who could not do without him, and the volunteers. His usual response is to encourage grateful clients to donate by swiping their fob over one of the many striped virtual collecting tins, which count donations in a little digital display, triggering a jolly tune when the income reaches a round hundred. My sterling allocation is really low until Lyn can get my allowance to me, but I swipe my digital loose change into the tin and make for the door. 'Don't go yet Zade, I have something for you, if you are interested?' He hands me a very old pamphlet, so deteriorated that it is kept in a transparent wallet. 'Upstairs they had a box of old papers from a house clearance but were throwing this one out,' he added, 'I thought of you because of your research into the history of education; you do what you want with it. It was only heading for the nuclear incinerator,' he finishes. I look avidly at the title, which means nothing to me; "The Art and Science of Selection, S. Herbert, Oxford, 2048", thank him, and vacate the room for a family waiting patiently in the queue.

I secrete the pamphlet in my zipped pocket, curious to read it, and set off for home. Every time I return now, I am relieved to find things as I have left them. Sam was reassuring but I still fear a visit from the bailiffs. A disorganised system, as I know, can throw up random acts, and it would be my luck if they did have Lyn's flat on their urgent list. Thankfully, today all is quiet in the courtyard, and I am relieved to get home, escaping the thick midday London air.

The pamphlet is typed in an old font which isn't used now, and isn't at all easy to read, but from a quick look, one word is repeated throughout. The pamphlet is all about scintillation.

Chapter 10

The Patel household was in complete disarray. At first Lucas was asked to speak to slick newsfeed journalists, which he did, his eyes sparkling at them and his high-pitched voice wooing their sensitivities. He watched himself on the big screens in the news reports. Then, suddenly, the flow of journalists stopped and was replaced by manic activity. Granny Patel came to stay for a few days, and collected him from school on the last day of term because his parents were in London. He had searched for London landmarks at school on the Mini-Prexia, and he and his friends had played going to London, drawing more maps and waving flags all the way. He loved Granny Patel, who brought presents for him and Noah, cooked cakes with spices, and sang beautiful, gentle songs at bedtime.

Mrs Patel was a teacher in a secondary Grammar Academy in the nearby town. Lucas had looked forward to attending his mum's school when he was older, but this seemed less certain now. Mr Patel taught in the local nursery school, which was located in an ancient manor house nearby, taking Noah with him each day. Sometimes Lucas went there before school too. He loved playing with the nursery toys which he had so enjoyed when he was younger and attended full-time. The main thing Lucas liked about the nursery school was that they could play all day. The other thing he liked was that the children were all so different, unlike at the Grammar Academy. There was a busy mix of children whose eyes sparkled, and children with plain eyes, and it simply didn't matter. He liked that.

Now it was the summer break from school, Lucas was looking forward to going to work with his dad. Last summer before he started at the Grammar Academy, he had played outside in the rambling gardens of the manor house for weeks, making dens, drawing maps and exploring with his friends. But things were changing by the day. Lucas knew that it was all because of Noah's eyes.

Last night he had found it hard to sleep, with all the disruption, and he had crept out of the bedroom. He was coming down the stairs to find his mum and dad, but something made him pause on the top step. They were talking about the family's problems, their voices rising and falling, sometimes angry, not at each other, he could tell. He sat on the step craning his ears, looking out of the window into the blackness of the night. 'It's not fair; they have us over a barrel,' his father said. He wasn't sure what "over a barrel" was. His mother then said that they had signed the contract and they were where they were. She said that they simply could not stay. They talked about going out to the Periphery to find work and maybe if they looked for somewhere by the sea, the boys might prefer it there.

Lucas liked the idea of living by the sea. He had been to the seaside on a Scintillation Club trip once when Noah was a baby, and remembered the crowds, the ice creams and the vast blue horizon. He loved digging in the sand pit at the nursery school, and after all, the beach was just one great sand pit.

His parents continued to talk in low tones, and he strained his ears. His mum was describing something called the Prophet Corporation Medical Plant. Was this a plant which grows in the garden, he wondered, but as they spoke more about scintillation, he began to realise that there was a factory where sparkling eyes were manufactured, and it seemed to be located near the sea. His father was speaking about a plan to turn off scintillation; it sounded exciting. He didn't want to add to his parents' worries, so he tiptoed back to bed and drifted off to sleep thinking of the sea.

The family did set off to seek work in the Periphery, planning to stay with a friend called Jeff for a week and then return home to make arrangements. The two boys had small wheeled cases decorated with characters from the Earlies. Lucas liked his because it doubled as a rucksack and he could play explorers. They left after supper, and their comfortable family driverless, filled with the biofuel of the Central Area, took them 150 kilometres at speed on the expressway, overtaking the lines of old manual cars all the way to the Isle of Ely. Then the delays began. There were three lanes of old-fashioned cars queuing for no apparent reason. They crept forwards at a snail's pace, Lucas and Noah watched the Earlies for so long that the episodes started repeating from the beginning, but they didn't mind. It was dusk when they eventually reached the massive illuminated gantry announcing, 'You are now leaving the Central Area.' As they drove through, two armed police officers waved them across into an inspection bay while the clanking old motors limped on through. 'Bother; why us?' muttered his mum, but they knew why. Their driverless drew attention to itself in the procession of older and less flashy vehicles. The police officers wanted to see their passports and evidence that they had accommodation to go to. They wanted to know why the family was travelling. They asked questions, becoming more and more agitated. Eventually they allowed the family to continue on their way, warning them that the return trip would not be easy as the gates for the reverse direction, from the Periphery to the Central Area, were very closely guarded by armed police night and day.

This experience, along with the darkness and the heavy rain, dampened the mood in the driverless. The Earlies had timed out, and Lucas and Noah were encouraged to sleep. The roads deteriorated and Lucas, pretending to doze, peeped out of the windows as they sped through dreary towns and past the odd illuminated diner, into the furthest reaches of the country. Eventually he slept.

When Lucas woke, the summer seemed to have returned, with the morning dawning unexpectedly clear and bright. He stretched up in his seat and gasped, for ahead of them, and to both sides, was the sea; not the sea he had seen before, but a wild sea with rugged cliffs and headlands. Birds were swooping in the thermals, and his mum and dad were standing on the headland, just outside the car, stretching in the way people stretch when they have been stuck in a driverless all night. Then they held hands, and gazed out to sea, before returning to the boys. Lucas always remembered that moment, when his parents looked hopeful and the family was poised at such a significant turning point.

Through the 2070s, all the holiday accommodation in the area had been requisitioned for the displaced families from the Central Area. Instead of being sparsely populated, as it was decades ago, the region was now overcrowded, and not only overcrowded, but experiencing extreme pressure on public services, as most of the migrating families came without work or resources. This had meant that securing accommodation for the week had been tricky, but thanks to their ingenuity, the Patels had contacted Jeff, an old friend from their teacher-training class, who not only offered them a room for the week, but also promised introductions in local schools.

After a morning exploring the cliffs and eating their picnic overlooking the surf, they switched the car to manual due to the uncertainty of the winding lanes, and Mrs Patel drove them to the small inland town of East Bridge, where the navigation system located their destination for the week. Lucas looked out of the driverless window in disbelief as they exchanged windblown coastal hedges for dirty streets littered with food wrappers, empty bottles and scavenging dogs. The streets were narrow, the buildings were dilapidated, and there were groups of rough-looking people on street corners. There was a menace in the air, which unsettled Lucas and Noah. It was as if they had entered a foreign country in a recession, or after a war.

As they drove slowly up to Jeff's house, a group of men in ragged clothes approached the car, glaring and gesticulating. Mrs Patel followed her gut reaction and drove off, anywhere, out of that accursed street. Sweating, she pulled over as soon as was practical, in a quieter area. While Mr Patel soothed the boys, she decided to drive round the block, and to look out for the other side of the property. After several circuits, they succeeded in locating not only the house, but Jeff himself, who was looking out for them. Mrs Patel turned to her husband saying, 'Thank goodness; now it will be fine.'

Jeff Stringer was a bearded giant of a man. He ambled out the front of his semi-detached renovated Victorian house in the older end of the town, and waved enthusiastically, guiding the driverless into his lean-to garage. He made them very welcome. Lucas took to Jeff from the outset because, as he had hopped out of the driverless, putting the Earlies rucksack on his back, Jeff had called out, 'Hi Lucas, the explorer.' Jeff had an easy manner, the antithesis of the groups they had seen in the back streets. He was cheerfully single, taught arts and metalwork in the local school – not described as a grammar academy Lucas noticed – and opened up his small house to a myriad of colourful characters. There were two teenage neutrals sharing the upstairs room. Lucas had not often seen neutrals in the Central Area, although he had heard talk of them. These young people looked like fun, he thought, with their bright red, green and yellow clothes, their long hair and ready smiles. There was another family, with twin baby girls, newly arrived from the Central Area and waiting for housing, camping in the back room.

The small lounge was at the front of the house, and when they arrived was inhabited by several cats. Noah was fascinated by these furry living playthings, and they entertained him while the family settled in. Jeff had provided sleeping mats and a pile of pillows and blankets which were to be brought out at night. Lucas and Noah would sleep top to tail, which sounded fun in daylight but proved less successful through the long night hours.

During their six-day stay with Jeff, patience was tested. They didn't sleep well, all packed into the one room, and although it seemed like an adventure, the insides of their heads became sore from lack of sleep so that each morning they felt worse than the night before. Even Lucas, who usually showed extreme equanimity, became short-tempered. Having said this, they battled on with their quest, visiting several potential employers, possible schools for the boys, and looking at accommodation.

They were completely unprepared for the way of life in the Periphery. Their comfortable lives in the Central Area had not equipped them for this. For them, the Periphery was simply an unknown fringe where people went and never returned. When parents raised a scintillated child, the Periphery was not talked about, and became an irrelevance.

Chapter 11

Alexandra Essex had submitted a literature request to the High Council Library for anything written by S. Herbert. She had also asked the Intern Pool to search the systems for any research by him, but they had drawn a blank. All that emerged were endless references to the work, but not the work itself. She had typed a sticky note reminding her to ask Michael when she eventually spoke with him. Surely, he would know where to find it? Meanwhile, she messaged Manya, but even her response was cryptic and unhelpful, saying that all copies had been destroyed for security purposes. Manya again urged Alexandra to visit the East with her. A date was set for the next week, as calendars were under less pressure in August. Alexandra was keen to see lessons in the Periphery schools, and Manya reassured her that in the Periphery, many services continued through the summer break, with schools opening every day for respite care, catch up classes, adult education and volunteer work. Alexandra had not seen this side of school-life, always having taught in grammar academies where the classrooms remained firmly shut through August, unless used by the Prophet Corporation Childcare programmes, which were money-spinners, mainly involving the supervision of children on Prexias.

After her recent tortuous trip to the West, she had decided to avoid the train, and had asked an Intern to book her a driverless from the Department. She chose to travel alone, and after a brisk walk, she swiped into the Department's Central London underground multi-storey. It was already hot; she did not enjoy the dry, stale heat of the city in August, and the air-conditioned garage for the driverless fleet was dim and cool. Her eyes adjusted and while she was scanning the rows of automatic electric vehicles, an early mechanic in overalls emerged. 'She's all ready for you,' he announced. 'Security and safety checks complete; just need your fob…' She thanked him, swiping the access pad which unlocked the doors and allowed her to programme her destination, which was the underground multi-storey in Cambridge. She would then travel through the gates at the Isle of Ely with Manya.

He peered in through the door saying, 'Have a good trip. You won't see me when you return. It's my last day today and I finish at 12.'

'Oh, have a good day,' she responded, automatically.

'Well, it's going to be hard. Travelling tonight to the Isle of Ely ready for my son to start school in the East next week.' His face was tense with worry. 'Don't know where we are going to live yet. They said to arrive and we will be allocated a cabin. I've worked here for ten years. Going to miss it.' His shoulders dropped and he slouched off, diminished, fearful. Alexandra put the code into the driverless and arranged her travel-coffee and cranberry yogurt beside her oat bagel. It was only when she was settled that his words registered, but it was too late to respond as he was disappearing sadly into the kiosk, ready for his final shift.

Did he know who she was she wondered? Would the driverless be safe? It wouldn't take much for a resentful parent to sabotage the usually mega-safe machine. She spent extra time checking the dash and the diagnostic lighting display but all seemed to be in order, so she thought no more of it, and the driverless launched, quickly building speed on the aerial expressway out of the capital, passing the City Airport and then heading north. Greater Southend was in her Area, so she often travelled out this way. The fences started at Maldon; it was messy, she thought, with outer Maldon being hers, feeding the Grammar Academy at Burnham-on-Crouch and the town school being Manya's. There had been so many letters of complaint from residents on both sides of the fences; a community divided they said, but the Periphery boundary had to start somewhere.

She opened her Prexia and searched the messages. Still no news of the S. Herbert research, so she sat back and began reading Michael's latest update from the North. The driverless performed impeccably and she was soon sailing through the outer suburbs of Cambridge. Although Manya's office and the Eastern Area Department was based in Cambridge, the schools in the vicinity were included in the Central Area. This had been agreed with senior academic figures long before Alexandra started teaching. It preserved Cambridge as an integral part of the Central Area, and allowed the officials managing services in the Eastern Periphery some comfort.

The driverless located the underground multi-storey and delivered her to the nominated parking space in very good time. She was familiar with the Cambridge offices and chose to walk around to the front of the building, pausing at the community garden which bounded the river. This small oasis of nature was valiantly clinging on, surrounded by noisy construction sites. The vast administrative blocks seemed to grow each time she visited.

Fortunately, she had arrived early, as the series of security checks, even for someone of her seniority, took an age. She eventually arrived in the busy reception area for EaSA, the main Eastern School Area offices.

Manya was visibly and genuinely pleased to see her; they hugged, and smiled, and behaved like two teenagers escaping from the classroom for the day. But the mood was not completely superficial as they both knew there was much to discuss while they were out of the prying eyes of Interns and officials. How far would they go? Each was nervous, and for different reasons. Manya still saw her friend and colleague as the ambitious but naïve new girl. She knew Alexandra had reached a level of knowledge of the programme which led to endless questioning, but she did not understand where her colleague's ethics lay. She wanted to chip away at the exterior and find out what she needed to share that would help Alexandra to continue in her role. It was in Manya's interests for there to be a strong Central Area of grammar academies as she was then left to work with the Eastern schools in her own way, unchallenged.

Alexandra approached the friendship with the assumption that the two were equals and that they shared certain basic beliefs about education that bound them together. She respected Manya's openness and had particularly valued the trusted interventions of a close colleague in her early days in the role. She wanted to ask Manya about the Herbert research, about scintillation, and she sought reassurance that she was identifying the right issues to put to Michael when they next met.

They set off for the Isle of Ely immediately, keen to maximise their time out in the Periphery. Unlike in the West, where the Marches formed a long, now heavily defended boundary, between the Central and West administrative school areas, the Isle of Ely was the only gate to the Periphery in the East. This was far from ideal. Recent clampdowns on security checks had minimised attempts by individuals to cross the high fences between Maldon and Ely, whereas the layered fences between Ely and The Wash had always been a more informal affair and so attracted criminals.

The border guards had been characteristically efficient through the night, and there were no queues, just a few stragglers; late and disorganised families with heavily loaded vehicles. Manya was telling her companion how, most recently in the East, hefty fines had been introduced deterring families from crossing in the daylight. The local councils liked to keep the clutter off the roads at peak times, and it gave some discipline to the potentially chaotic migrations, especially in August. As soon as the fines started, mass crossings became largely nocturnal, except for peak times. Alexandra thought of the parking attendant's hunched shoulders; tonight, he would be in the queues crossing, ready for the start of term next week. 'There is always increased volume in late August,' Manya commented, asking, 'Why don't they get their act together earlier, after all, parents have over three years to get used to the idea, and to plan.' Alexandra seized the opportunity,

'I have never understood why the Four Plus is scheduled so long after scintillation. I mean, all the pre-schools in my Area are mixed, which doesn't help transition into the grammar academies.' Manya had all the answers.

'Well,' she started, 'Firstly scintillation occurs before the melanin in the infant iris is sufficient to maintain the child's permanent eye colour, which is usually between about six and nine months old, and secondly, we cannot possibly maintain a funded school system any earlier than age four; it would simply be too expensive. So, the policy was agreed decades ago; scintillation (or not) by nine months and final grammar selection ready for a school start at age four.'

The driverless drew up at the first security barrier, and routine checks were undertaken which fast-tracked the two senior officials through the enormous gates. As the driverless slowly proceeded, threading its way through the checkpoints, security gantries and heaps of twisted metal, Alexandra studied the massive construction. The blackened lettering declared, 'You are now leaving the Central Area.' She noted the armed guards, alert and ready for the slightest unusual move.

As soon as they entered the Periphery the landscape changed. On this bright summer's day, it was already hot with the heady combination of the sun's rays and the pollution layers clinging to the earth's crust. Alexandra was surprised to feel immense relief once she was away from the high-rise skyline and the anthill of interminable urgency with its persistent pressures. She could detect that Manya relaxed once in the Periphery and commented on this. 'I love being out in the East,' Manya confirmed, 'Now, let's see my schools!'

Their first visit was to a typical primary school near the border, a "community school". Surrounded by a shanty town of tents and vehicles, the small dilapidated building appeared completely insufficient for the demand. As they parked and opened the driverless doors a stench rushed into the air-conditioned interior. Alexandra was used to this when she visited the Periphery, and reached for her neat white paper face mask. Her colleague offered a small minty pellet from a pocket-sized tin, which she took gratefully.

Manya seemed to have grown taller and more elegant out here, walking with poise and purpose, dressed not in the central fashion of tailored white summer-wear, but flowing in her loose Indian-style dress. Whilst Alexandra was encumbered with the face mask, her shoulder bag, her Prexia, security devices and office paraphernalia, Manya carried nothing. It was deliberate, she said, to put the families at ease.

The headteacher, a polished and beaming young man, lit up with joy on seeing Manya, and shook Alexandra's hand warmly, pumping it up and down.

They peered into an adult literacy class, with fifty or more parents packed into a small classroom, their children were running freely outside, some playing a makeshift football game, others foraging in the hedges and happily making dens under the trees.

The headteacher showed them the childcare with pride. Hordes of unscintillated children were busily playing in a brightly coloured and disorganised whirl. A group of older children were working on out-dated tablets, preparing posters to place around the shanty town. A tall, serious boy showed Alexandra his striking design, with the wording: 'Education is the most powerful weapon which you can use to change the world.' He explained that he had chosen to quote Nelson Mandela to inspire the parents to come to the summer classes at the school. His knowledge of the life of his hero was extensive, Alexandra was humbled; the stereotypes of unscintillated children which she had harboured for so many years were seriously challenged in the five minutes she spent listening to the boy. Manya smiled. She hadn't stage-managed her colleague's visit to the Periphery, but this was a helpful start.

As they walked across the playground, they carefully avoided straying too close to a group of children of various ages ranging from four to fourteen years old, who were painting a large mural with joyful enthusiasm. The two Interns who were supposed to be supervising were having as much fun as the children. A previously blank wall was being covered with a vast array of jungle animals now being surrounded by lush wet undergrowth. 'We have an artist in residence funded by the Department for one year,' the headteacher explained. 'This will be the infant playground next week. The children will be thrilled when they see this.' Art was no longer on the curriculum of Central Area grammar academies, although some older students could opt for Commercial Design in their final year.

They walked past a room filled with crates of food items, milk cartons, biscuits and tinned vegetables. 'What is this?' Alexandra asked curiously. The headteacher explained that the school recouped rejected food items from the nearby factories for distribution to the most-needy families. Cushioned by Central Area affluence, she had no idea that enterprises such as this existed.

After their tour of the school they landed in the headteacher's small air-conditioned office, the atmosphere enhanced by e-perfume in an attempt to overcome the background peripheral reek, but they were not able to stay because a nurse arrived with her collapsible digi-kit for weighing the babies and young children. A queue was already forming outside the door. The headteacher explained that on arriving from the Central Area children usually experienced rapid weight loss, as food was far less plentiful, and it took parents time to learn to cook from scratch. The Eastern Weight Measurement Programme funded a nurse two days a week to support families in keeping their children above the "emaciation" weight threshold. The nurse opened her suitcase to show them a variety of small demonstration baby products in vacuum packs, which had been rejected in the Central Area as "seconds". She gave the samples to her most-needy families and she stocked up from the depot up each time she visited Cambridge for meetings.

Finally, the headteacher took his visitors to a classroom where he had assembled six members of the School Council from the secondary school next-door. Manya knew that this was risky but had condoned his plan, provided the meeting was not recorded. The six students rose respectfully when Alexandra entered the room, and shook her hand politely, one by one, telling her who they were and what they hoped for. 'Good morning, my name is Ishmael, I am sixteen years old and was in the first unscintillated cohort. My parents brought me and my younger siblings to the East from London in 2068. I attended this primary school and then the High School over there,' he gesticulated out of the window, 'I am studying hard because I intend to qualify as a lawyer. It is my hope that I will be able to challenge the oppression of displaced families.' Alexandra shook his hand and forced a smile.

The headteacher facilitated a spontaneous question and answer session. Alexandra bravely asked the students if they could change anything in society, what it would be, nervously expecting them to say "scintillation" or to focus on unequal wealth. They surprised her by overwhelmingly advocating that all children in the Central Area should experience the rich and empowering education that they had received in the Periphery. They asked her whether she had any intention to review the curriculum in the Central Area, learning from the success of the Periphery. They were very well-informed. Again, this dumbfounded her as she had never even considered such a review. They asked what her aspirations were for the new generation of young adults coming through the education system, and then asked whether she thought that parents in the Central Area would welcome support in controlling the weight of their offspring through diet rather than only through the compulsory physical exercise programme in the grammar academies. She gave suitable bland on-message responses, and shook their hands with great relief when the time was up, thanking the keen headteacher for arranging such an enlightening visit.

'Let me take you for a coffee now,' Manya offered with a knowing smile, seeing her friend battle with the unexpected and possibly unwelcome revelations, and they returned to the driverless.

Chapter 12

The two women settled in the driverless, Manya quietly pleased at having disturbed her colleague's long-held assumptions, and Alexandra presenting a cool, detached demeanour while her brain was frantically generating questions. Manya programmed the driverless to accelerate to an independent diner nearby where she often picked up a coffee. The Prophet Corporation hadn't expanded into the East because customer buying power reduced once you left the borders of the Central Area. In the East, there were a few isolated Chateau-Privees in historical areas on the coast, where the original residents had purchased as many properties as they could, to fend off the encroaching tide of migrants. Manya knew there was a black market in scintillation from these areas, with illicit outward migration to the Central Area increasing, and she had decided to turn a blind eye at present. The driverless drew up outside the diner, which was hidden from the expressway and not frequented by migrants. They agreed to sit in, rather than take-away, and settled at a table outside in the shade.

'Well?' enquired Manya of her colleague.

'To be honest, I have so many questions that I am not sure where to begin,' Alexandra responded honestly, deliberately postponing a fuller response as she checked their itinerary, 'Did you say we would head for the coast this afternoon? Ideally I would like to back in London by the evening.' Manya described their next destination, a successful primary school near the coast which was bursting at the seams and where they would be able to see some summer holiday Four Plus booster classes. She explained that the large influx of migrants in the summer months meant schools struggled to accommodate so many new starters in September, and also that skilled counsellors were needed to support parents with displacement anxieties and anger management. She was proud of the East of England Counselling Service which played a major part in smoothing potential peaks in civil unrest and criminality, and wanted Alexandra to see it in action today. Manya explained how the displaced children from the Central Area generally arrived unprepared for the active learning of the Periphery, and booster classes helped them to acclimatise before the start of the new school year.

Their Blue Mountain Coffee arrived, steaming in china cups, which was quite unusual these days. They inhaled with a deep satisfaction and Manya coaxed, 'So, where shall we begin?' The cooler shade, the fragrant coffee and relief from the oppressive London air soothed Alexandra, who had not realised how stressed she actually was each day.

'It is good to take a step away from all the meetings and papers,' she started, thanking Manya for organising her visit. 'It puts things into perspective. I wanted to ask you about scintillation, how and why, but now I am more interested in the role you play out here in the Periphery. I had assumed the Central Area grammar academies were the pinnacle of the educational system. Their results are streaks ahead of all other schools, and they deliver annual cohorts of suitably prepared professionals into the labour market. In the Central Area, the Periphery is seen as second class, chaotic, and a place where those who are not blessed with academic potential can be accommodated en-masse. But this morning I have seen that this is not always the case. Manya, why are you are out here in the East, and what you are striving for?'

The question was carefully posed, to persuade Manya to talk openly, and Alexandra was not disappointed. 'I believe in the power of education to transform lives,' Manya began. Her glib and outmoded approach was not generally mentioned in the Central Area these days as education was clearly about building future success. She continued, 'Scintillation does us a favour in the Periphery. It removes the vast upper tiers of trainee bureaucrats from the picture so that we can work with the genuinely talented and aspirational youngsters, with the misfits and the thinkers, and with all those whose personal challenges, or circumstances, have meant that they cannot achieve at the high academic level expected in the Central Area. Here in the East, headteachers, teachers, psychologists and counsellors derive a deep fulfilment in picking up each rejected family and supporting them so that they can fly. My regional Board tracks long-term state benefit rates as our main success criteria. They start high, and massively reduce over time. All migrants arrive and claim benefits; there is little work for the parents out here. As families become established, the need for counselling reduces, our adult education service picks up the parents, whose lives can be turned around, and the children find their strengths through our less-oppressive curriculum. You will see this afternoon, the arts, and music play a huge part out here in the East. As children transfer on to their secondary school, they develop aspirations to greatness. Some falter, inevitably, and we have the support services in place for them, funded,' she added, 'by your Central Area Compensation Fund.'

They finished their coffee, and Alexandra contemplated Manya's upside-down world, where the dregs of society were seen as having the potential to rise above the levels of the superficial Central Area. 'So, you welcome scintillation?' she summarised.

'Well, it does us a favour out here! Now, come on Alex, let's see the sea!' They continued their conversation as the driverless made easy progress on the expressway to the coast. The toll system had been introduced in the early 2050s when tourists trouped out to see the spectacular views, the remaining wild birds and the quaint villages. There were no holidaymakers today, but the road was maintained through the tolls so officials like Manya could by-pass the clogged minor roads.

As the driverless skirted the migrant camps which had accumulated in a band close to, but not on, the coast of Suffolk, Manya showed her guest the prefabricated townships which were being built. Hundreds of pastel-coloured single-storey cabins were arranged in multiple rows around community buildings. Some were already inhabited. Others were nearing completion. But the driverless sped past these, off the expressway now, through some smaller villages, and into a town, drawing to an eventual halt right on the seafront. 'Have you ever walked along Southwold Pier?' Manya asked. Alexandra had not heard of Southwold. 'The pier is preserved for posterity. This is not really work,' Manya added, smiling, 'but I wanted you to breathe better air and see wider horizons…'

The driverless parked and the two immaculate women walked on to the ancient wooden structure, the waves of the sea pursuing their relentless obscure purpose under their feet, as they had done for nearly two hundred years since the steamships of the early 1900s. Alexandra turned and looked back towards the driverless, small and incongruous in the historical scene. She saw a mural on the back of the entrance to the pier. Screwing up her eyes she could make out a massive face surrounded by graffiti. 'Have you read anything by the writer George Orwell?' Manya asked, as the delicate flowing folds of her dress caught the gentle sea breeze, adding, 'The mural is a memorial to him, preserved from the early years of this century. In the East, teachers often use quotations from Orwell to prompt debate.' Betraying her experience in the legal system, she paused to recall his exact words, resuming, 'For example, "each generation imagines itself to be more intelligent than the one that went before it, and wiser than the one that comes after it".' Alexandra, who had not read anything written by Orwell, felt uncomfortably out of her depth, but smiled and grunted in vague appreciation.

Manya took her colleague's hand and gently ushered her around a preserved but boarded-up hut constructed of white clapboard sitting half-way along the pier. They now faced an odd metal structure about four metres high, supporting sculptured iron figures, topped with an old timepiece, frozen at twelve o'clock. It was a bizarre sight, partly vandalised, with twisted metal, grinning figures and the remains of a sculpted bath and toilet. Manya laughed, and explained that it was once a water clock; on the hour the copper figures used to pee into the toilet. She had seen footage of the clock working and said it was delightful. For Alexandra it symbolised the Periphery, odd, broken, and historical. She began to long for the predictability of the technologically advanced Central Area, despite the beauty of the vast blue horizon in front of them.

They reached the end of the deserted pier and stood together, two senior national figures who had momentarily escaped, looking out to sea, past the wind farm and the moving specks of shipping, towards the Netherlands, lost in their individual thoughts.

Manya's soft voice drew Alexandra's attention to the landward view. What had once been a string of gaily painted beach huts was now inhabited by squatters. These bedraggled migrants had travelled as far as they could, and were presented with the immense challenge of the ocean with its hidden security ring and surveillance systems linked directly to the High Council Coastal Enforcement Centre. As she peered through the intense sunlight, Alexandra saw two small children dressed in grey throwing pebbles into the sea, behind them were several roughly dressed figures shouting and piling something on to an old truck.

It occurred to her that there was no security here; they hadn't even needed to swipe their fobs to walk the on the pier. It was reminiscent of her childhood when free movement was taken for granted. She couldn't remember a time when children dug channels and built sandcastles on beaches, but she had seen nostalgic photographs, and she knew about the Scintillation Club Seaside Trips where the sand had been manufactured in Prophet Corporation Plants to assure its hygiene.

It seemed insensitive to ask about S. Herbert at such a beautiful moment, and Alexandra was just deciding where to begin when Manya broke the silence, gently quoting again from Orwell: 'If liberty means anything at all, it means the right to tell people things they do not want to hear.'

Manya confessed to her colleague, 'I asked the Intern to switch your challenges paper last week. Actually, I had to bribe him with a Chateau-Privee cappuccino; he was rather nervous. Alex, there is so much more to it. I wanted you to see and feel before diving into the debate. I am sorry, do forgive me?' The concept of forgiveness was not often used in the Central Area, and Alexandra needed to enter a dusty ethical chamber in her mind. Instinctively she knew that Manya had been right, and had been acting in the best interests of her friend.

The two women embraced, spontaneously, and then drew apart, pleasantly embarrassed, laughing conspiratorially. 'Of course, I not only forgive you, but thank you; I start to see now…' Alexandra spoke genuinely, in a voice she no longer used, overwhelmed by something she did not fully understand.

They walked comfortably together back along the pier, and took the driverless to their second school visit of the day.

Chapter 13

The afternoon is far from quiet and I can hear the continuous whine of driverless vehicles beyond the courtyard, as well as drones and air taxis above the flat. The high pitch troubles my ears, and I am feeling sick with anticipation as I take The Art and Science of Selection, by S. Herbert, from my pocket. The sun is high in the sky, visible through the bedraggled curtains, lighting up the dusty air in the flat. I know that this could be a seminal moment, not only for me, Zade, but for all those poor unscintillated children condemned to the Periphery.

I lay the flimsy publication on the kitchen table, and take a deep breath. The faded dark green cover is simple and indicates an academic pamphlet rather than a public document. Although the author is clearly announced as S. Herbert on the front, as I start to read the foreword, and flick gently through the pages, there is no mention of him, or her. The foreword is written by someone called Maximillian Morgan, and the final page is signed "MM", but there is no explanation of his role or identity.

I read on: 'The objective of the scintillation programme is to maximise academic achievement in the Central Area and thus improve productivity of the national powerhouse in the longer term.' There is a lot of unfamiliar jargon from the 2040s. On the second page, scintillation is explained: 'For academic potential to be formally and effectively assessed before entry to school, there needs to be an unequivocal indicator; scintillation provides simple visual proof. It therefore avoids any contention, and parents are forced to accept the designation of their children. Scintillation is derived from an analysis of the factors contributing to later success, primarily but not exclusively parental earning power.' I start to become interested; here is the root of selection to the grammar academies.

The text continues, 'Following detailed analysis of risk factors, it has been agreed by the Department of Future Success that only infants of medium to high earning parents will automatically proceed to the scintillation programme.' I am now alarmed; this document is justifying discrimination on the grounds of parental earnings. But it becomes even more unsettling: 'The following sub-groups have also been eliminated from the scintillation programme due to heightened risk-factors affecting chances of later success; all children in foster care, recent international immigrants, children identified with significant cognitive delay soon after birth...' the list ran on to half a page. It seems to me that through this propaganda, the state had ruled out the possibility of high academic performance by any child in groups statistically less likely to achieve highly in education. Surely not?

The most significant clue to the process of scintillation follows, as MM continues, 'The classified scintillation process is initiated by the Department for Future Success. Prompt weekly downloads of post-natal cohort risk data are shared with the Department for Wellbeing. This digital uploading process is automatic and will populate the Health database used to inform infant eye screening checks by one week old.' Reading ahead, I gasp audibly, although no one is present to hear or to see my stupefied anger: 'Wellbeing Officers routinely use Cyclopentolate to dilate the pupils in infant eyes during the one-week old eye screening process. Scintillation can only be achieved through a specific (classified) addition to the Cyclopentolate in the eye drops. Batches of scintillated drops are provided for babies designated by the Department for Wellbeing as "A" following digital upload from the Department of Future Success, and all babies not designated as "A" receive routine Cyclopentolate.'

The author then considers the possible impact of the policy, proposing actions to mitigate adverse publicity; not adverse effect on children or families, but adverse publicity! Whoever actually wrote this displays the classic weakness of a social engineer who fails to consider the impact of their policies on ordinary people.

If this pamphlet is authentic, it could provide vital evidence that the scintillation process is actually engineered by the state, but who will be interested to see it? Certainly not those currently presiding over education in the Central Area. The value of the pamphlet is undeniable. There will be many who would seek to destroy it, ironically it would have been incinerated had it not been for Sam thinking of me. I grab my phone, thankfully on maximum charge, and systematically capture images of the cover and each page, checking the wording is clear in each shot.

I had felt vulnerable before, due to being under-age and alone, due to the possible Landlord's Association visit, because I was illegally absent from school, and because I knew I held beliefs that were not encouraged by the Central Area establishment. Now I feel a hundred times more vulnerable; I have in my possession what seems to be an important piece of evidence which many people far more powerful than me might like to destroy.

Also, I am clearly a scintillated child, in foster care from birth; I know of no other child who has been fostered at birth who scintillates like me. As the pamphlet says, we are not designated as "A". Moreover, my eyes are unusually bright. I am a living antithesis of the policy. Who am I?

Chapter 14

I picked up a phone message from Sam earlier, asking me to come into the Advice Bureau this afternoon, and am treating it seriously as he hasn't messaged me like this before. I am curious, but wary. I secure the scintillation pamphlet and my personal documents in my rucksack, covering it carefully with old blankets in the back wardrobe. Before I slip out, I check my pockets thoroughly, choosing to travel light in case this is a trap; no paper identity on my person. Double-locking the door with my fob, not letting my nervousness get the better of me, I cross the courtyard quickly, trying to look innocent. I don't feel comfortable leaving the flat when so many people are on the streets; there are eyes everywhere.

It is refreshing to be out, despite the midday fug, and the wider horizon cheers me up. Lengthy incarceration in the dusty concrete casing of the flat can be depressing. Although being handed the information in the pamphlet, if it is genuine, was a massive breakthrough, I am finding my mind is going around and around in circles without making progress, as I try to solve the profoundly serious conundrum of scintillation.

Deliberately varying my route to the Advice Bureau, I choose to follow the path along the river past St Thomas's, where my life began, and across the barricaded Westminster Bridge. I dislike the heavy security measures here. I swipe my fob in front of the reader and the barrier rises automatically, the vast illuminated hoarding telling me that 100% of pupils in Central Area grammar academies achieved their expectations in 2080. As I walk across the bridge, I wonder if that really is good news, to share on a public bridge so close to the breathing heart of our democracy. After all, doesn't it suggest that expectations might have been too low? We are not meant to ask questions like that. I raise my arms as the android security guard scans and pats my pockets. Free to move again, I skirt the old Parliament buildings, cut across the green, past Westminster Abbey, and hurry to the Advice Bureau, with its blackened brick and boarded lower windows, appearing oddly historical nestled amongst the high-rise buildings. I feel more at home here.

As usual the corridors are full with raggedy customers; the residual and diminishing underclasses of London seeking help. I suppose that, as scintillation works its way through generations, the Central Area should see the underclasses gradually disappear as cohorts of new bright sparkling young people emerge. I push politely through, and am welcomed at the reception desk. 'Ah, Zade, excellent; Sam was asking after you. He said if you arrive, you must go to community room D on the first floor.' I thank the receptionist and take the stairs, wondering what or who I will find there. I knock on the door, and as it is opened, I can faintly smell violets, light and refreshing; reminiscent of a time lost. A volunteer, who I have seen on many occasions, invites me to sit down next to a very old and strangely beautiful lady.

'Zade, this is Danielle, she will not mind me sharing with you that she has recently celebrated her hundredth birthday! Danielle, this is Zade, who I was telling you about,' he speaks very slowly and plainly to the elderly woman.

Since the late 2040s, life expectancy has dropped dramatically. Scientists say this is the result of a combination of over-medication and air pollution, as well as euthanasia having been legalised, Lyn said to solve pension fund deficits. Obesity is definitely a factor in the Central Area, but not in the Periphery, where Lyn says people eat more healthily.

It is very unusual to see someone aged over a hundred these days, especially in London. I focus on her wrinkled face, her thin wrists and her pure white hair, so white that it looks unnatural. She is dressed in colourful layers of Lycrene, with scarves and ribbons, as if she is playing a part in a screen drama.

She holds her gnarled hands out to me, silver rings on her swollen fingers, and I respond in kind. She clasps my hands, smiling, and starts speaking in an unexpectedly sonorous voice, putting her infirmities to one side. 'Hello Zade, I was told by this charming young man that you are interested in the history of education, and I want to share some of my knowledge with you. I was a primary school teacher; I trained between 1998 and 2001, and taught for over forty years. By my reckoning I taught well over a thousand children, although I don't remember them all as well as I did in my younger days. What I do remember well is the rise of the academies, and the central grammar academies of the 2040s. I was an active member of my union, and we fought tooth and nail for our beliefs at the time, until we were outlawed, and that didn't stop us. I am too old for the fight now, but that doesn't prevent me speaking my mind to those who wish to listen.' She pauses for breath. She hasn't mentioned my eyes, like most people do, which I appreciate.

The volunteer raises his eyebrows in my direction, as if to say, is this okay? I nod. He tells us that he will leave us to our conversation, and will ask someone to fetch us a pot of tea. There is a digital display on the wall, which he switched off before we began talking, to reassure us of the informality of the occasion, but he flicks it back on now indicating the time and says clearly to Danielle, 'Your driverless is booked for three o'clock, in an hour.' We thank him and he departs. Danielle rises slowly, causing invisible strands of the gentle violet perfume to weave around me. She picks up her walking stick, which she pokes energetically at the switch for the digital display. It turns off, and the surveillance cameras stop buzzing. She seems incredibly independent for her age.

'Now, before I begin, tell me about yourself,' she invites. This makes me nervous, and to show willing I share the minimum, in a slow, clear voice; my name, my age, and that I am interested in finding out more about scintillation, for my studies....

Her eyes twinkle and she says, 'I have been tidying my books and papers. I gave several boxes of old things to the bookshop upstairs. Sam tells me he rescued a pamphlet which he gave to you.'

At this point a knock on the door announces the arrival of the tea, which is delivered by a young volunteer not much older than me, who shyly places the old tin tray beside Danielle. There is a cracked green china teapot with approximately matching cups and saucers, a milk jug, and a small plate of biscuits. 'Thank you; just how I like it,' she beams, patting the girl's arm. We are left alone once more, and she presses, 'So, you are not at school today?'

Can I trust this old dear? Can I trust the Volunteer Centre not to have a secret camera or recording device? On balance I decide that I can, and I explain my position to her, 'I haven't attended school for over a year now. To be honest, I learn more on my own, from my time in the Biblio. I read, I observe, and can therefore hang on to my clarity of thought. The grammar academy didn't suit me.' Lowering my voice, and placing my mouth by her scented ear, I add, 'What they teach is indoctrination.' She has no difficulty hearing this, perhaps because she is in tune with my struggle, and she nods and chuckles.

I am used to fighting secretly, and to concealing my anger. I am used to a solitary and unsupported existence, so when she speaks kindly to me, washing volumes of empathy over me as she prepares my cup of tea, I am surprised. It is nice.

'Now Zade, let me talk. You will have questions, but let me talk… In the 2020s the academy programme gained momentum with more and more Council schools converting to become academies, either voluntarily or being forced because they were not deemed good enough. Imagine, back in those days Central Area teachers were very morally driven. They wanted to make a difference to children's lives, to open doors for them, to share their passions for art, for literature, for history, their fascinations with numbers, and their desire to solve problems to make the world a better place. The teaching profession had always been spirited, as long as I can remember, and when the Government of the day, like the High Council now, started to control the content of the curriculum, earlier than the 2020s, disaffection set in. Many teachers left the profession each year. Children, especially older students, were bored, and behaved badly. Schools, including academies, became stressful places, and there were big problems with absence from school and forced exclusions, when headteachers banned disruptive young people from the classroom.'

She reached her hand out towards me, and continued, 'Some schools closed on Friday afternoons in protest at under-funding to address these issues. The toxic mix, combined with the increasing control of academies by highly paid bureaucrats, meant that things built up to a head. Drugs and knife crime were rife then, especially in cities. I was teaching in the South of England at the time. Even in primary schools, some young girls and boys secretly carried knives, bullying was an everyday occurrence, desperate children harmed themselves when they were alone, and those with genuine learning needs were often excluded. Despite the Government's attempt to reorganise assessment, pupil achievement in secondary and primary schools plummeted. Too many schools were inspected as "inadequate" caught in a downward spiral.'

These historical events are obviously still very real in her mind and I can understand the anger in her face as she paints the picture for me.

'So, once the High Council was formed in the early 2030s, they acted swiftly. The politicians in power had gained increasing control in the Central Area, and the concept of the "Periphery" emerged. Even before scintillation, there was a steady migration to the Periphery as laws were tightened in the Central Area.

'The Department for Future Success was the brainchild of Maximillian Morgan, a wealthy businessman who had amassed personal wealth as a director of the Prophet Corporation, and then moved on to running his own concerns, which included turning around failing academy trusts by employing unqualified teachers who were ex-military and ex-police officers. My view is that he started the repression in schools. He controlled the curriculum and examination arrangements in the Central Area, outsourced contracts to his own companies, and turned the whole experiment into his good news story. The trouble was that teachers, like me, could see through the sham that it was. Children were not being educated; they were being controlled. It made me sad and angry at the time, and still does so now.'

She continues, checking I am still attentive, 'Experienced teachers like me chose to move to the Periphery where we were left to our own devices. There we were not only free to teach what we believed in, and what we knew gave our children the best tools for their future lives, but we could teach real children, not the drugged automatons in the Central schools. Morgan only controlled the Central Area. That was our saving. The biggest barrier to his success was that, however he organised schooling and assessments, children from poorer families didn't achieve highly enough. He tried many techniques, but the Periphery always topped the league tables for this. These "tables" named and shamed schools with the worst examination results. Until he altered the calculations underpinning the tables, schools in the Periphery in the 2040s were always at the top. He was also concerned that...'

She pauses to drink her tea, offering me the plate of biscuits. 'He was concerned that there were groups of pupils who he didn't want in his Central Area schools because they caused trouble and didn't achieve as well as their more wealthy and obedient friends. He worked closely with the Department for Wellbeing and in the 2050s he introduced the pupil medication programme, using products from his chemical plant on the East coast. This programme is still used in the Central Area today. His Corporations then compulsorily bought up all the smaller Academy Trusts in the Central Area and he formed one massive Trust, which became CenSA. At this time many of the local trusts shifted to the Midlands and the North, to preserve the schooling they believed in. This is why the current rebellion in the North is holding so firm.

'Then, in the 2060s he introduced the Four Plus and converted all his trust schools into primary and secondary grammar academies, using his ground-breaking scintillation programme as the selection mechanism, and you are a product of that.' She stops; she is still feisty at her age, but now looks utterly exhausted. It is as if she is apologising to me for the proliferation of a system which she has not been able to prevent.

Her words land in my receptive mind and begin to ferment. I realise how ashamed I feel as a willing participant in Maximillian Morgan's social experiment. Now, instead of feeling shame, I know I must act, but how?

She finishes drinking her tea, and seems to be revived, asking me, 'Zade, do you want to know anything else; I will answer if I can?'

My brain is aching; I need more time to think about all of this. I have one crucial question: 'Is Michael Morgan anything to do with Maximillian?' She nods, 'He is his son.'

I am about to ask about the pupil medication, and how he engineered scintillation, but the volunteer returns to collect Danielle for her driverless taxi and there is not enough time. I squeeze her hand and thank her as she hobbles out of Meeting Room D. She winks at me and presses something into my hand; something small and hard wrapped in paper. I think it may be an old-fashioned sweet. and I slip it into my pocket after they leave, along with the remaining biscuits.

Chapter 15

There was no need for Education Enforcement Officers in the Periphery, but a large service of over three hundred trained employees worked for CenSA and liaised closely with the Police and Crime Commissioners in the Central Area. In addition, a recruitment round had been initiated by Sue Sutton to boost capacity in the North. The advertisement, which was circulated to all grammar academy leavers through the newsfeed, asked, 'Do you value the integrity of your education? Could you apprehend those who do not?' and continued by stating, 'If you enjoy playing e-games like Ace Detective or Border Enforcer, and you have an appetite for discipline, look no further…this job is for you.'

Many of the Enforcement Officers were school-leavers who were not only cheap to employ, but who valued the prestige associated with such a position. They were encouraged to defend the grammar academy ethos with a zealous enthusiasm. Central Area Enforcement Officers for Education, Parking, Waste, and a number of other high profile potentially anti-social activities, were provided with smart black creaseless uniforms, the latest technology in stab protection vests, and state-of-the art protective helmets. The main tool of their trade was the Prexia. They simply acted as a physical presence out on the streets and had legal powers to enter homes, reporting illicit activity through the dedicated confidential reporting mechanism, which in Education, was called "CenSAForce". They were not armed, but carried a standard self-defence pack provided by the Police and Crime Department. This included the latest in stun weapons made by Taser Technology, various canisters of gases, and shrill alarms to be set off in an extreme emergency. The pack acted as an incentive to new recruits who revelled in testing out the various items, which were only available to Enforcement Officers and the Police.

Access to CenSAForce was strictly controlled, and was coordinated in a command room at the Department for Future Success. Here, banks of screens displayed colour-coded cases in real-time, as they were entered by Enforcement Officers out in the field. Red denoted urgent cases which were added at the top of the priority waiting list. Amber indicated that a case could wait, and black was used for serial offenders. Live data informed managers how many red cases were being addressed and daily targets were set on the officer's individual screens and personal Prexias.

There was once a green category for investigations that would be likely to result in no further action, but as workload increased and Enforcement Officer capacity diminished, cases in this category simply accumulated on lengthy virtual lists. This had led to large backlogs which were officially written-off after six months. In 2078, the Statutory Instrument was amended, and the green category was removed completely.

The fervent and forbidding Education Enforcement Officers were allocated a daily caseload through a completely different system called "CATCH" which had been developed by the Department for Wellbeing. A public portal encouraged good neighbours to report any illegal education activity on the grounds of "unhealthy behaviour". It was surprising how many referrals came through this route, although many resulted in no further action because they were either vindictive, or by the time an Enforcement Officer scheduled a visit, the family had disappeared. Office-based administrative staff attempted to filter these out, resubmitting only bona fide cases to the system.

The vast majority of referrals to the service were from attendance officers in the grammar academies themselves. Many related to families attempting to circumvent the Four Plus, such as through false scintillation. A considerable number of families, who were desperate to remain in the Central Area, resorted to illegal use of a range of black-market scintillation products for their four-year-olds. These were sold in the digital underground at exorbitant rates but did not produce convincing results.

Other cases related to pupils, particularly older teenagers, refusing their medication and absconding. Absence from grammar academies was forbidden unless in the case of severe illness. There was also an increasing line in detecting unscintillated teenagers who had obtained illegal places at the grammar academies at the age of fifteen or sixteen, and who had returned from the Periphery to re-join family members, once the scintillated eyes of their peers faded.

In recent years, the underground home education movement had strengthened. It had been illegal for parents to withdraw their children from school in the Central Area for many years, but some had persevered, especially when younger children did not scintillate. Home education of unscintillated children in the Central Area was punishable by deportation to the Periphery and large fines. Parents were often unable to pay these, and so had monthly levies removed from their benefits to cover the debts until they were fully paid several decades later. The underground home education movement had documented cases of malnutrition, and even death, of infants resulting from the effects of this lengthy debt-recovery system.

Enlightened parents, who were dedicated to home-educating their children, tended to move to the Periphery voluntarily as there were support services in the West, the East and the South West enabling such practices to proceed in harmonious liaison with local schools. These teams were funded through a historical grant from the Central Area to the Periphery called the "Peripheral Relocation and Home Education Fund". Recent attempts to introduce a complete ban on home education in the North were faltering due to fierce opposition from voluntary bodies including the Northern Home Education Alliance, hence the latest recruitment drive focusing on the North.

The motivational motto, signed off by the Department for Future Success, had been devised by the Education Enforcement Office managers. It was proudly emblazoned on all messages sent by the service, "efficient and sufficient".

Zade Better-Smith had been listed in the CATCH system by her Grammar Academy Attendance Officer, but, as an "amber" case which was now over a year old, had been dropped down the list and then deleted as having timed out. Her grammar academy had taken her off their roll to avoid being fined for her absence by the Department for Future Success.

The Department for Social Welfare, which operated separately, had coded Zade as "FP" which denoted a foster child in the Periphery.

So, as an individual, she was genuinely off-the-radar at present. However, the Landlord's Association was working through repossessions, and Lyn's rented flat had risen to the top of the ever-growing list.

Chapter 16

Alexandra was sitting in her office high above Great Smith Street, dressed in an impeccably cut light-blue linen suit in readiness for the heat of the day. She was preparing for the week ahead but was dogged by nagging doubts prompted by her visit with Manya to two schools in the East in August. She was convinced that her colleague, friend and confidante had deliberately tried to open her eyes to the hidden successes of the two Periphery schools which they visited. However, she remained adamant that her clean, organised grammar academies, with their rigour and exceptional pupil data, embodied Michael's vision, the High Council's vision, to build successful schools ready for the approaching twenty-second century. Manya's schools were still operating to an out-dated model. On reflection, when out in the East, she had seen dirt-ridden overcrowding, and a curriculum that was far too focused on enjoyment to produce the workforce of the future. This said, the visit had unsettled her.

She studied her packed calendar for the week ahead, thinking that she would need to take stamina pills, and retrieved the blister pack from her bag, swallowing two with the Intern's apology of a coffee. The first week of term in September was always busy, she reflected. Today she was opening a new school out towards Watford, followed by attendance at a senior Education Enforcement Manager's presentation back at the Department, two routine meetings in the late afternoon, and then her long-awaited appointment with Michael Morgan at the end of the day.

A group of middle-ranking officials and two security guards accompanied her, in a driverless mini-coach, to the magnificent new buildings of the Secondary Grammar Academy LXIV, Outer London. Earlier in the century, academy trusts had grown in an ad hoc manner and had been named with a confusing multitude of aspirational words and phrases, but when the High Council approved amalgamation of all trusts in the Central Area, forming the CenSA Grammar Academy Trust, it was decided to name all Central schools in a less emotive and more business-like manner, and Roman numerals had been officially adopted for all CenSA academies.

The expressway was slow due to the extra security checks required at the start of term. Doting parents did not trust their scintillated progeny to the Academy Transport until they had settled into their new schools. As a result, in early September, there were thousands of extra vehicles on the expressways at the start and end of the day.

Arriving with seconds to spare, she strode with dignity to the podium where the new headteacher, aglow with pleasure at this long-awaited opening ceremony, welcomed her publicly. 'On this special day for the Secondary Grammar Academy LXIV, I am delighted to share the stage with Alexandra Essex, School Commissioner for the High Council, in the Central Area. If it had not been for her vision and drive, this school would not be ready for you today,' he announced.

She puffed up with pride and addressed the staff, the students, the front row of parents who had paid for their seats, and the newsfeed journalists standing around the edges of the vast school hall. She was not overwhelmed by the rows and rows of polished young faces, all scintillating; showing their potential to shine, all drilled through seven years at their primary grammar academies, each one appearing attentive and supremely ready for the academic year ahead of them. The Academy was opening with two cohorts of a hundred and eighty students, and would grow until 2084 when it would be fully operational.

'You have been chosen for greatness,' she began confidently, rattling out the mantras of the Department for Future Success. 'The High Council has invested over £100 million sterling in this magnificent Secondary Grammar Academy; your Grammar Academy. You will benefit from amazing state-of-the-art facilities, the latest in individualised Prexia technology, extensive laboratories for developing commercial acumen, the Cutting Edge hospitality training facility, classroom suites providing individual study screens, a highly sanitised Health Suite for medication purposes, and this fully air-conditioned examination hall, where you can meet together as an Academy, to hear key messages as you are today. Here you will spend five years preparing for your professional and academic future so that you can return our investment in you by becoming adults for future success. The future is in your hands.' There followed not only the expected wave of applause, rhythmical and reassuring, but three hundred and sixty pairs of glittering eyes closed and opened, closed and opened, in the required and startling adulation.

During the applause, Alexandra spotted a small disturbance near the back of the hall. A student was becoming agitated and started shouting. She caught two repeated words piercing the drumming of the applause, "exploitation" and "suffocation", the fighting talk of the education underground. A security guard swiftly intervened and injected the offender, who fell immediately unconscious and was briskly removed from the hall. The headteacher bent towards her and whispered,

'We anticipate a few of those; he refused medication this morning...' and she smiled with understanding, impressed by the prompt action taken to remove the offender.

On the driverless mini-coach travelling back to the office, she continued to attempt to obtain the S. Herbert research before she spoke with Michael later, but she still could not locate it. She began to wonder if there was a conspiracy.

They arrived back at the Department and she took the lift up to her office where an Intern was preparing for the Education Enforcement presentation in five minutes time. Alexandra lacked detailed knowledge of this one of the many services under her leadership, but she found the manager, Stacey (she couldn't remember her surname) to be brusque, verbose and sometimes unintelligible, so she was not looking forward to the next hour and a half.

While the attendees arrived and fussed with bags and Prexias, slowly assembling around her meeting table, she placed her light blue linen jacket on the back of her chair, excused herself, and headed for the Intern pool downstairs. She caught as many Interns as she could and galvanised them into further searches for the S. Herbert material. She really needed to locate it. She visited the bathroom, freshening up and spraying a top-of-the range fragrance liberally over herself to combat Stacey's cheap perfume, and returned to the presentation. It proved to be as tedious as she feared, and she didn't learn much more than she knew already. The Education Enforcement Officers did seem to be vital for maintaining order, and expansion into the North was inevitable. If high standards were to be maintained, attendance and participation must be controlled. After a dreary ninety minutes, the guests departed and she switched on her screen-share ready for an hour with the Finance Officer, directly followed by an hour with a colleague from the Promotional Data department who talked her through the end of year results, and how they were planning to present them to Michael ready for Scrutiny in the High Council Committee in October, before the usual displays in public places.

Alexandra was proud of her work ethic, her ability to think on her feet, and her endless capacity for assimilating widely varied subjects in short periods of time. She organised her days like a clockwork toy, wound up and ready to run, but by the end of this afternoon, she needed a breather, and some space, to prepare for her conversation with Michael. Avoiding various people who were hoping to catch her for a quick word, she took the glass lift down to street level, scanned out of the building and headed for the Chateau-Privee at the end of the street.

Chapter 17

I am returning from my meeting with Danielle, the centenarian, and am entering the familiar courtyard in front of Lyn's flat, when I suddenly become aware of three uniformed and helmeted but unarmed Property Enforcement Officers clumsily inserting a crowbar into my front door. Splinters of the old wooden door frame are spraying across the paving stones and the hinges are tearing from the screws which have held firm for a century.

'Hey, stop that,' I call, flashing my eyes at each of them as they turn, startled. I can see from their build, and through the visors of their helmets, that two of them are women which may be my saving grace. I approach them conveying supreme confidence. 'What's going on?' I demand. 'Who ordered this?'

They draw out their Prexias, and access the system. 'Landlord's Association; vacant property,' one of them reads out.

'Well, you can see it is not vacant,' I assert. I know that they are unlikely to ask me for my documents because of my eyes. While the scintillation lasts, I have my own in-built branding, proving my social acceptability. 'Go back to your office and check the system, but re-attach my door before you leave,' I order, adding, 'I'll get my parents to contact your office.'

One of the women comes over to me and gently takes my arm. 'Sorry love, we'll check,' she reassures me. As the other two officers find tools and screw the door back in place, she asks curiously, 'Why aren't you at the grammar this afternoon? Where is your school uniform?' Thinking on my feet I say, accurately,

'It's in the wardrobe,' adding the lie, 'I'm on work experience today. I'll show you.' I don't want her to cross the threshold. Taking control, I ask her to wait while I fetch it. I need to prove my legitimacy, to reassure them and for them to leave, promptly. I dive inside, retrieve the old grammar uniform, shaking it violently to remove any dust, and reappear in the doorway. She glances at the badged blazer, the shirt, the trousers, and is satisfied. They check the door latches and all three slope off.

My heart is beating faster than it did after I once ran a marathon at the grammar academy. My lips are dry. I fight tears, and win. Keeping my head as cool as I can, I throw the uniform on a chair, scan each room with a sad nostalgia, and unearth my rucksack from under the blankets. I knew this moment would come sooner or later, and it is a relief in many ways. They will, of course, return, maybe even today, and they may alert the Education Enforcement Service.

Living with the constant nagging threat of being discovered, and losing my freedom, is crippling.

I relocate all documents, the pamphlet, my cross in its box, the St Thomas letter, to the zipped pocket in my coat, and firmly re-tie the rucksack. I pause, asking myself what I have forgotten, indulging in a final few minute of peace. I stuff my uniform into a refuse sack, not wanting them to use it to identify who was living here.

Lyn's flat has served me well, but it is time to go. I close the door for the final time and walk briskly towards the river.

I dispose of the refuse sack containing my uniform in someone's bin store, under some relatively clean bags of rubbish awaiting nuclear incineration. I wipe my hands on my coat and stride along the pavement, my rucksack on my back, hiding my eyes under my black peaked hat. I have a pair of dark glasses handy to wear during school hours. I just want to minimise suspicions. The traumatic and unexpected situation at Lyn's flat has taken it out of me and I head for the Chateau-Privee where I will eat and recharge my batteries.

Crossing Lambeth Bridge, I join the river of scintillated children returning routinely from school, all with nice homes to go to, all loved and comfortable, but without the joy of learning in their eyes which Danielle had talked about. Our earlier meeting didn't seem like the same day. I am thinking once again of William Blake's mind-forged manacles, and am again hastening past the street-sleepers sitting now begging on the benches in the park. This time my mind is in turmoil.

Reaching the Chateau-Privee, sweating from the necessity of wearing my coat on such a hot afternoon, I stand tall, swipe in, and make my way through the throng of chattering executives holding late-afternoon informal meetings. I collect the cheapest and most nutritious-looking sandwich and a coffee, swipe my payment and land with relief at a small table in the corner by the electricity supply. I take off my heavy rucksack containing all that I own, and rest it carefully against the mirrored wall, setting up my phone to charge as I have a chance to do so. I sigh with a strange mixture of relief, anxiety and anticipation of something unknown. I feel uneasy about the unknown journey ahead of me. It is certainly good to take stock, and I begin to plan my next move.

At that moment my attention is drawn to stylish businesswoman, who I think I have seen here before, in an impeccably cut light-blue linen suit, immersed in a phone call on her state-of-the-art Haptic device. I am alerted to her presence because I think I hear her mention the name S. Herbert, and this is confirmed as she says, 'No, no, it's about the Four Plus; I need it for my meeting with Michael at six. It is by someone called S. Herbert.' She has not taken the precaution of removing the identity badge attached to her jacket. It broadcasts to anyone mindful to read it that she is Alexandra Essex, the CenSA Commissioner, and she is talking about a meeting with Michael Morgan, son of Maximillian. I reflect that opportunities often place themselves in my way at the most unlikely moments. Trusting my instincts, while she signs off from her call, I calmly poke my fingers into the zipped pocket of my coat and draw out the pamphlet allegedly by S. Herbert. Without a further thought I remove my glasses and my hat, turn my eyes in the direction of one of the six most influential Education leaders in the country, and strike.

'Excuse me. I couldn't help hearing the name S. Herbert and wondered if you might be searching for this, The Art and Science of Selection?' Her face displays extreme disbelief. She looks at the pamphlet, and at my alluring eyes, and back at the pamphlet and asks crisply,

'Who on earth are you?'

Chapter 18

When it becomes clear that I am not prepared to part with the pamphlet without some tough negotiation, Alexandra Essex invites me up to her office in the tall building of the Department for Future Success in Great Smith Street. She is very taken by my eyes, and I know they are helping to persuade her to engage with me. It is really unfortunate that I am burdened with a large rucksack and heavy coat, but I am making light of this. My baggage is being taken into the guarded cloakroom near the entrance, and I am holding the pamphlet in my hand. Now my photograph is being taken and I am issued with a time-limited access pass linked to hers. We move into the lift, and she asks me how I came to have a copy of the pamphlet in my possession. I simply say that it was rescued when a very old lady was clearing out her books and papers. As the lift passes through a series of floors, I ask her if she knows who really wrote the pamphlet. She has no idea, except for Herbert. When I quietly mention Maximillian Morgan, she is stunned. She not only looks beautiful, smart and successful, but she smells delightful. I feel very clumsy alongside her.

We are inside the warren of desks and offices, glass panels and people looking busy. On entering her office, she overrides the auto-record system, effectively switching off the recording of our conversation. It is now close to 5pm and she tells me that she must attend an important meeting shortly. She doesn't mention Michael Morgan but I know, from overhearing her call, that she is meeting him at six. I can see she doesn't trust me and I begin to question my recent actions. There is only one exit from her office and I could easily be apprehended. I don't reveal my anxiety, and respectfully wait for her to begin a conversation.

'So, who are you, and what will it take to persuade you to part with S. Herbert's pamphlet?' she begins.

I find, honesty can cement a tricky relationship, and that is what I opt for on this occasion. 'My name is Zade. I was fostered from birth, which is why I have no fixed surname. I don't know how I came to be a scintillated child; it shouldn't have been possible. My most recent foster carer was Lyn Better-Smith. She was…' I started to say "forced" but decided it might antagonise my illustrious companion, so continue, 'She migrated to the Periphery with her daughter who failed the Four Plus, and so I was left behind.'

Alexandra seems interested, asking, 'How long have you been living alone?' and I tell her well over a year, nervously aware that she is ultimately in charge of the Education Enforcement Officers. I then decide to demonstrate my knowledge. I don't want her regarding me as some poor waif or stray.

'This is tricky for me because you are the Director of the CenSA Grammar Academy Trust, nearly 10,000 schools, and soon you may be Director for the North too. It is tricky because I know from first-hand experience that your grammar academies are...' I force myself to avoid using stronger language, '...are a sham. You will know that all pupils are regularly drugged, through the legalised medication programme, to control their behaviour. This results in living human beings becoming drug-dependent automatons. From my years being taught in grammar academies, I can say that your curriculum is indoctrination. It may work for batches of young people destined to become passive professionals, officers, academics, but it did not work for me. I have learnt more about Shakespeare from spending hours in the Biblio, more about our country's wealth of literature, and history, from reading by torchlight.'

My words tumble out uncontrollably as, given this opportunity, and in the heat of the moment, I lose my restraint. Surprisingly, what could have become a tense conversation leading to me being unceremoniously bundled out of her office, starts turning into something delicately meaningful. She listens to me, staring deeply into my scintillating eyes.

'I have visited the Periphery,' I add, 'And the schools there are far more alive with aspiration than in CenSA. I have seen a Periphery school bursting at the seams as more and more rejects are sent away from the prosperous Central Area. The schools out there are more like community hubs, supporting parents to rise out of their poverty. They have such a tough job, but they are more successful than here.'

'I, too, have seen this,' she responds unexpectedly.

'So,' I wind up, pulling her into my argument, 'We both want to understand how this situation came about, and you think that S. Herbert can provide the answer. Having read through the pamphlet, which seems to be written by Maximillian Morgan, Michael Morgan's father, and Michael's predecessor who established the Department for Future Success, I now want to find answers to my questions about scintillation...'

'Yes,' is her simple answer, as she processes this conversation. She continues, 'You know more about me, and my work, than I know about you. I can promise you one thing in exchange for the copy of the pamphlet. I can find out for you who your parents are, or were, if you are willing to lend me S. Herbert.'

She had not only listened to me, but she had quickly pinpointed my one major personal vulnerability, and is prepared to exploit it. She has won me over with her astute offer.

I hold my hand out to her, my rough swarthy hand clasping her thin white manicured fingers. We shake in agreement and I pass the precious pamphlet into her care.

'Thank you Zade,' she says softly. 'I give you my word that I will return it to you.' We agree that we will meet again in the Chateau-Privee tomorrow at 5pm.

As she walks me down the corridor to the glass lift, and accompanies me to the guarded cloakroom, she tells me a little about her recent visit to the East, and a student who was making posters to display around the school to encourage parents to attend the adult education classes. Arriving at the cloakroom she says, 'His poster quoted Nelson Mandela, 'Education is the most powerful weapon which you can use to change the world.'

She watches me out of the security zone and does not return upstairs until I am on the pavement with my baggage.

'Education is the most powerful weapon which you can use to change the world,' I reflect, wondering if the great Nelson Mandela ever envisaged such deliberate and endemic misuse of the powerful weapon as I was seeing in the Central Area. And I have just met the person with the influence to change that. Wow.

My next challenge is to find somewhere safe to spend the night.

Part 2

Chapter 19

I know that I must enter the Underground tonight. I have been down there before to meet friends, on two occasions, but not to sleep myself. It is a daunting place, mainly because of the six-hour lock-in down in the bowels of the city. I put on my dark glasses as it is certainly not the place for scintillated children like me to be visible. Sam has told me about the voluntary patrols policing the underground at night. In fact, he used to volunteer down there himself until he got his job in the Prophet Café. He said to make sure that you get a spot near the patrol assembly point, and check your electricity is working before you settle, as the power cables down there are old and unreliable. He also says don't use the toilets. There is limited plumbing and up near the surface levels, the bucket facilities are said to be appalling. Underground wash-room attendants are at the very foot of the social hierarchy, but are the hardest-working in one of the most unpleasant jobs in the City.

The overnight sleeper system is first-come, first-served, and so the earlier that you go down, the better chance you have of securing a decent berth for the night. The gates close to entrants at midnight and open again from 6am. A few stations offer a free-flow sleeper service for night-workers, through a guarded revolving door, but not Embankment where I am heading.

Westminster is best avoided because of its proximity to the new High Council building; I have seen streams of frustrated activists disappearing noisily down the steps at twilight, and I have heard that an angry underclass causes trouble there. I am walking towards the Embankment now. I know that the upper-level platforms are close to the surface and better for casual sleepers like me.

Single people not dressed in the silver and gold of the executives, carrying lumpy canvas bags and weary from endless nights of semi-sleep, lurk nearby hoping for an early opening time. You can never be sure when the disused stations will open, as the arrangements are discretionary and opening times depend upon the beneficence of the night warders. It is the closing times that are set, and rigidly adhered to. There are frightening tales of weary "new sleepers" trapped down there all day without air. The terms and conditions specify that you enter at your own risk, and emergency services refuse to go down while the underground is locked during the day. I am told that people are left to suffocate, and the bodies are removed before the gates open again in the evening.

Even at a distance, I can hear the metal grills in the disused station being dragged back with squeals and groans. As I turn the corner, I see warders in boiler suits entering their security booths ready to oversee tonight's nocturnal hibernation of the homeless, but not completely destitute, masses. Daylight is fading, and I really don't want to be on the streets after dark, prey to the gangs. I join the queue for the android body and bag scan, lowering my eyes so the cameras do not detect my scintillation. There are four old androids stationed where the ticket barriers used to be. I remove my coat and place it in a tray with my rucksack and it trundles through the scanner. The android's makeshift hands slowly pat my head, my shoulders, my body, hovering over rectal and genital areas in case of hidden packages, my thighs, right down to my feet. The warders watch the screens. Once I am cleared, I can collect my belongings. Mercifully the rudimentary scanning equipment didn't reveal the emergency food bars stashed deep in my rucksack, or I would have lost those to the charity collection which re-uses any legal contraband.

Where there used to be maps of the underground network on the walls, there are now posters declaiming, 'Zero tolerance; no children, no food, no drugs, no alcohol, no weapons.' You can bring bottled water down, that's all. I swipe my fob across the reader pressing the button for one night, which costs five pounds sterling, and a digital ticket appears on my phone, once I have agreed the terms and conditions. For some reason the system hasn't clocked that I am under-age. I guess it is "purchasing technology" rather than "surveillance technology" that is in use down here.

I join the mass of weary people riding the ancient escalator which takes them into the bowels of London, reading the homespun notices posted down the walls, which now replace the illuminated advertisements of the 2070s. Unknown voices form an eclectic poem of the underground: "conception aids", "reclaimed accommodation available now, call me", "Inner London Neutrals Association meets every Wednesday at 7pm, Prophet Café on The Strand", "life-prolonging essential oils", "need an abortion, contact us", "invest wisely" and "funeral plans; put your loved-one's anxieties to rest". The last one is a covert advertisement for euthanasia.

Reaching platform level, I breathe in shallow gasps as I acclimatise to the heat and the rank stench of living bodies sweatily impregnated with the pollution of the streets above. Without trains to circulate the air anymore, the atmosphere is endemically stale. They say that when you breathe down here the air has already passed in and out of the lungs of thousands of people. This is why they use grills and not security doors, in a feeble attempt to introduce freshness while we sleep.

It is as Sam described; the platform is used as an orderly walkway, overlooked by a bullet-proof cabin, which is a purpose-built assembly point for the patrols. The people settle where the tracks used to be in delineated rectangles; they are called the "new-sleepers", not "the poor", "the desperate" or even "the underclasses", but the "new-sleepers". The irony is not so funny when you are faced with a night down here. Each rectangle has a power ring; this is how they justify the cost by saying that it pays for the electricity. The old underground lines were purchased after the closure of the network, and are owned by separate companies. The newsfeed recently looked into the Prophet Company's bid to take over the running of them all, but although they do seem to turn a nightly surplus, especially in winter weather, apparently the margins were not attractive enough. The underground "new sleepers" are a London phenomenon, due to overcrowding as scintillated children grow up and seek work. Many other cities have partially emptied due to the migrations, so housing isn't such an issue elsewhere.

I clamber down into the disused track bed and place myself in a fairly clean empty rectangle, one that does not smell of urine, immediately opposite the security cabin, testing the power supply, which seems to work okay. There is no need for bedding because it is so hot. I set my rucksack up as a pillow and lie on my coat. Already, in the dim security light, I can see lines of supine figures holding devices which are draining the power supply. They are charging Prexias, and old-style phones, from the power ring, as well as the sophisticated Haptic devices, and they have their own personal lights. A man is shaving. Two companions are playing a game with one Prexia illuminated between them. Many use headphones. The thick air seems to hold the light from hundreds of personal screens in a trembling homage to technology.

All the berths in the station area are soon taken and new arrivals plod on down the platform and into the dank tunnels where there is overspill. I can only see random blue and yellow lights through the brick archway, disappearing round the bend where trains once ran.

An unsteady calm settle on the "new sleepers" around midnight and wardens patrol with torches, intervening to try to avoid any antisocial behaviour. Drunkenness, casual sex and drugs are rife; dubious noises rise and fall, punctuated with screams and groans, and I sleep sporadically, unable to fully overcome my anxieties. Alongside my fear of my fellow new-sleepers, I hate our incarceration. If there was an emergency would we manage to escape?

The alarm was set on my phone for 6am, but I don't need it and am up and ready to leave. I cannot describe the utter relief I experience as I emerge from the escalator into the sunshine, free once again, along with many unknown ragged night-companions; fellow prisoners. I am going to the Biblio today, once it opens, and then I will head for the Chateau-Privee to meet Alexandra at 5pm.

Chapter 20

Once she had seen Zade off the premises, Alexandra hastened to her office and copied each page of the document reputedly authored by S. Herbert, saving the e-documents in her confidential area. Only then did she pause to read it, her eager eyes hurrying, as she was due to meet Michael Morgan upstairs in ten minutes. In many ways the contents of the pamphlet were not a surprise to her. She had guessed much of the information through her two years in the Commissioner role, but seeing it in black and white was seriously troubling. The bolt of lightning for her was the name Maximillian Morgan, and the obvious link with Michael. She had not suspected that.

She paused with concern over the sentences that had so alarmed Zade: 'Only infants of medium to high earning parents will automatically proceed to the scintillation programme,' and the description of the groups that are eliminated from the programme by statistics. She had been naïve, supposing that scintillation provided opportunities for social mobility; it was the opposite.

Forever a victim of the clock, she knew that she must now take the lift to Michael's impressive floor at the very top of the building. She locked the pamphlet in her desk drawer as a precaution. She had not yet decided whether to return it to Zade as promised, or whether she should destroy it and rely on her digital evidence if needed. Zade had no doubt taken a copy too. Alexandra wondered, with concern, whether Zade would have shared it with anyone else.

She glanced suspiciously at the advertisements for the Prophet Corporation gracing the walls of the lift, her brain working flat out. Who was S. Herbert? As the lift doors were opening, she suddenly realised; S. Herbert did not exist at all. It was simply a displacement device to divert inappropriate readers away from the truth. She had laughed to herself at first as it nearly spelt "sherbet"; the medication programme for infants, from age five to eleven masqueraded as sherbet milk. This was no coincidence; it was a sick joke by the author, the father of the genial gentleman who now sat in his office awaiting her arrival.

'Hello Alexandra,' he greeted her with affection in his deep and beguiling voice, pulling out a chair for her and asking his Assistant to bring coffee. 'We haven't had time to catch up for ages. That was good work in the West; I have stepped up the surveillance on Sean,' he added, glancing to check his auto-record was switched off. She wondered how much surveillance was focused on her.

Alexandra could play this game with skill and charm, and she started the meeting by asking him a string of superficial questions to bolster his ego. Their easy eye contact, and relaxed body positions signalled to the Assistant, as she brought the coffee, that she was seeing two senior colleagues who trusted each other implicitly, and that Alexandra was, as everyone said, Michael's protégé; his "favourite".

As he spoke, earnestly and with animation, she watched his familiar furrowed face, wondering what Maximillian had looked like. Michael had been on the verge of retirement from the Department for some time and several of Alexandra's supporters had told her that she was being prepared to take his role in due course. She guessed he wasn't ready to retire yet. His standards continued to be impeccable; no stray grey hairs, piercing blue eyes which penetrated into your mind, an expensive hand-tailored suit which signalled success, and always a slightly but not too eccentric tie. Most men didn't wear ties in the summer months but he persisted and as a result appeared to his employees never to take a break from his work role, never letting anything slip. She wondered what he did at home; he didn't talk about that side of his life, just as she had never told him how she started her adult life as a teenage parent. Was Michael a parent himself, she wondered. He sometimes joked about his wife, saying, but not asking, 'Now, what would Mrs Morgan say to that!' She normally liked his emphatic dominance, his no-doubt leadership, but today she was unsure.

He detected a hint of something cross her face; was it doubt? There was a short pause as he reflected, 'You wanted to ask me about the "challenges" in the system?' he invited, sounding puzzled, and with a slightly mocking air. Any facial evidence of her recent doubt had disappeared as quickly as it had arrived, and she took the floor with her characteristic calm assurance.

'Yes, thank you,' she started, continuing, 'Having now spent two years immersed in the Department, I find myself asking some key questions. Michael, I want my understanding to be as comprehensive as possible so I can fine-tune my communications strategy, especially with parents. Take the recent Noah Patel case as an example. It's not pleasant to pay-off parents. The publicity before we became aware of the situation, was potentially damaging. I need to know how we can ensure there are no more Noah Patels Do you know what went wrong in that case?'

Michael nodded, 'I completely agree; if you look at the statistics, we really do have a very high scintillation success-rate, but there are still the odd non-compliant cases and these must be eliminated; they are not good publicity for an otherwise exemplary system.'

He mused on possible reasons starting with genetic differences, and moving on to societal considerations. 'We have already eliminated all children with unmarried parents at birth from all scintillated cohorts, and the marriage register is 100% accurate. There is, of course, always a very small possibility that the post-birth DNA check doesn't pick up if a child was in fact the result of a liaison with a different man; not the father of the family. So, brothers perceived as siblings may only be half-siblings, and thus the younger infant would not automatically scintillate.'

'Did you see the photo ID of the two boys?' Alexandra interrupted. 'They are very alike; it would be odd if they were not full siblings. The younger brother's polygenic factors will be different to his scintillated sibling I suppose?'

'Yes,' he continued, thinking aloud, 'So maybe it was the older child who scintillated uncharacteristically. Perhaps it was something connected to the melatonin and an aberration in their genes; they are half-Indian after all.'

Suspicious, Alexandra baulked as she realised the implications of his casual remark about half-Indian genes. She then realised he had also said, 'We have already eliminated all children with unmarried birth parents,' in keeping with the approach in the scintillation pamphlet. To date, in his conversations with her, he had firmly presented the view that the scintillation process itself produced the lists for the Four Plus, not that someone, or the system, had actually programmed the result. She again reflected on scintillation as a form of post-genetic engineering. She was very concerned about his unguarded comment about Noah Patel. She had often noted that most scintillated infants came from white families. Was her once trusted boss presiding over not only a massive social engineering programme, but also a strategy for white supremacism?

She mustered all her patience, and pushed him further, 'Are you saying we must improve research into the Four Plus so that, if the odd aberration occurs, we can remedy it efficiently, or are you saying we need to focus on the scintillation programme itself and ensure no more irregular cases slip through?'

Michael agreed emphatically with both of her suggestions, but was starting to look very slightly uncomfortable. Alexandra then voiced an out-of-the-box thought as it entered her mind, 'What if we re-engineer the Four Plus in the Central Area so it is a…well, a One Plus. The benefits would be great; parents would be in no doubt as to their children's potential at the earliest opportunity, earlier investment always pays dividends, and we could establish pre-school grammar academies rather than the current compromise?'

Michael relaxed at this welcome refocus of the conversation on to safer ground. He did rate Alexandra highly; she cut through the complexity to the bare facts, and came up with possible solutions. He wondered how open he would need to be with her about the programme, but for now simply agreed with uncertainty that a One Plus could possibly be the answer. He added that it would provide more time to address the few anomalies, but he would be very concerned about the cost to the Department of funding pre-school grammar academies. As she knew, currently historical arrangements for childcare, and for education before young children start school, were low-cost. The running costs were low, staffing costs were low, and now the national database for administration of place-allocation was so slick, the Department could simply let it run. But he would be open to an exploratory paper, including the potential costs, if she wanted to draft one for him to consider before any wider circulation. She would need to compare the cost of changing the system with the current cost of the occasional pay-off, like the Patels. 'On this level, the current system seems to me to be vastly preferable,' he concluded.

She nodded, and persisted with her line on scintillation, 'Okay, say reforming pre-school is not cost-effective in the short-term, is there any way that we can check the biometrics underpinning scintillation to prevent anomalous cases?' Michael gave nothing away, saying,

'The biometrics are sound and I am not aware of any new scientific possibilities at the moment.'

This presented Alexandra with her opportunity, 'We do, of course, refer to The Art and Science of Selection, by S. Herbert as the underpinning scientific rationale. Did S. Herbert write any follow-up, or is there any more up-to-date scientific rationale I wonder?'

'Ah, Samuel Herbert,' he laughed. 'I knew him when I was a young boy in Oxford. He was elderly then. A genius. Yes, total genius. He died soon after, and so there is no follow-up. Thinking in the Department has been that it is such a seminal work that it stands alone as the basis for the whole programme in the Central Area. Your colleagues in the West, the East and the South West might not necessarily agree of course,' he chuckled.

She felt brave, and sipping her coffee, asked, 'Is there a copy of "The Art and Science of Selection", which I can read? I have been trying to find a copy but have had no luck.'

'Well, my dear, that is one of the few things about which I cannot help you I am afraid. Academics in the 2040s were still very paper-bound. The significance of the work was not appreciated until after Samuel had died, and by then there had unfortunately been a fire in Sherrington Hall where all the scholarly papers were stored.' He droned on with excuses and historical anecdotes.

She didn't push any further on this occasion, but she was appalled that such a massive educational programme, with such far-reaching social and economic implications for so many people, was based upon a piece of research which no longer existed, and which was no longer available digitally or in print.

Without flinching, she continued by asking Michael about Sue Sutton in the North, needing to re-establish his view of her as totally on board. 'Do you think Sue will be able to prepare the North for a CenSA take-over – it is what is needed?' she asked. She listened to his long and wandering account of his recent visit to the North, and noted Sue's difficulties with the headteachers. When he stopped talking, she offered to work more closely with Sue, which he welcomed. On this positive note, she decided it was politic to draw the conversation to a close. Thanking Michael for his time, she took the initiative and rose from the table. He stood too, towering over her, clasping her hands before she left, he reassured her,

'Try not to worry about the Patels, they have already been paid and will start a new life. With a fair wind there will be no more anomalies. Meanwhile, my door is open; come and find me anytime, and decide whether you will write the paper bout the One Plus. It might be the right time to air the debate. You would have many supporters for a plan to invest more in the youngest children I am sure.'

'Okay, thanks,' she squeezed his hands with enthusiasm, and left, beaming at him as she went, to leave a lasting positive impression.

Alexandra was beginning to be worried about many aspects of her current role. Why had she taken so much for granted, assuming that the system in the Central Area was right because the data told her so? Why had she been lured into trusting Michael Morgan? Self-doubt nagged at her usually supreme but now brittle self-confidence.

She knew that she needed to speak again with Zade. The wild-looking bright-eyed teenager seemed to hold more knowledge of the forces underpinning the education system than she did. Reluctantly she admitted to herself that she had not felt so humble in the presence of a teenager for many years.

Chapter 21

On the first day of term, in the Central Area Primary Grammar Academy CXIX, racks of children's coat pegs lined the sanitised corridor and the doors of small air-conditioned lockers lay open, awaiting the arrival of the lunches carried by their new owners. At eight thirty, the mass of scintillated children filed in, eager in their smart new school uniforms, and particularly keen because, in the second year of primary school, they would be entitled to sherbet milk each day at break time. They were thinking about this as they arrived, seeing their friends, and looking forward to the sweet, fizzy milk that they had been told would give them strong muscles, and would make them into super-heroes. Young academy pupils coveted the sherbet milk. As they entered their classrooms, and the noise in the cloakrooms abated, only the coat peg which was labelled "Lucas Patel" hung empty. The only locker left with a flapping unlatched door was also labelled with his name; an empty peg and an empty locker. His first dose of sherbet milk would be left undrunk.

Meanwhile, a hundred and fifty kilometres away, near East Bridge, the Patel family was settling into a new morning routine in the prefabricated cabin that was their temporary home. They hadn't been able to bring many belongings with them, but had amassed essential items from the old-fashioned store in the nearby town. The parents had deliberately created a holiday atmosphere, relieved that the family had not been split up over the scintillation fiasco.

Mrs Patel was already firmly established on the teaching staff of the nearby secondary school where Jeff Stringer taught metalwork. She had led some catch-up English classes in late August along with a colleague of Jeff's, and had enjoyed the experience much more than she had expected. The students were enthusiastic, rowdy, spirited. She couldn't quite put her finger on it, but they seemed more alive than the troops of blank-faced young executives-in-the-making who she had taught in the Central Area. The curriculum was very different, and she became more interested herself. The books were mostly rejects from CenSA, with curled covers and original wording, not the modern versions which she was used to. She was actually looking forward to the term ahead.

Mr Patel had quickly found work in a nursery located in East Bridge Primary School. Years back it had been a small village concern, but now it served the migrant town nearby. Families willingly walked the half mile out and back in all weathers, and the collection of brick buildings provided sanctuary for many migrants. Lucas and Noah had made several new friends in the last two weeks of the summer break, before Lucas started his new school.

The Patels had received their settlement figure from the Department for Future Success, after a swathe of legal fees had been deducted, and were going to look into more permanent housing in due course. As Mrs Patel said, there was no hurry.

At first Lucas found it difficult at school because he was different. His eyes scintillated unlike every other child in the school. Some adults seemed to see him as an unwelcome outsider. Children fussed over him, older ones petting him, and they called him names like Bright Eyes and Sparkler. He didn't like this. After a few weeks, things had settled down, his sunny nature had endeared him to the staff, and he had made many friends. He simply told the adults that his brother had normal eyes and they had moved here so he and his brother could go to school together. This simple narrative made sense, and they forgave Lucas his unusual appearance.

There was no sherbet milk here, which disappointed Lucas at first, only half a small bottle of ordinary milk because there were too many children for a full bottle each, but that was okay. He was more interested in the Forest School which took place once a week in the nearby woods. They could make maps and follow tracks, laying sticks as arrows, and when they had successfully followed the routes through the trees set by their teachers, they were rewarded with the lighting of a fire in a pit. Then they cooked treats which they ate with their morning milk, sitting on logs in the fresh air; pastry twists one week, and toasted marshmallows the next. There was nothing like this at his old school. He told Noah all about it when he got home.

Chapter 22

At the same time that Zade was sleeping fitfully in the underground, Alexandra was in her bedroom, bent over her Prexia typing furiously, and searching image after image. It was past midnight and she was due to see Zade at the Chateau-Privee the next day. She could recall a newsfeed cutting featuring the arrest of a renowned education activist in the early 2060s. At the time, she was a trainee teacher, and had followed the story keenly. The son of a high-ranking churchman had become a popular hero amongst teachers, and had led the illegal smuggling of vast numbers of trained teachers out of the Central Area into the newly developing Periphery. It was a massive story at the time, with footage of the underground passages which enabled the hordes of rebellious teachers to relocate against the regulations of the High Council. She had found reports of his dramatic arrest by armed police, but not the photograph which she remembered.

Varying her search terms again and again, persistently thorough, she was finally rewarded as a copy of the blurry black and white photograph from her memory appeared on the screen. 'Got it!' she exclaimed to herself, triumphantly.

Peering, she zoomed into the image as far as possible before it melted into a blur. Her memory was correct. The picture showed a man being brutally arrested in the mountains; his arm being forced behind his back by a heavily armed police officer. Behind him was a woman, strikingly beautiful with a brooding complexion and long, jet-black hair. This woman was visibly distraught. She was reaching both arms out to the man, and she was heavily pregnant. At the time, Alexandra wondered what had happened to the child. Zade had reminded her of this woman.

She read the text, 'Owen and Matilde Beaufort finally arrested; yesterday the outlawed insurgents were discovered after an extensive police operation throughout the Welsh Marches. The pair is responsible for the illegal smuggling of nearly five thousand teachers over several years from Central Area schools into the Periphery in the East, West and South West. Their apprehension is a triumph for the security services.'

It was a long shot but the timing worked; what had happened to Matilde Beaufort's baby? She stretched and yawned, knowing that she should sleep, but instead focused back on her search. She logged into the Department database which included search facilities in records such as births, deaths and marriages. She found the marriage of Owen Beaufort and Matilde Fury in 2062, and took a screen shot. Better not download or it might be tracked. Zade was such an unusual name, and she was scintillated. She should show up on the confidential scintillation database, although in the first year of the programme records were being developed, and were not as comprehensive as now.

It was nearly 2am before she succeeded in bringing Zade Beaufort up on her screen. Oddly, there were two Zade Beaufort's, one assessed on 23rd December 2064, and the other the day after, on Christmas Eve of the same year. The assessments were apparently conducted in completely different places, the location line on the first one being blank, but on the second recording "St Thomas; Maternity". It, therefore, seemed that eye drops had been administered to Zade on two occasions. Alexandra reflected on this; a "double-scintillation" was likely to have caused Zade's to sparkle even more intensely than other scintillated children. It would also explain why Zade's scintillation was not fading.

She noted that the first entry listed Zade's parents as Owen and Matilde Beaufort. Triumphantly, she took screen shots of both entries, covered her digital tracks as best as she could, closed down and fell into bed, where she slept deeply until the alarm woke her at 5am. As morning dawned, she felt rough. Going through the motions of her early day, swallowing two stamina pills, she emerged from the security doors of the apartment block and headed for Rochester Row. The early morning breeze cleared her head and she slipped into automatic mode, preserving her unusually diminished energy for the day ahead.

She survived a string of meetings through the day, keeping frantically busy and thus successfully steering her mind away from the intense tiredness which lurked within reach. Arguably one degree less immaculate than usual, despite having taken more stamina pills, just before 5pm she collected the pamphlet from her locked drawer, donned her chic all-weather pink raincoat and headed for the Chateau-Privee through the drizzle.

***

I am sitting in a quiet corner of the Chateau-Privee watching the secure entrance doorway, hoping to see that bright and perfect face, hoping to catch a waft of her delicious fragrance, hoping for the confidence that a second rendezvous can sometimes bring. Alexandra Essex is invading the part of my being that usually allows no one entry. My rule of thumb is never to get too close, or you risk being hurt. Even with Lyn, I keep an emotional distance. I don't understand what it is about Alexandra that compels me; I don't think it is actually about her, I think it is the power which she holds. I know that I need this second meeting to be a success. She is wavering, unsure whether to fix her loyalty on all that she knows, including Michael Morgan and his Department, or on the potentially dangerous possibilities which I am revealing to her. No doubt the persuasive Michael Morgan will have cast his spell over her at their meeting last night. My triumph, I suppose, is that she is even considering the unethical nature of the very system which she espouses. I have planted the seed of doubt and am waiting.

If she turns up, it is my aim to achieve three things from our meeting. I want to have the pamphlet back in my zipped pocket, despite the burden of holding it. I want some information about my parents, and finally I need a date to be fixed for us to meet again.

It seems a long wait until she appears at the security entrance, a pink blur, swiftly waving her fob over the keypad and looking for me amongst the patchwork of professional heads filling the Chateau-Privee. As she approaches my table, I see that she looks tired, but I can also tell that she is eager to see me. I reward her by removing my dark glasses and scintillating at her, which she appreciates and we laugh, breaking the tension. She sees that I have no drink and bustles off to collect coffees, her pink clasp bag firmly across her shoulder. Is my copy of the pamphlet in there? She returns with expensive coffees and a cake box. 'Do you like frangipanes?' she asks. They are way out of my price range, and I peep into the box. A delightful almondy waft escapes.

'I have never eaten one,' I respond politely, 'But they look, and smell amazing.'

As I demolish the delicious tartlet, closing my eyes with every bite, she laughs again nervously, a tinkly laugh, which cuts through the tension. 'Now Zade, we cannot meet here for long. It's not safe, so we must be quick. I have two items for you…' She extracts the pamphlet, exactly as I gave it to her, in the biodegradable cellophane wrapper and hands it to me, checking that I, like her, now have a digital copy. She counsels me to keep it secreted somewhere safe as it is probably more valuable than either of us can guess. She has no idea that I spent last night underground as a new sleeper and that I have nowhere I can call home just now, let alone a safe place to lock a much sought-after pamphlet. My first expectation of the meeting is realised.

The second item is a large crisp brown envelope. 'I said that I would find out about your parents, and I can tell you what I have discovered,' she begins. I am not ready for this. Having spent nearly sixteen years resigned to ignorance, and craving information, I have not let myself believe that she would come up with anything. Fearing disappointment, I muster my emotional strength.

'I have checked with the Register of marriages, and I have used the Department's scintillation data. I have also brought you a copy of a newsfeed article, which you can find online yourself. I am telling you that I have consulted the Department's data to reassure you that my information is bona fide.' She scans the restaurant and lowers her voice, 'I can see confidential records for any scintillated child in the Central Area, but I would appreciate it if you keep that to yourself because, technically, I must never access data to compromise my professional role. I have signed the High Council Secrets Act and am bound to abide by certain requirements in my position.' She seems to have taken a significant risk in obtaining information for me, and I respect this, reassuring her that matters are completely confidential with me. She appears to be repaying my trust, rewarding the risk that I took in approaching her yesterday.

I place my hand cautiously on the brown envelope, not enjoying the feeling of emotional vulnerability; 'This is a big moment for me; please, just tell me what you have discovered.' She speaks slowly, softly and dramatically;

'You are Zade Beaufort.'

I have never heard my real surname before and I repeat it again, and again, 'Beaufort, Beaufort…'

'In the December of 2064, your parents were arrested.' I had feared my scintillation was a mistake, and that I had a murky and unfortunate past. At least my parents seem to have been married.

'Arrested?' I query.

'They were arrested for acts against the High Council. Your parents were seen as freedom fighters. They campaigned against the grammar academies in the Central Area. Over many years, they fought for the rights of teachers to relocate to the Periphery where they could follow their historical methods, teaching in the ways which they believed worked best. They led many protests, but failed to change laws and so went underground. Here, read this from the newsfeed.'

I am stunned, immensely proud, and confused by the new identity which is presented to me.

She opens the envelope and takes out a printed article. I see a blurred photograph of a man being arrested, and a woman stretching her arms out towards him. I quietly read the text aloud, 'Owen and Matilde Beaufort finally arrested; yesterday the outlawed insurgents were discovered after an extensive police operation throughout the Welsh Marches. The pair is responsible for the illegal smuggling of nearly five thousand teachers over several years from Central Area schools into the Periphery in the East, West and South West. Their apprehension is a triumph for the security services.'

'Five thousand!' I marvel, studying the blurry image, dumbfounded, intensely proud. I turn to Alexandra and whisper, with tears pricking my sparkling eyes, 'I look so like my mother.'

'That is what set me on this train of thought,' she says unemotionally. 'I remembered this photo from my time as a trainee teacher. I followed the story back then, and when I saw you yesterday, I remembered the woman in this photograph. It took some finding I can tell you. She is pregnant, with you.' I had not noticed my mother's huge belly, but now she points it out, it is obvious. What an amazing and yet bizarre image for me to take on board.

I ask if she is sure, and she is, completely sure. She has not only brought me a screenshot of my parent's marriage certificate, but also of my post-birth medical checks, which confirm her story. 'Why are there two records?' I ask.

'That puzzled me, too. You will need to check but I am guessing you were born in one place, perhaps a prison hospital or detention centre, and then were taken from your mother and moved to St Thomas' here in Westminster.'

I gather my thoughts. She offers me a scented tissue, and I dab my wet eyes. Changing the subject, she asks, 'You alerted me to Maximillian Morgan. Have you worked out the enigmatic identity of S. Herbert?' She pronounces the name several times, emphasising the initial "sh".

Of course, *Sherbet*; I remembered the coveted little glass bottles of soda provided in the grammar academy at break-time, with their sweet addictive taste, and the assistants supervising the drinking of every drop so we should grow up strong and heroic. The colour would vary from day to day, bright pink, green, and orange, but not the flavour, although we gave them names like "sizzling strawberry" or "luscious lime". In the older classes, we were given paper straws to add to the novelty of the drink.

Alexandra is starting to look agitated. It is not ideal meeting in such a public place near to the Department. She turns to me, lowering her eyes, and says, 'Next time we meet I think we should choose somewhere else. It is too convenient here, far too many people from the Department come and go. We need a narrative…'

'I can provide the narrative,' I volunteer, and I suggest that I am working on writing the history of education, for a homework project, and met her here by chance, which is true. When I recognised her, I boldly asked about her role as CenSA Commissioner. She agrees we should use this back-story, and rises to depart. At least we are to meet again.

I want to thank her, but it seems oddly inappropriate. She probably wants to thank me, or does she? I am presenting her with possibly unwelcome truths. Her future life would have been so much easier had we never met. Maybe this is over-dramatic; she was already seeking the work by S, Herbert, and so I have simply helped her in her own quest for truth. I know that we must cement our future; I need to know her commitment.

'What now?' I ask.

She is decisive. 'Zade Beaufort,' she begins, 'I need you to write down for me – write I mean, with pen and paper – all that you already know about scintillation. Treat it like a project.' Should I trust her? In response, I assert myself, brazenly saying,

'I will do this for you, but in return, I need you to share with me all that you know. Then, the next time we meet, we can bring the two together and settle on our next steps.' I deliberately start to talk in the first-person plural. It is no longer me, and her, but "us".

We are an incongruous pair. If we plan to meet in a high-end establishment, I stand out as oddly and inappropriately dressed. If we plan to meet somewhere that I feel at home, such as the Advice Bureau, she would turn eyes with her smart suits and professional manner. She rises from the table, tidying the cups, and asks, 'Do you know the Rooftop Chateau-Privee in The Strand, opposite the Art Gallery?'

'I know the Gallery well,' I responded, 'I will find the rooftop Chateau-Privee.'

'This Friday at 10am; you can give my name,' she states, consulting her Haptic. She swipes, and my ancient phone buzzes in my pocket. Then she leaves.

Looking at my phone I see the eye icon again, the one that appeared momentarily once before in the Chateau-Privee. This time it shows a reminder for our Friday meeting, scheduled for precisely one hour, which she has called "research student". I smile in silent satisfaction at a morning's job well-done, my three hopes for the meeting all achieved.

A waiter approaches my table carrying a tray bearing an expensive coffee in a tall mug and a plate of six shortcake biscuits, drizzled with chocolate and nuts. He smiles at my sparkling eyes; my dark glasses still in my pocket, and goes to place the tray on the table beside the brown envelope brought earlier by Alexandra. 'It must be for someone else,' I say, but no, he beams, pointing to the door, telling me in broken English

'Your friend; she paid as she went; there.'

Alexandra's small, symbolic gesture is welcome, not least because it promises unexpected sanctuary. As a "paying" customer, I now have a further two hours in the sumptuous Chateau-Privee, and can read and re-read the newsfeed article and the copies of the certificates, while I work my way through the biscuits.

Chapter 23

It is Friday morning. I admit that I am not in a good state right now. After two successive nights as a new sleeper in the underground, I am worn thin for lack of a satisfying rest. My clothes are starting to hang limply with grime. A quick wash of my face, and clean of my teeth in the bathroom of a Chateau-Privee is not proving sufficient. I feel dirty and frayed at the edges. I have, even so, written ten pages about scintillation, the Four Plus, state medication and grammar academies, ready for Alexandra today. It was a useful exercise, bringing all my scraps of knowledge into one coherent account. I wrote by torchlight in the underground, drafting the piece several times before arriving at the final version which I have in my small shoulder bag today. As a precaution, I copied each of the ten pages on my phone for my own records. I stored the rough drafts, written on paper, in my rucksack, knowing that I somehow need to destroy the packet of notes confidentially.

We are due to meet at 10am, and I am just making my way past the heavily guarded Art Gallery. Earlier I stowed my rucksack and my coat in the secure luggage facility at Charing Cross, and attempted to smarten myself up in the washrooms there. I am trying to contact Lyn for the next instalment of my allowance as my sterling is low and I have absolutely no back-up. She is not answering my messages, which is usual as communicating with anyone in the Periphery is generally a challenge. The cyberspace connecting the Periphery to the Central Area is heavily protected, and communication is not reliable or entirely secure. Also, the historical system used in the Periphery is not fully compatible with those here, so messages often fall into a metaphorical pit. Someone from the High Council once described this as a digital cess pit, but I know there are many ordinary people like me who rely on their messages getting through, and in my view, this is not acceptable, and should be addressed.

Depending on how this third meeting with Alexandra goes, I may visit the Art Gallery afterwards. As a scintillated child I am entitled to free access. But now I am focusing all my remaining energy on making a success of our imminent meeting.

I am arriving early, and will need to use my powers of persuasion, as access to the exclusive rooftop restaurant is by invitation only. My scintillated eyes could prove an issue this time as they might declare me as under-age, and I put my dark glasses on. It is a bright day, and I do not feel out of place.

After I spend five minutes observing others come and go through the gate, swiping their fobs with nonchalance, I move forwards. There are two private uniformed guards inside the doorway. One, a man, is assiduously checking each person's identity as they enter. The other, a woman, is waving people through more readily. As the queues for entry build up, I notice the woman is answering a call on her Haptic. This is my chance. I breathe slowly and plant a genial open smile on my face, swiping my fob, which allows me through the barrier and inside the doorway. I push into a gaggle of customers, bustling past the woman, and slipping through, following the affluent customers up the series of escalators, all overlooked by security cameras. We ascend four floors and at the very top there is another barrier with more uniformed guards. I am expecting this, and extract the folder of written sheets from my shoulder bag, holding it in an obviously student-like manner. I access the meeting invitation sent by Alexandra, on my phone, and show it to the guard, saying, 'Alexandra Essex, 10am.' He checks his booking screen and nods, then signalling for my shoulder bag, which he searches at length, and finds nothing. Next, I am subjected to the routine body scan. He bends down to me, talking loudly over the noise of the "tasteful" music.

'You are early; please wait over here. The attendant will call you when your host arrives.'

Success; I am finally in the Rooftop Chateau-Privee! I sit on a pristine armchair to wait. There is a steady flow of professionals who are dressed smartly in contemporary fashions and carry the latest in Haptic technology. They all ignore me, speak in loud voices, and are intent on impressing their companions. A group of younger neutrals enters. They are dressed carefully in the current accepted non-conventional dress. Their chatter fills the space so quieter pairs sitting at tables glance round, and then resume their important business. My mind turns again to my parents; I expect they would have felt as out of place as I do here.

The attendants, dressed in very tight white uniforms of vaguely translucent fabric, take orders on pocket-size Prexias and then disappear off to the left, into the kitchens. Here they process the orders, and collect silver trays bearing glasses and decorative cups full of sweet-smelling drinks, fruit teas, sparkling sodas and daytime gin cocktails. Some guests are eating pastries and expensive morning snacks, leaving half-eaten crusts and corners. These morsels are later scooped up and tipped into bags which hang on the trolleys of the staff who clear the tables. No doubt the discarded food is going into the nuclear incinerators. I reflect that there are plenty of street beggars or even "new sleepers" in the underground who would relish these high-end scraps for their lunch.

It is now ten minutes past the time of our scheduled meeting, and I am still sitting on the immaculate armchair, a lonely observer. Tiredness starts to nag at my eyes and the confidence that I mustered to achieve entry is ebbing. Where is Alexandra? I recall how, when we met last, she looked nervous. Maybe she is in trouble for meeting me. Maybe she has met with Michael Morgan and has decided not to pursue the reasons behind scintillation anymore. Maybe she is attending to an emergency, or ill, or just running late? I glance around the room.

The views from the far windows across the high-rise layers of London are fantastic. Guests who have not visited before are drawn to the window as if it were a magnet. They exclaim and point. I am used to seeing civilisation from street-level these days, or even below-ground as at night I am now incarcerated in the tunnels of the underground. It is helpful to be high up, seeing the streets way below, as I feel more in control of my destiny; less downtrodden by circumstance.

My phone buzzes, and my heart misses a beat. I peer at the screen through the dark lenses of my glasses, and all I can see is that the appointment has disappeared. It seems to have been cancelled, or has it just timed-out? I turn my head for the hundredth time and scan the arrival corridor, but do not see the person who I am looking for.

I can't have misunderstood the place, or the time, because the guard who admitted me checked his booking screen.

A swaggering older man, dressed in a smart beige suit is arguing with the guard, who does not seem to have a booking for him. The man is raising his voice and says he will complain, but he is not admitted, and finally returns angrily down the escalator. Two women in suits arrive and wave at a group already seated in the restaurant area. They are delayed as the body scans pick up various small metal items in their pockets, tweezers, paper clips, and a shiny metal pill case. The guard places the items in a secure tray for the women to collect as they leave. Security here is tight, and yet I was admitted, but unfortunately, I cannot yet make any use of being inside. I start to feel disappointed, let-down and foolish. There is no message from Alexandra; she does have my contact details, but I realise I don't have hers, as the appointment was set up from a confidentially blocked contact number.

At half past ten I accept she is not coming and leave as anonymously as I can, dejected, tired and unusually for me, feeling lonely.

Chapter 24

Back out on the pavement, I have to confess that this is a low point, and I really do not know what to do for the best. I feel duped by Alexandra Essex, tricked and used. Perhaps I was too naïve when I approached her on the spur of the moment in the Chateau Privee. Now I have compelling reasons to fear detection by her Education Enforcement Officers. I need to be more vigilant, and it is dawning on me that I need to leave London. My supply of sterling will run out in a few weeks if I do not hear from Lyn soon. At the moment I can afford a train ticket to the Periphery rather than throwing money literally down the drain on the nightly underground. I have resisted leaving for the Periphery so far, as Lyn's flat was an excellent refuge, and I know this locality so well, but without my own accommodation, I am realising that I am far too vulnerable.

Taking myself in hand, I start to develop a plan. Firstly, I need a good nutritious meal. Seeking companionship too, I decide to head for the Advice Bureau café via Charing Cross where I must retrieve my rucksack, and my coat. That was a waste of money too. A brisk walk in the autumnal streets is therapeutic. I like to be moving and purposeful. I walk through crowds of slick professionals with money to burn, who weave in and out of the street-dwellers. I pass a grammar academy, which is deathly quiet as the students are all inside, no doubt drugged into behaving with passive uniformity.

It is a relief to be walking unencumbered by my heavy rucksack, but not for long. Entering the busy over-ground station, I join the inevitable queue at the luggage storage depot and retrieving my phone from my pocket, I access my left luggage e-ticket. The supervising officer behind the transparent panel is young, but, of course, is unscintillated. He must be a little older than me and would have been born before the scintillation programme started. I muse on this; you never see scintillated adults because people's eyes return to their natural state, usually at the age of fourteen, sometimes up to sixteen. Scintillation seems profoundly unnatural to me; it is an invasion, a visible label, condemning the young child to soda control and the dull mechanistic curriculum of the grammar academies. Strength starts seeping back into my veins along with my anger at these injustices. I scan my e-ticket and, with relief, I see my familiar rucksack and coat sliding down the chute. The supervisor just looks, not pulling them over for further inspection.

My belongings travel on a moving belt through the armoured archway. Above the opening there is an illuminated advertisement, in flashing script, for Prophet Corporation Baby Showers, "Celebrate your baby's scintillation;

autumn discounts". It makes me feel sick. I could throw something at it. I want to smash the sparkling words. I want to shout out loud to all the gloating parents, 'You have been tricked; it is not what you think.' Instead, I collect my coat and put it on, press my shoulder bag and the papers which I didn't give to Alexandra into my rucksack, re-tie the drawstring, and head for the river. I will walk along the embankment to the Advice Bureau.

The powerful mellow tones of a saxophone weave in and out of the structure of the bridge, and as I pass the bedraggled musician, I swipe my loose change into his collecting tin. He looks like he could do with it even more than me, and the penetrating notes of his melody raise my spirits, restoring a glimmer of faith in the beauty of mankind.

As I emerge from the shadow of the bridge into the autumn sunshine, I see one of my true heroes staring at me, Joseph Bazalgette. The monument is striking if you take the time to pause. The day after Lyn had moved to the Periphery, I dulled my loneliness by talking to Mr Bazalgette, as he stared back out of his monumental plinth. He looked like the sort of teacher I would have liked. I found out more about him in the biblio that day; what a man! Rudimentary Latin had been on the grammar academy curriculum but I couldn't work out what the chiselled phrase meant at the time. I now know it says something like, 'He placed the river in chains.' I think they just mean he conquered nature when he designed and oversaw the completion of the original sewer system in central London. He solved the biggest problem of the day. While we "new sleepers" lie anxiously under the ground, we need the reassurance that tonnes of sewage aren't going to flood down, engulfing us in their wake. Marching on along the pavement, I reflect that Bazalgette was ultimately dealing with substance; stone and water, waste and pipes. Our challenge today is harder to pin down; it is more ephemeral, more abstract, but still potentially catastrophic. We are being socially engineered, generation by generation.

As I approach the old Parliament buildings, I turn away from the river, and am soon facing the dilapidated but cheerful frontage of the Advice Bureau with its yellow paint and bright posters covering the shuttered lower windows. I do not see Sam as I pass the reception and the busy public interview booths. I take the old staircase down into the basement and enter the volunteer café, removing my dark glasses. Even before I find a table space, several people who I recognise say "hello" to me. The old man who clears the tables calls me over, and through his long-yellowed beard croaks,

'Zade, try the pie today it is great!' The food served here is wholesome. There is an agreement with the Prophet Corporation for any food past its best to be collected by volunteers and re-used within 24 hours. There is no mark-up so it is very affordable, and I often choose to eat a hot meal here when I need to.

With relief I lean my rucksack against a vacant seat close to the servery, hanging my coat over the back of the chair, and collect the dish of the day, a slice of t-beef pie (actually make of tofu) with a mound of steaming potatoes, some cooked green vegetable leaves and gravy. I know this is the best medicine for me as I attempt to overcome my earlier disappointment, and tuck into the steaming food at speed, not wasting a single morsel. Revitalised, I collect a mug of the free coffee, which tastes pretty bad, but finishes off the meal and gives me time to plan.

Taking myself in hand I face the inevitable; I must relocate out of London, possibly out of the Central Area completely. Migration to the Periphery is relatively easy, but once there, your chances of returning to the more prosperous Central Area are slim. The irony is that it is only a matter of months until I am legally able to live here independently. Even then, my scintillated eyes will cause issues if they continue not to fade. But is independence my only goal? I am determined to find out what is behind scintillation, and to expose Michael Morgan. My anger at Alexandra Essex starts to seep back, but I push it away.

I think of the ten pages of notes which I wrote so thoughtfully, plucking out the key facts for her to read. That was not time wasted. I run through the main points in my mind; firstly, the eyes of babies scintillate before they are a year old. This enables them, in time, to pass the Four Plus assessment, which entitles them to a grammar academy place. Roughly a quarter of babies do not scintillate and they are condemned to education in the Periphery. There seem to be strict criteria for this, as listed in the Herbert pamphlet. Children only scintillate if they were born to married parents in the earning classes, without a list of predisposing factors. Education in the Periphery is widely perceived as inferior, but in my view is a real education, and drug-free. The old lady, Danielle, was convinced of this too. As I think back to the hour I spent with her, I remember our parting, and that she pressed something into my hand, which I put in my pocket. I had totally forgotten about this!

Fumbling in each of my coat pockets, I hope I haven't let the mystery item slip out, but I locate it quickly and explore it carefully with my fingertips, removing the paper wrapping. It seems to be a fob or digital key, a small round metal case with a directional arrow protruding. I can feel writing inscribed in the metal. Casually looking around me to check I am unobserved; I bring it out and study it. Yes, it is a tiny key fob, and a miniscule red light is actually illuminated. I cannot read the inscription with my naked eye and quietly focus my phone's magnifier over it, reading, and photographing "scintlab2".

I drain my gritty coffee, re-wrapping the fob in the scrap of paper and putting it into the safer zipped pocket in my coat. Do I really need this complication just now? I should be focusing on finding a better bed for the night, and migrating to the Periphery myself, but instead I am being enticed to play detective. What and where is scintlab2? About to put my phone away, ready to move on, I see the eye icon flash up on the screen. It is a message, no sender, confidential, and no apology. It says, 'Appointment rescheduled 8pm today, meet outside Art Gallery reception.' I wrangle with my anger but decide that I will go.

In the time available to me before this rescheduled appointment with Alexandra, I visit the nearest Biblio, which I know well. I use my fob to secure time on a static Prexia, risking the surveillance, and hoping no one is interested in checking the sites accessed by a schoolgirl with scintillated eyes. Sitting within sight of my pile of belongings, I tap and swipe the small screen, seeking information on scintlab2. Access to any meaningful references to scintillation is blocked, but my searches keep returning to the Prophet Corporation Medical Plant pages. A map directs me to an area on the East coast in Suffolk. I am then offered a link to a page to which they do not allow access. Brazen, I proceed, reading the sentence, 'The Scintillation Programme emanates from the main Prophet Corporation Medical Plant in Suffolk in two dedicated laboratories. The first focuses on medication and the second on scintillation. Access is...' The screen flashes the standard alert of an unsafe site and closes the pages. I am used to this, and quickly access a safe page about the history of education in Suffolk before the Commercial Enforcement Officer struts up to my booth to check what I am doing. I flash my eyes at her and apologise, explaining that I am researching for a project on the history of education. She moves away, but I am on her radar now.

So, it seems I now have some sort of access fob to the scintillation laboratory in the Prophet Corporation Medical Plant out in the Periphery. Time to leave the Biblio and kill time on the streets until my late meeting with Alexandra.

Chapter 25

The solid foundations of Alexandra Essex's world were being undermined, and she was not comfortable. She liked to present herself as principled, as ethically driven. She believed in providing the best possible education for new generations, and in preparing young people for success in their adult lives. She had signed up to Michael Morgan's Department for Future Success. She knew, of course, about the impact of the selective Four Plus on those who were unsuccessful, but had simply justified it as necessary, so young children with the most academic potential were provided with the best education possible. She hadn't often paused to consider the longer-term plight of those sent to the Periphery.

She believed in the medication programme, knowing from her experience as a teacher, how disruptive children's poor behaviour could be. The Central Area soda products simply gave every scintillated pupil the chance of an uninterrupted education, and meant that teachers could focus on the craft of instruction rather than the behaviour management which was necessary in the earlier decades of this century. The human race, she had believed, was using its intelligence to develop the right products to promote the right behaviours. She filled with pride when she saw a crowd of obedient scintillated children, their sparkling eyes symbolising all that is good about life; hope, enthusiasm for learning; little lights of the future.

However, doubts were beginning to creep into her mind. Her eyes had been opened by the trip out to the Periphery in the East with her colleague and friend Manya Gray. She was also having to handle the fallout from aberrations. The Lucas Patel case was the most recent in a long list which included the student who protested at Secondary Grammar Academy LXIV. And now Zade Beaufort; what was she going to do about her? The blurred newsfeed image of Zade's parents kept returning to her mind. Zade's fierce determination and her amazingly scintillated eyes kept sneaking into Alexandra's consciousness when she least wanted such distractions from her vital and valuable work.

Sitting alone in her comfortable living room, late on Thursday evening, after two days of rumination, she had weighed up her options carefully. The easiest plan of action was for her to continue to lead CenSA and to alert the Education Enforcement Officers to Zade's whereabouts, ensuring she was returned to both foster care and to school. End of story. Then life could carry on as it had done last week, and the week before. She wondered, if Zade had been her own daughter, would she have wanted that for her? Success? Defined by whom? The irony of the situation struck her. In some ways, Zade was behaving with a maturity beyond her years, and yet her eyes were still scintillating like a younger teenager. Alexandra could see Zade was desperate for an education, but knew that she had rejected the grammar academy experience so vociferously that returning her to it would probably not work. Was Zade a genuine casualty of the programme which she sought to expose, was she simply a nuisance teenager, or was she right? Are isolated cases of rebellion inevitable when a ground-breaking, and prescriptive, system is established?

She pulled her mind back to the purpose of her reflection. Perhaps she should consider resigning, thus side-stepping the whole contentious scenario. She had significant savings and had always wanted to travel abroad; given her current role, she would be granted enhanced travel permissions. She fancied spending time in some of the more advanced jurisdictions like Iceland, the centre of the successful global programme to combat climate change, or Singapore, where the post-modern education system had already matured. But she knew this would be the coward's way out, and apart from not wishing to be seen as a coward, something was tugging at her moral core. She was currently in a position to act decisively and possibly even to change the system herself. Or was she? With Michael Morgan in charge, so obviously believing in the maintenance of the status quo, the chances of her succeeding would be slim.

What should her next step be? Should she meet with Zade or set the Enforcement Officers on her? Unusually for Alexandra, she was still unsure.

The next morning, when she was due to meet Zade, the decision was taken out of her hands as the Department was on high alert. Michael Morgan had been called away to the North, to another disturbance, and Alexandra was asked to cover his morning meetings. In a whirl of appointments and e-papers, she missed her 10am booking with Zade and didn't realise until too late. She had asked the Interns to cancel or rearrange all her meetings, but as she set up the rendezvous with Zade herself, it had been overlooked. It wasn't until later in the day when she realised this embarrassing error, and desperately rescheduled to meet Zade after work, mortified for letting the girl down. Having become nervous about meeting at the Chateau-Privee, she now preferred to keep her liaison with Zade low-key, and had suggested they stage a chance meeting on the pavement outside the Art Gallery.

Alexandra could tell she would struggle to make the 8pm appointment as she was still deputising for Michael, and the incessant flow of semi-urgent messages needed responses. However, in accordance with her earlier booking, a private taxi arrived at the Department at a quarter to eight in the evening. Fortunately, traffic on the expressway was flowing well and she was able to arrive on time.

The fading light was placing the three-hundred-year-old frontage of the Art Gallery in shadow. Under the gaze of the stone sages, the pavements were still heavy with the frantic daily bustle of the earning classes as well as noisy groups of professionals leaving their offices for the day. Zade was leaning on the iron railings, her rucksack on her back, her face hidden under her hat. On the stroke of eight o'clock Alexandra sprang out of her private taxi, neat and bright. She picked her way between the pedestrians and startled Zade. Onlookers would have thought they were simply seeing a maternal businesswoman and her student daughter rather than two strangers building a fragile bond, a bond based on a still-confused shared commitment to the success of future generations.

***

At last, on the dot of eight o'clock, Alexandra suddenly appears and greets me in a waft of pink perfume. She starts speaking at speed, explaining why she had missed our earlier appointment, not really apologising. I take off my dark glasses and wait for a pause, pointing my deeply scintillating eyes at her with calculated deliberation, and cutting to the chase, 'Because I am meeting you now, and not earlier, I will have lost my usual place in the queue for underground sleeping. There will be no safe berths left by the platform and I will have to sleep in the tunnels. The disruptions and the noise are greater there and I will not feel safe.'

She takes some time to comprehend. I can see that she is not at all familiar with London's underground sleeping. She sees the glint of genuine fear in my sparkling eyes, and is decisive, saying, 'Come home with me; now.' She hails a passing private taxi, with a driver, one of the expensive ones used by executives, and she ushers me, and my baggage into the rear seat with her. Should I trust her? She asks the driver to take us to The Jugged Hare on Vauxhall Bridge Road. In silence, we speed south of the river, very close to Lyn's old flat, no doubt now encased in security screening before they requisition it for re-letting. We pass the rear railings of St Thomas's, already patrolled by the night warders with their dogs, and we slow as we cross Lambeth Bridge. The late evening sun sinks below the glass panes of high-rise London, and once more I think of Whistler, and I think of Blake. She is studying my face with a combination of brittle pride and yet anguish. We do not speak while the taxi navigates the one-way systems in the small streets, and draws up at our destination, where we alight. She swipes the fare and adds a generous tip, asking the driver to wipe the trip from his itinerary, thinking that I don't notice.

She ushers me through the automatic security barriers, using her key fob, and into a lift where I take off my rucksack in anticipation of our arrival. We do, indeed, arrive at the front door to her apartment where she double-unlocks, and we enter. 'Make yourself at home,' she says.

I feel like a prisoner who is being released. I am on the threshold of a comfort which I have not known for some time, and I am within touching distance of a feeling of safety, which is rare at present. I have not spoken much since we met, and now, standing in the small hallway, my words come tumbling out. I thank her for trusting me, and I acknowledge that this is difficult for her. I tell her about the underground sleeping, and about the left luggage, but not about the small key fob which I have been given by the centenarian Danielle. That can wait.

On her home patch she looks different, more relaxed, less on-show. She kicks off her heels and takes charge, showing me her spare bedroom, which is extremely tidy with a desk, chair and a neatly arranged bookcase. She pulls a folding bed out of a fitted wardrobe, complete with sleeping bag and pillows, and says, again, 'You make yourself at home,' adding, 'This can be your room tonight. Would you like a shower? There is some urgent work which I must complete, so I will be in the lounge. Help yourself to my things if you need anything; towels, shampoo, shower gel.' And she disappears into the room at the end of the hallway.

I take my rucksack into the bathroom and lock the door. I extract my small wash bag and place it on a stool. It looks pathetic amid all the comfort. I cannot describe the intense pleasure of the once normal activity of having a shower. I am embarrassed to see lines of grime on my skin as I undress. I am filthy with the dirt of the streets as a consequence of having had no running water for months. Taking Alexandra at her word I squirt various sumptuous-smelling potions on my body, languishing under the hot water jets, and scrubbing with my old faded flannel. Then I tackle my hair, which has become long and matted, retrieving my hairbrush and working my way through it in sections, the way Lyn showed me years ago, then washing it thoroughly using some expensive-looking pink shampoo. I fetch my spare, and fairly clean, clothes from my rucksack and scoop up all the dirty items for washing. I sit on the stool and breathe, not wanting to end the sweet-smelling privacy which I have so enjoyed.

I unlock the door, return my belongings to the spare room, and pad into the lounge in my last pair of clean socks, saved for an occasion such as this, which I could not have foretold. Alexandra is bent over her Prexia, as I have seen her several times before. She raises her head asking cheerfully, 'Is that better?' I smile, thank her again, and ask whether I can clean my clothes. She swiftly loads the digital air-washing machine with my grimy garments, then cleans her hands, and switches it on. She soon has me sitting in a large armchair festooned with cushions, providing strong milky coffee and a plate of cheese and tomato sandwiches. She eats too, and we ease into a more relaxed mode. I am keen to impress, and ask her if she has read *Les Misérables*. It is the longest book I have ever read, by torchlight, when I couldn't sleep at Lyn's flat in the early days last year when I was alone, and it captivated me. She says she has seen it on the screen, and read chapters in French when she was at school. She tells me about a trip she made to France, to a place called Arles, when she was my age, and she visited the house where Victor Hugo lived. I would love to travel abroad. I say that I feel like Jean Valjean when he escapes and is offered sanctuary by the priest, but that I have no intention of stealing her silverware, and we both laugh.

Her face becomes serious, and she tells me that even though she is ultimately in charge of the Enforcement Officers, she promises that she will not betray our confidences; she will not alert them to me. This is reassuring, and means I can sleep more soundly tonight. In return I shyly hand her my ten-page essay on scintillation, written in longhand, nervous of her reaction. She flicks through and says that this is just what we need; she is impressed. I note the use of "we". She gives me nothing in return, but sanctuary when I most need it, which I value beyond measure.

We have oiled the wheels for future conversations about our quest, about scintillation and how we can stop the injustice, but now she needs to finish some work, and I am longing for sleep. She finds me a hairdryer, and parcels me off into the spare room where I dry my hair and sink into the soft sleeping bag. I close my eyes, and know nothing more until I wake on Saturday morning.

Chapter 26

By midnight, Alexandra had finished fielding the messages of the day. Then she entered a summary of progress she had made earlier, on a variety of projects, and sent it to Michael. He would want to know, and she needed to keep him sweet. She sent the message and received an immediate acknowledgement, wondering what he would think if he knew who she was sheltering in her spare room. She tiptoed up to the door, silently peering in, seeing Zade, clean and deeply asleep. The poignant scene awakened memories of her earlier life as a young mother.

She was not ready for sleep herself, and spent the next hour reading Zade's essay, which was well-structured and clearly written. Zade developed a strong, reasoned argument against scintillation, raising the same questions that had been in Alexandra's own mind. They were both asking how scintillation actually worked?

Alexandra and Zade had now read and re-read the Herbert pamphlet, which described how babies were selected for the scintillation programme based on predetermined factors, but neither of them understood exactly how eyes were scintillated. It seemed to be a Department for Wellbeing secret and was connected with the Cyclopentolate used by Wellbeing Officers when conducting their checks on new-born babies. Alexandra didn't doubt that Michael Morgan knew exactly how scintillation occurred.

In her current role, Alexandra knew she had an important part to play, but she was adamant that direct collaboration with Zade was out of the question. It would contravene her conditions of employment and, if discovered, she would not only be blacklisted, losing her access to inside information, but would probably be sacked for misconduct. Her entire career could be compromised. She must not be seen to feed any information to Zade, and she must not get too involved. Out of human kindness, she would give the girl shelter for a couple of nights, and help her on her way.

She started to map out a plan, which she intended to share with Zade in the morning. Although it was late, she messaged Manya Gray requesting an off-the-record meeting. They communicated briefly and cryptically, careful not to reveal the actual nature of their digital conversation. Manya was intrigued. She was planning to be in Cambridge on Sunday, and so, partly to demonstrate the strength of her bond with Alexandra, but also to satisfy her curiosity, she suggested they should meet at the Downshill Country Hotel Spa. They had met there once before as it was conveniently half-way between Cambridge and Westminster.

***

It is the first morning for a very long time that I am waking up feeling refreshed. I am momentarily surprised not to be suffocating in the stale air of the underground, and as I get my bearings realise where I am. I lie still for a while, savouring the moment, and wondering what is expected of me next. I am, of course, well-used to relocating in my life, and have often camped in other people's homes, sleeping on settees, floors and camp beds. I begin to realise it must be later than I imagine as the street is bustling with noise below. I reach for my phone, but in all the excitement of last night I forgot to charge it. Reprimanding myself, and stretching to wake my limbs, I fumble for the charge-boost and set it up beside an array of printing and copying equipment. It is past 11am. My previously filthy clothes are barely recognisable. They have been successfully air-cleaned, folded and placed on a chair. I get up, brushing my hair with ease for a change, and marvelling at my transformation. This morning I do not need to put my shoes on. I quietly check my coat pockets, specifically the zipped pocket, and am reassured nothing has been taken. I think I can trust Alexandra now. In fact, I find I am caught up in her spell of comfortable affluence, attracted by the way in which she has bravely opened her mind to new possibilities. I wonder where she is; it is so quiet inside the apartment.

I emerge cautiously from the spare room, use the bathroom to freshen up, and pad into the lounge, which is quiet. I peer into the small kitchen, and see a pot of coffee is keeping warm, and there are various dainty breakfast items on a plate, covered with a small transparent dome. I also see a note written on a leaf of rose-scented notepaper. It tells me that Alexandra has gone to the gym and will be back around midday and gives me a personal number to contact her on her Haptic. I stroke the scented paper, not used to luxury, and return to the spare room where I enter Alexandra's number into my old phone and secrete the fragrant piece of paper in my rucksack.

The next hour is precious time for me to plan ahead. I know that Alexandra cannot shelter me for long, not in her position. Firstly, breakfast and coffee, and then I must empty my belongings, check and tidy my rucksack and coat, and prepare to leave. The coffee is deep and rich, and I eat each of the pastries on offer, returning to the spare room where I empty my belongings from my rucksack on to the luxuriant carpet.

One of my earliest memories is packing a small case with my favourite toy, a soft white mouse with little pink ears, a few clothes and my flannel, toothbrush and hairbrush. I am not sure whose home I was leaving and where I was moving to. I must have been no older than two or three. I was moved so many times it is now a blur, but I remember the mouse being stolen later on by another child. One time, when I was placed with a totally unsuitable drug-dependent couple, who were violent towards me, I escaped, taking no belongings at all. I learnt from that experience. I started to store belongings in my locker at the Grammar Academy in case I was moved again, but the teachers discovered this and confiscated my things.

Today I am older and wiser, and I check my kit meticulously, moving all my papers together into a zipped pocket in the rucksack, with my passport and fob in my coat. I extract the packet of scribbled notes which I know must be disposed of confidentially, and seeing a document disposal unit beside Alexandra's desk, feed each sheet carefully through. I charge my torch from the ring. I fill empty water bottles. I wipe down the rucksack and repack it. Satisfied I return to the kitchen where I sit on a high stool and pour more coffee. At this point I hear the click of Alexandra's fob double-unlocking, and she bursts into the kitchen glowing with exercise, wearing a top-of-the-range silver and pink sports suit. I am embarrassed at how pleased I am to see her, and just say, 'Hi.'

She asks if I slept well, and checks that I have all I need. I tell her that I slept better than I have for a very long time, thank her for my clean clothes, and for the breakfast. We exhaust these pleasantries and she says that she wants to run her plan by me. She sounds enthusiastic, but I am wary that she is taking control of my life for me.

She lets me down gently, which is not unexpected. In fact, I know it is the wisest way forwards. She says that she cannot be directly involved; she is happy to provide comfortable accommodation for a couple of nights, but it cannot continue. We both know it is too risky for her, but now I see that she is not at all nervous about sheltering me, she is more concerned about keeping her professional access to information and influence. She is obviously well-in with Michael Morgan and says that we need this to remain so.

The surprise for me is that she has more to offer. Tomorrow, Sunday, we will travel northwards and will meet her friend and colleague Manya Gray at an expensive Spa. I say that I know of Manya from my research; she is the School Commissioner in the East. Manya will take charge of my accommodation for a while, and we will go from there. I ask whether I am being sent to the Periphery and will find it hard to return, but Alexandra has thought this through. Manya is based in Cambridge, which is actually in the Central Area, and she passes in and out of the Periphery daily, through the gates at the Isle of Ely, so I shouldn't get trapped out there. This sounds like an excellent plan, and I say so, telling her that I have actually travelled in, and back from the Periphery once before as my previous foster carer relocated in the West. She looks relieved that I am in support of her plan. I do not mention, but think to myself, that the Prophet Corporation Medical Plant is out on the East coast. For this reason alone, I agree readily to her proposal. I want to be able to access the source of scintillation.

Thinking of this, I move our conversation on to scintillation; at last we have time and privacy to discuss matters confidentially, adult to adult. Alexandra says that Manya has contacts in the Department for Wellbeing who may be able to help us. She asks me if I have any contacts in the education underground, but I have not. Maybe I have been naïve in trying to fight this battle alone. There are others who are deeply unhappy about the grammar academies, about scintillation and the effect it has on families with unscintillated children. She says there is also an underground movement of parents against medication in the Central

Area. She is fed information from the Education Enforcement Officers, who regularly convict miscreants.

I understand that she cannot be seen to be briefing against her own programme, and try not to place her in a difficult position. There are tensions in our conversation, but not between us.

Sitting face to face in the comfort of her lounge, we talk honestly and openly, wrangling with the difficult ethical questions emanating from the medication programme, and from scintillation. I tell her about my hour with Danielle, the centenarian. Although she seems to be aware of most of the historical details, she dismisses Danielle's views as typical of teachers at the time, explaining to me how credible the whole Central Area education programme now is to most participants. She emphasises the risks of even contemplating major organisational change in CenSA. She says we are talking about a need for long-term change not overnight resolution or a quick fix.

She asks me what I actually want to achieve, possibly thinking I will share my personal academic goals, but I am still adamant; all that I want is to see the end of the manipulation of generations of children. I want to put an end to the discriminatory practices of scintillation, and to re-establish an open and empowering education system for all pupils. She challenges me, asking, 'It is always hard to take things back in time; how do you think the teachers in the grammar academies would take to change? They like having compliant pupils. And parents of scintillated children like the system too?' I agree that these things need to be carefully thought through, but I am adamant that we must uphold a moral imperative. I remind her of the quotation from Nelson Mandela, 'Education is the most powerful weapon which you can use to change the world,' and ask her if she really believes our education system is safe in the hands of Michael Morgan. This causes her some consternation and I can see she is torn between presenting a front of professional loyalty, and a quiet, even private, pride in her strengthening ethics.

At this point she becomes pragmatic. She takes my hands in hers and looks deeply into my sparkling eyes, saying, 'Zade, you need to continue your fight. Manya Gray will provide you with more practical support than I can. Meanwhile I need to focus on my work, and my ultimate goal, to replace Michael Morgan as the High Commissioner for Future Success.' She only alludes to this ambition on the one occasion, but it is sufficient to open up a whole new scenario for me. Now I understand. I have a responsibility to leave her to achieve this. With the High Commissioner's powers, Alexandra could "change the world".

I vow to myself to remain loyal to her however long our fight against scintillation might take.

Chapter 27

It is Sunday morning. I am up and ready to leave early. Revitalised by my short stay with Alexandra, I am keen to push forwards in our quest. My host has hired a private driverless which draws up outside the apartments and we leave together. She is business-like this morning, intent upon the trip and seems keen to get me on my way. I lay my rucksack and my coat in the secure storage area in the rear of the driverless, and she locks it, then programming the route. The expressway is relatively empty at this time and we sweep round central London with ease, heading northwards, shadowing the old motorway 11. We sit in a comfortable silence, both with our minds on our own business, slightly anxious, and now keen to part. Although I have lived in the homes of many people over my fifteen years, and I have travelled further afield for short periods, I have never lived outside London, my stomping ground. I do not fear the unknown, but this morning I know that I will need to step up my vigilance.

What if I don't take to Manya? That is unlikely; I looked her up last night on my phone and found out about her past radicalism when she was training to be an educational lawyer. Unlike Alexandra, she opens her media statement with her principles, and talks about the importance of equity and educational opportunities for all.

After only twenty minutes travelling at speed past Chigwell and Epping, towards Hertfordshire, Down Hill Country Hotel and Spa comes into view. The long driveway leads up to the mansion, but is so crowded with security cameras and checkpoints that its stately ambience is lost in a cloud of unsubtle surveillance. We sail slowly up the driveway, bordered by manicured grass lawns, and small hedges. With Alexandra's professional ID, we are waved through each time we slow down. We pass ornamental fish pools and grand marquees, and draw to a halt at the final security point, joining a host of luxury driverless vehicles already parked neatly around the hotel entrance. I am not familiar with such affluence, and it grates on my conscience as I recall the world of the "new sleepers" risking their lives under the ground each night in the stale air.

Alexandra turns to me as we leave my belongings locked in the driverless, saying that I should not worry, they are safe, and she counsels me to "be myself" with Manya. She tells me that we are booked in for the "All is Calm" beauty package, reassuring me that this spa is used discreetly by senior officials; there are no listening or security devices once you are in the house. "All is Calm" is a mystery to me; I am used to a quick scrub with flannel and water. She can see my mild distain and laughs. 'Manya and I meet here occasionally. We will have our nails shaped and polished while we talk. Just try to blend in!'

At the grand entrance we pass through the body-scanners which are supervised by smart assistants in dark green uniforms with peaked hats; no android scanners here. I have left everything I own in the driverless and feel anxious about this. Massively under-dressed in my, now clean, jeans and top, I use my sparkling eyes to divert the attention of the assistants. As soon as they glimpse the powerful scintillation lighting up my face, they relax and smile at me.

We pass through long and luxurious corridors, the décor combining a deeply traditional style with the latest in technological wizardry. I am fascinated by the glowing blue-lighted signs which are projected on to white panels from miniscule, virtually invisible projectors. Soothing messages appear and fade out; "all is calm", "join our Elysium" and "season of mists". Alexandra seems to feel very at home here. She leads me through the wide passageways with confidence, and we finally arrive in a grand lounge area, the high ceiling festooned with chandeliers. Manya has arrived ahead of us and is sitting elegantly in a private corner, two empty golden chairs alongside her.

I stand back as the two women hug each other seemingly with genuine affection. Alexandra draws me forwards, introducing me to Manya as Zade Beaufort. I have never been introduced as this before and it seems strangely grand. I like the way Manya speaks to me as an adult and ignores my scintillated eyes. She is respectful. When Alexandra pronounces the name "Beaufort", Manya raises her eyebrows and smiles knowingly.

Alexandra asks a uniformed waitress for morning tea, and an elaborate pot of tea, three cups and saucers, with a plate of wafer biscuits arrives. We talk in low tones, sipping the hot tea. For me, there is an uncomfortable hierarchy, with Alexandra and Manya at ease in their lush surroundings, obviously used to blending small talk with important matters, and me, unusually polished and actually feeling proud that I am out of my depth. I prefer the honest streets to this artificial comfort. Although Manya is very focused on her colleague, she is surreptitiously observing me. When Alexandra leaves for the bathroom, Manya turns towards me, urging me not to worry, saying that occasionally attending places like this can oil the wheels with Central Area chiefs. She asks me what I have read, suggesting authors who are definitely not on the CenSA curriculum; Zola, Steinbeck and poets like Blake and Eliot. I forget the stilted affluence of our surroundings, and by the time Alexandra returns, we are deep in conversation about leaders in literature who stood up for their principles.

I am secretly dreading that they will take me to the sauna, or the massage rooms, and leaf nervously through the glossy brochure on the tea tray. Manya says that time is of the essence, and it seems they have an appointment for their nails in a few minutes. I hide my hands in my lap, as my nails are short and stumpy compared with their long, elegant talons, and notice a lifesaver in the brochure. There is a hair salon. I suggest that I would benefit from a haircut, and they agree readily. I guess they would like some time without me tagging along, to talk about me, and to consider what they will do next. Alexandra takes a small piece of scented paper from her bag and jots a series of numbers on it. She smiles saying, 'Give them my ID and enjoy; see you in an hour.'

***

'Well?' Alexandra asked Manya, when the two women were alone and awaiting the attentions of the manicurist. 'What do you make of Zade?'

Manya responded insightfully that Zade was clearly her mother's daughter. As Alexandra had not explained anything of Zade's background to Manya, she was surprised at this comment. Manya continued wryly, 'She provides an interesting dilemma given that the basis of the scintillation programme is a belief in genetic educational potential. Her eyes are amazingly scintillated, but she is the biological child of not only two convicted criminals, but the two most effective leaders of the education resistance in recent times. She has, I expect, attended grammar academies since the age of four. What were we doing admitting her to a grammar academy instead of sending her to the Periphery? I find her fascinating, and a touch challenging; she never knew her parents, and yet she rejects the education of the Central Area. My friend, what do you want me to do with her?'

Alexandra defends the programme, saying, 'It was the first year of scintillation, 2064, when she was born. These days any children born to the education underground should be automatically unscintillated. I agree she is a puzzle. How did you know about her mother?'

The silver-clad manicurist arrived and started her delicate work, allowing the women to talk, while she coloured, buffed and polished, but they were constrained in her presence, and started talking about their day out in the East, remembering their escape to Southwold Pier. The attendant took great care, and paused over each nail with precise attention to detail. When she offered a sparkling glitter-finish called "scintillation", she looked surprised when both women said simultaneously, 'No thank you,' opting for the pearlised look instead. She applied scented oils to their fingers, and offered further hand massage, but they wanted to talk, and dismissed her as soon as they could.

'I recognised the name Beaufort,' Manya explained.

'I see,' Alexandra resumed, 'I am growing fond of Zade; she is so refreshing, and so…brave I suppose, no; so resilient, so special. Do you know she was sleeping in the underground stations! She came up to me out of the blue in a Chateau Privee. She lent me a copy of S. Herbert's "The Art and Science of Selection".'

Manya very rarely swore, but she couldn't help saying, 'Shit, how did she get hold of a copy of that? I was told they were all destroyed to protect the programme?'

'Zade is on a mission,' Alexandra responded.

'She is liaising with the education underground, I assume?' Manya asked, and was surprised that Alexandra denied this, saying,

'She is working alone; we need her on-side. I couldn't turn her out on to the streets. I contemplated handing her over to the Enforcement Team, but I couldn't Manya, I simply couldn't.' She paused, thoughtfully, and resumed, 'I told her about her parents; they are her vulnerability. Do you think they ever resurfaced? Can you get her into school? She will be more comfortable out in one of your Periphery schools; I think she will repay investment, and we don't want her to be a loose cannon…'

Manya asked, 'Does Michael know?'

'No,' Alexandra reassured her, adding, 'That wouldn't be wise.'

'Just checking; I know how close you two are,' Manya observed with a smile. In low tones, the two friends and colleagues agreed their plan for Zade.

***

Alone at last, having left Alexandra and Manya in the nail salon, I walk along the grand corridor with my head held high. At the reception desk I ask for directions to the hair stylist, who I am told works on the lower ground floor behind the entrance area. I have never been to a hair stylist before, having just let my hair grow in its own way, avoiding the alarming android booths at railway stations, which provide a cheap cutting service. You sit in the booth and select your style, close your eyes and after much whirring, the job is done.

Today I enter an underwater-themed room without windows. There are no other customers to enjoy the whale music playing gently in the background, and I press a bell on the desk. A young uniformed girl arrives promptly and sits me in a scallop-shell throne where I perch, and explain that I just want a nice short practical cut. She takes me at my word and combs and snips my thick dark locks into order, showing me in multiple mirrors as she cuts. Piles of black strands fall on to the sparkling floor, and are sucked into an automatic floor-sweeper. As she finishes off, an older woman arrives and is seated in some sort of curling machine. I am offered a multitude of sprays and polishes but decline them all, thank her, present Alexandra's number, and leave, looking older and taller than when I entered.

Eager to make progress, rather than hang around much longer, I head for the nail salon where I find the two ladies deep in conversation after their treatment. I can see they are pleasantly stunned by my new look, and they make suitable exclamations. I just know that it is far more practical; I should have thought of it earlier.

Relieved that we seem to be leaving now, I follow them out, pausing while Alexandra swipes her fob and settles the bill, and we return to the parking area. Clouds have massed behind the stately building and the security notices are creaking as they blow idly in the breeze. The guards are armed and alert. It is a strangely pathetic scene, the ancient building engulfed by the need for security, now populated with "successful" figures taking a break from their responsibilities, seeking comfort and reassurance in alcohol, cakes and bodily comforts. Alexandra unlocks the driverless and I lift my rucksack and my coat out of the storage area. She smiles at me, for a moment holds me tightly, and wishes me all the best. She says that she will see me again. I wonder where and when.

I walk over to Manya's driverless, load my belongings and we head for the East.

Chapter 28

The unexpected and welcome lightness after my haircut is making me shake and toss my head. It is good to be on the move again in Manya's personal driverless, which seems to be clear of surveillance devices, and I can see my belongings this time if I glance backwards, which is reassuring.

Manya is both kind and challenging simultaneously. She ignores my scintillated eyes, treating me as a fellow adult, but she is demanding, asking me all manner of questions about my life, my foster carers and why I left the grammar academy. In return she openly provides a wealth of information, mainly about schooling in the Periphery; "real education" as she calls it, not the dispiriting CenSA grammar academies which she treats with as much disdain as I do. She talks about "her" schools in the East with warmth and enthusiasm, telling me about the volunteer programmes and the parenting work, and about the difficulties in planning for the extensive annual inward migrations.

I ask what her views are on scintillation, and there is a silence while she decides how to answer. Eventually, she volunteers that morally, scintillation is abhorrent, but given we are where we are, she focuses on her responsibility to provide the support needed for the fall-out from scintillation. She is obviously really committed to her work in the East, and I respect her for that.

We speed on our way and pass a large event in the open fields, on the edge of Cambridge. This briefly interrupts our progress, although there is only a short delay on the expressway. While we are stationary, I squint down to the scene below, trying to make out what is happening. There are large marquees, many old cars and hundreds of people looking like tiny ants from the height of the road. 'It is the Prophet Corporation Fast Forward Festival,' Manya volunteers. 'People actually drive those old cars themselves, with the historical engines. I went to watch once with a friend, and it was entertaining.'

As the driverless accelerates out of the traffic, she starts to explain her plan. She lives in a small room in Cambridge by the week, close to her EaSA office, and owns a house by the coast where she stays most weekends. Apparently, Alexandra asked her if she could provide me with accommodation, and a school where I can complete my education. I frown. I am amazed that Manya has already organised contact with Lyn, through her liaison with Sean Price in Wales (I found contacting Lyn to be virtually impossible), and from tomorrow she has organised payment to me, not only of my foster carer's allowance, but also the back payments which have not been received. She tells me that in the Periphery these matters are routine, unlike in the Central Area where scintillation has effectively outlawed all children who are looked after by the High Council. She says that I will find survival much easier out there, waving her elegant arm in the direction of the East coast. As long as I am linked with her, she tells me, I will automatically have free passage in and out of the Periphery through the Gate at the Isle of Ely.

'So, Zade, this week you can stay in my home, in a village called Aldness, on the coast. You will have a week of freedom, and when I come home next weekend, we will decide upon a school for you. It is not a case of grammar academies out in the Periphery.' Smiling encouragingly, she adds, 'I can also introduce you to the leaders of the Education Underground. They may know where your parents are.'

Having assumed that my parents, who I never knew, were either incarcerated in one of the Central Area high security prisons, or had died in their fight against injustice, it was strange to contemplate meeting them one day. I had confined them to history. It was even stranger to hear Manya talk of them.

I am nervous that my freedom is being compromised by these two high-powered women and am determined to take back some control. I grill Manya, extracting as much information as I can. Investing my voice with a degree of innocence, I ask her how she can plan for the influx of migrant children to her schools, does she use the Four Plus, or scintillation data? She laughs, responding readily, 'We just accommodate all who arrive. We turn no one away. Our schools in the East, and indeed in the rest of the Periphery, are totally inclusive.' I ask her if she is comfortable ignoring the discrimination of scintillation in the Central Area, and she seems to like my directness, telling me that her role is to ensure the best possible lives for the families, and the children, in her area. No, she is not comfortable, she insists, but she quotes Bentham's greatest happiness principle as justification. I had forgotten that she is a trained lawyer. I know a little of Jeremy Bentham from my reading about human rights in the biblios, and I counter her comment by asking whether she supports complete transparency, like Bentham. Scintillation, I say, is a covert method of discrimination, indeed, it is a form of apartheid. I turn my scintillated eyes upon her and glare with the passion of my argument.

She responds by stating, 'I am a pragmatist, and am in a position to make a difference to many people's lives. I admire your ideals, your principles, and if I can help you to achieve your goals I will do so. If there is ever any threat of takeover of the proud Periphery by the Central Area, I will fight. I despise the immorality of scintillation, of the medication programme, of the way of life in the Central Area…' This time it was her eyes which glared with passion.

Mischievously I add a post-script to the conversation, saying, 'Although you take orders from Michael Morgan…' Manya throws a wry smile in my direction. We now know exactly where each other stands.

She reaches over and touches my arm, kindly, suggesting we take a break after we pass through The Gate. We have encircled Cambridge and are nearly at the border now. The roads around Ely are all either circuitous or dead ends except the main expressway which heads for the gate. There are no depressing queues of migrants today, instead just a few older cars waiting for clearance. Manya has higher level ID, and asks for my passport, showing both as we cruise down the premium lane, through the towering stone columns, past the armed guards and out into the Periphery. She makes it seem so easy; the advantages of privilege. We both sigh with relief, leaving the tension of the guarded fortress and the high razor-wire fences behind us.

On this grey autumnal Sunday afternoon, the Periphery looks restful, a brooding landscape, free from the towering high-rise conurbations of the Central Area, but cluttered with the mess of years of migrations. Abandoned cars litter the roadside below the expressway and loosely organised groups of people, dressed in drab colours, come into view, and then fade into the distance behind us. Manya taps away on a mobile phone, messaging someone, seemingly receiving an instant response.

'Good, we will stop off at a special place I know,' she tells me, cryptically, and when I ask where, she winks. 'It is called "The Barns". They are usually there on a Sunday afternoon and today they want to meet you.' She re-programmes the driverless and it promptly pulls off the expressway and on to smaller roads, bounded by high overgrown hedges and riddled with pot holes. She briefs me, 'We will move your things, just in case. I have heard of undercover border guards tracking a premium driverless from The Gate, and searching before the owners return. Central Area Security has the technology to blast through most locks, but they should know my driverless,' she adds.

We pull into a small dusty layby. As the doors of the driverless open, the rank smell of the Periphery takes me by surprise and I cough. Manya hands me a small tin of mint sweets, and I take one, recovering, as I stow my rucksack and coat into the boot out of sight. She double-locks the driverless and I follow her down a barely perceptible track, ducking under overhanging boughs and watching where I tread, to avoid mud and decaying rubbish.

Manya's delicate flowing skirts must be made of expensive fabric as she glides along the overgrown paths with ease and dignity. I tromp behind, trusting her, but anxious and wary, looking to each side and constantly checking behind us. This terrain is new to me, you can smell the damp turf, as well as the reek of the Periphery, and there are birds flitting in and out of the bushes. We do not walk far, and soon approach a clearing where I can see a collection of old brick-built agricultural buildings.

As we approach, a middle-aged man comes out of the doorway and greets Manya like a long-lost friend. He starts by shaking her hand, respectfully, and then as she grasps his hand with both of hers, they stand intimately. I cannot hear what they are saying, and hold back, unsure. Manya quietly calls me over and introduces us, explaining that the man is called Rebel. He doesn't look much like my image of a rebel, clean-shaven and well-organised wearing tidy jeans, a shirt and an ancient, but smart leather jacket, but I soon realise that appearances can be deceptive. As he hears a rustling in the bushes behind us, his hand darts to his jacket pocket, where I can now see the shape of a small pistol. My heart beats faster as I begin comprehend the very different way of life in the Periphery. The rustle turns out to be a bird. He offers me his hand to shake, with an odd formality. I take his hand and he says, in a deep and respectful voice, 'Zade Beaufort, I never thought I would be meeting you, and certainly not here.'

Manya explains to me that she represented Rebel in a high-profile legal case many years ago, and that, before that time, he had known of my parents in the education underground. Bewildered by this turn of events, I follow them into the large barn-like building and discover a group of roughly clad adults sitting on long wooden benches around a makeshift table all pouring over one small, ancient tablet. They raise their eyes from the screen and greet us enthusiastically. Rebel asks if we want coffee, and strides across the beaten earth floor to a small kitchen area, with a table and methane burner, where he pours a steaming black liquid into china mugs for us. I wonder if the black coffee is an initiation challenge as it is so strong that it makes me cough, but it is welcome, and I drink it to demonstrate both resilience and gratitude.

Rebel is clearly the leader of the small group of twenty or so adults, men women and neutrals aged from around twenty to fifty or sixty. They seem to regard Manya in high esteem; she is familiar to all of them, and they hang on her every word. They ask her about a new programme she is running on behalf of the Department to provide work placements with legal teams for young people of my age. There is funding for over a hundred placements and she is asking the group to put forward some of their student members, not present today, but seemingly part of a wider network. Rebel stands up to her, questioning, bargaining, asking for more places, for more funding. The atmosphere inside the barn is completely alien to my previous existence. I can feel the intense trust in the barn. I can discern that these people are strongly bonded, but their determination is tinged with fear. There is also so much dirt, ingrained and depressing, tinging their fierce optimism with sordid reality.

Manya is keen that we continue our journey to the coast, so we gulp down the coffee, and Rebel leads us out of the barn, moving close to me and murmuring that he hopes we will meet again. He says that if I ever need someone at my back, I can message him; Manya has his number.

We walk briskly back along the narrow, beaten path to the driverless and Manya tells me that she wanted me to see how different life in the Periphery can be. I reflect that all my survival skills, learnt on the streets of London, can come into play here. I am not daunted, indeed I am grateful to her for taking me into The Barns, and for being introduced to Rebel, although the bitter taste of the dark coffee still lingers on my tongue.

Chapter 29

Fortunately, Manya's driverless is waiting for us in the layby exactly as we left it, and we prepare for the last leg of our journey to her house on the coast. Sitting back in the air-conditioned vehicle is a relief in itself. I am not yet used to the smells of the Periphery. While she enters the route into her navigation system, I try to locate our position on my phone but it is not working properly. It was fully charged last night. 'There is an incompatibility in the Periphery,' she says, showing me her two phones, 'A top-of-the range Haptic for Cambridge and an old-style phone for out here. Don't worry, I have a periphery phone for you.'

The driverless reaches the entry to the expressway and I relax as the wide road provides some semblance of civilisation, more familiar than the ragged side-roads to The Barns. Manya hands me a small second-hand mobile device which looks even more out-dated than mine. She has entered her numbers, and a contact number for Rebel. It is easy to use and I take it gratefully, thanking her, working through the commands and checking whether I can operate the out-dated technology. I will hang on to my own phone for when I return to the Central Area. She also hands me a small bag full of "loose change" and a wad of worn paper sterling notes, which seems to be the way to operate in cafés and on buses out here.

We are travelling on an old, wide toll road which is virtually empty and we therefore make speedy progress. Periodically we pass through derelict toll booths where electronic signs hang with blank unlit screens and kiosks have been stripped bare of their fitments, including the doors. Each time we approach a toll, I notice Manya tensing up. She explains that you have to be wary of bandits at the toll booths as they can seize the opportunity to hold up cars and strip them of anything worth stealing, particularly a passing Central Area driverless.

I watch as we pass the immense shanty towns below; rows and rows of pastel-coloured cabins, lines of washing, guard dogs and young people, disappearing into grey dots in the distance. The culture-shock is hitting me. No one puts their clothes outside in London nowadays because the indoor drying facilities are good, and the outdoor air is too stagnant to freshen anything. I ask Manya about the provision of water. It is unlimited in the Central Area, although we are all educated to conserve it. She explains how, in the Periphery, grey water (basically the rain, caught in guttering, large vats and pipes) is used routinely for sanitation including washing. I tell her about my system in Lyn's flat once the water was turned off, catching the drips in bottles, and flushing the toilet using rainwater. She chuckles, saying that she is impressed, and then starts talking about the re-use of filtered water in the Periphery for cooking and drinking, with the purified water from the Prophet Water Plants only being used for medical purposes. I question what she means by "medical purposes" and she talks about the health plants on the coast where medications are prepared for the Central Area. Only the purest water can be used there, for health reasons.

The high expressway comes to an end and the driverless navigates on to smaller roads. When I visited Lyn in Wales, or the Periphery in the West as it is called by residents of the Central Area, the terrain was mountainous and the migrant camps huddled in the valleys. Here you can see for miles. The sprawling shanty towns are interspersed with patches of farmland, and there are small villages too, where the original inhabitants protect their gardens from the influx of Central Area rejects. As we drive down the escarpment from the expressway to the flat plains, far away on the horizon in the seaward direction, I see rows of factories, or industrial plants, sheltering behind belts of tall trees and ask Manya what we are seeing on the horizon. 'Oh, they are the Prophet Corporation plants; for food and clothing for the Central Area. The large block over there is the Prophet Corporation Medical Plant,' she says, with significance, pointing way in the distance.

She starts to talk about her home, in the small village called Aldness. As we draw nearer, she says that there is a cat called Aldous, and I can do her a favour by feeding him each day. She usually leaves food out on Monday and by her return on Friday the cat is really hungry. Sometimes she drops back home midweek if she is in the area for work. Pets are not permitted in the Central Area; only working animals are allowed, and this is a novelty for me. She gives me a fob which she says will lock and unlock the front door. 'Never leave the house without double-locking,' she insists, telling me to keep the place tidy. She plans to message me when she gets back from the office each day, around six in the evening, to check I am okay.

The driverless negotiates the winding streets into a small costal village, and I glimpse the sea, infinite and magical, through a gap between two old buildings. We drive out on to the seafront. Wooden crates and piles of colourful fishing nets litter the pavement alongside rusted cranes and small boats. If I wasn't here under such circumstances I would be captivated by the mystique. It could be so idyllic, the picturesque harbour and the waves slapping on the sea wall. 'If you go out for a walk, do be careful of the tides,' Manya urges. 'The water can come in really quickly and you need to be able to reach dry land.' It is a world I have never known.

We draw up on the edge of the street outside an old terrace of painted cottages. I tell Manya that I have stayed in many people's homes but nothing like this. She says she is very happy here, when she has the time, which isn't often at the moment, and retrieving my belongings, she leads me up the stone steps and through the bright red painted front door. It feels as if I am entering a museum; the ceiling is so low, and everywhere is so dim. She shows me each room, drawing my attention to the small fixed surveillance cameras which she uses for security when she is in Cambridge. We enter the tiny lounge, at the back of the house, crammed with books; no screens, and I smell incense and stale woodsmoke. Here I see Aldous the cat, asleep on a cushion. I want to work hard all my life and save up so I can live in a house like this one day.

The stairs are so steep that you have to hold on to the wooden rail to steady yourself. Upstairs there are two very small bedrooms and a bathroom. Manya invites me to leave my rucksack in the guest room which is under the eaves of the roof overlooking the road. You have to watch out not to hit your head on the ceiling. There is just room for an old-style wooden bed and a bedside table. It is the most delightful, simple room I have ever stayed in, and so quiet. She takes me across the narrow landing to the window in her bedroom and we stand in silence looking out over the distant sea. A watery sun emerges from behind the clouds and dapples the waves with a magical scintillation. She sighs, looking into my sparkling eyes and saying, 'This place is very special to me. I am trusting you to take the utmost care here. Alex insists you are responsible. She is very taken with your strength of character, and I love your spirit. I would like to think this is the start of a lifelong friendship.' I have absolutely no intention of betraying her faith in me, and say so. She then warns me further, 'Don't trust anyone, and bring no one back into the house. The Periphery is a strange mix of the wonderful and the historical, but it accommodates the fallout from a cruel and violent world. It is very different to London, and you must stay as vigilant as you were there, actually more so.'

After we share a pot of tea in the lounge, and she has shown me the food that I can eat during the week ahead, saying, 'There are no prophet cafés or Chateau-Privees here,' she surprises me by announcing she will now depart for Cambridge. She has work to finish tonight and is straight into meetings early in the morning. My stay with her was arranged at the last minute and she cannot put her myriad of work commitments on hold. This suits me.

Looking out of my bedroom window, I watch the driverless disappear around the corner of the street.

Chapter 30

Four hundred kilometres to the south-west, on a Saturday afternoon in a small second-hand bookshop, a paper note was handed by the proprietor to a stocky gentleman with a full head of silver hair. He looked old before his time. 'This is not the usual,' the shopkeeper said, adding, 'I was told it is personal.' The gentleman frowned, fearing problems. He thanked the shopkeeper and moved outside on to the street. He scanned ahead and behind with his piercing blue eyes, and only when satisfied that he was unobserved, opened the scrap of writing paper so he could read the few scrawled words. He wasn't sure what to expect; they didn't contact him much nowadays, in fact he discouraged it. Expecting the worst, a warning of imminent arrest, or the discovery of his latest minor subversion, he focused his eyes on the three words, and the signature "Rebel". Standing stock still, he held the piece of paper delicately as if it was a jewel, tears welling and silently spilling down his rough cheeks.

What now? he wondered, desperate to know more, but confined by circumstance. The note was from Rebel. He had never met the man, but he knew that he was totally trustworthy. This would not be a hoax; surely not a trap? Fetching a cotton handkerchief from his pocket, embarrassed, he wiped the tears from his cheeks and took a deep breath. He had not visited the book shop for a couple of weeks; the note may have been waiting there for him for some time. If only Rebel knew; this could be too late. Too late.

Reminded of the time by a chiming church clock, he put the piece of paper safely in a secure pocket in his old leather shoulder bag and hurried to a bus stop in the square. Fumbling for his bus pass, he realised that he was trembling. He was used to this, and started to breathe deeply and rhythmically, calming himself. Buses were notoriously unreliable, and his daily trip of a few miles into town straight after work often took much longer than it should. As today was a Saturday, time was less pressing.

He travelled daily to visit his wife, as he had done for the last ten years since her admission to the hospital, five years after their dramatic escape to the Periphery. Her condition had deteriorated in recent months and now she was heavily sedated, but he convinced himself that she knew he came every day, as he had promised so long ago. Mercifully the nurses were extremely busy and therefore inadvertently discreet, never asking too many questions.

He didn't have to wait too long and a heavy old-style bus drew into the bus bay. He showed his pass and took one of the few vacant seats at the back, next to a teenage girl wearing headphones, like the hundreds of students he taught during the week. The engine ground into life, the girl looked blankly out of the window, and he placed his leather bag on his knee, shielding his hands from view as he extricated the scrap of paper, and read again, to be sure, 'She is found.' He stroked the paper with reverence, and returned it to its hiding place in his bag.

The bus stopped on the corner of each street and was soon full with standing passengers who were used to the inconvenience, but on reaching the suburbs, it emptied, and the gentleman alighted, walking the well-worn route to the hospital. It was a large long-stay establishment for the most severe mental health cases, and he felt at home there despite the harrowing stories harboured within the walls. The staff were always changing, which suited him as he could come and go with relative anonymity. It had once been a prosperous mansion with stable blocks and outhouses. Having fallen into disrepair in the 2050s it was eventually requisitioned to assist with the ever-increasing demand for mental health beds. Even in the far reaches of the Periphery, overcrowding and mental illness had become the norm. Some people travelled as far as they could away from the Central Area, and on reaching the edge of the land, simply accumulated; traumatised, angry and frustrated. He had assisted several to obtain passage by boat in earlier years, but increased offshore surveillance now rendered such escapes too risky.

He arrived at the imposing stone gateway and showed his identity card to the uniformed warder who opened the large iron gates which were now intended to keep residents in, rather than prevent outsiders from entering. Once inside he took the laurel-lined walkway to the main house, passing a group of recovering residents who were gardening, clipping the hedges and tidying the rather sad end-of-season flower beds.

Once in the reception area he enquired from the duty officer where he could find his wife today. Yesterday, she had been moved into a more intensive support ward and she was still there, he was told. He made his way up the sweeping stairs, along a corridor where he deliberately avoided glancing into the shaded rooms, to Ward 113. He always looked in through the reinforced glass in the door before he entered, in case he could see her, but today all he could see was a row of drably curtained beds. He pressed the buzzer and an unfamiliar seemingly efficient nurse checked his identity and ushered him in. He asked for his wife Janie, Janie Martine. Only the most discerning observer would have detected the flicker in his eyes as he knowingly lied. They had been given new identities after the escape. She had hated her new name, and now didn't respond to any name, so maybe it didn't matter anymore. He told himself that it did matter to him, and as the nurse directed him to the same screened bed as yesterday, he gathered his strength for what he might find as he pushed aside the curtain.

She was lying in much the same position as the previous day, sprawled on the pillow, her wild black hair unkempt, her eyes closed, her fists clenched and her face bearing the pallor of heavy medication. He approached slowly on the side of the bed where there was a panic button, and he took her clenched hand in his. 'Mathilde,' he whispered, 'I'm here; it's Owen.' There were no chairs for visitors, perhaps for reasons of safety. The beds were bolted to the floor. He perched on the edge of the bed, holding her clenched fist in his gentle fingers, murmuring to her, soothing, as he had done when he had managed to conceal her in his small home, before she became so violent. He believed she heard his voice as there was a small tremble on her face, and she opened her eyes, uttering a weak moan. He continued to talk, quietly, about irrelevancies, coaxing her into his space, seeking the smallest signal from her.

They were interrupted by the nurse who thrust aside the curtain with no warning and started talking to him, ignoring the patient, 'We have increased the medication today, so she is more comfortable. She continues to fight the feeding tube. To be honest, if we cannot get some nutrition into her, she will deteriorate further. You are next of kin?' He nodded in confirmation and she bustled back to her desk.

He started whispering again, luring her back with his soft words, his gentle touch. Sometimes it worked. He never gave up trying. He sat at her side for nearly an hour and saw no more recognition. He only stayed for an hour each day, and it was nearly time for him to leave. He bent his head to kiss her cheek, wary in case she flared up, but she was too weak today. He whispered in her ear, 'They think they have found her; I heard from Rebel. He says that she is found. I will try to find out more for when I see you tomorrow.' She did not respond, and he kissed her gently, rising from the bed and walking backwards out through the curtain.

Chapter 31

So here I am, on a Sunday evening, in a beautiful retreat by the sea, trusted with the fob for the door, a cat for company, plentiful recycled water in the taps, a quiet and comfortable bed and food in the cupboards. I know that I have one week of freedom until I am likely to be placed in a school, if I cooperate, which I think I will, and therefore every minute counts.

My obsession is the Prophet Corporation Medical Plant, some forty kilometres away. Ever since Alexandra, and then Manya, mentioned it, and I glimpsed the place on the horizon, I knew I needed to find out more.

The cyberspace out here in the Periphery is slow and unreliable and I am struggling to obtain information. I glance up at Manya's shelves and see a section of local history books and paper maps. I have never used paper maps before, and unfold one with interest. They provide a wealth of detailed information, but seem to have been made for a previous age. I search through each map in turn, opening it up and looking for a date.

There is a map which Manya, or someone, seems to have used for walking as it is tattered, a bit muddy in the corner, and there is a well-thumbed patch with an "x" on the small coastal village of Aldness. It seems to have been printed in 2050, before the more traditional mapping companies were subsumed into the Prophet Corporation and digital became the only mapping medium, in the Central Area anyway. The map is older than me, and will be well out-of-date. However, without the benefit of satellite navigation out here, it should give me the information I need.

In the bottom right-hand corner of the map is the innocent label "Prophet Medical". I can see a shaded rectangular area right on the edge of the land. I have heard accounts of cheap coastal land in the East, when scientists started to realise the true impact of the warming climate. In the grammar academy we were provided with a case study called "The triumph of the Prophet Corporation over Nature" which detailed the brave decision to purchase swathes of threatened low-lying land, and the introduction of ambitious drainage schemes. The constant erosion of coastal cliffs seems to be more challenging to control. When I was younger, we were shown digital models of a retreating coastline in an economics exercise to calculate deteriorating land values.

My Periphery phone buzzes with a message from Manya. She says, 'Arrived in Cambridge; message me if you need to.' I reply, to reassure her, and notice a message from Rebel, which must have arrived earlier. He gives me the location code for a community café in nearby East Braunton and tells me to ask for Ninia. Now I have a plan for the morning.

It has been a strange, long day, and I am keen to sleep, so head upstairs and lie down. I will sleep in my clothes, now a habit of mine in case I have to leave anywhere in a hurry. There is a faint glow from the moon in the small room. A few lights glimmer across the street, and there is a deep, velvety quietness which I never experienced in London.

I wake with the daylight at nearly seven o'clock and feel deeply rested. Forgetting to stoop, I bump my head on the low ceiling as I rise and walk out on to the landing and across to Manya's room, drawn to the sea. Gazing from the small window across the serene grey water in the early light, I plan my morning. I will head for East Braunton on foot if needed, or by bus if there is one. I saw an old-style bus stop in the village as we passed through yesterday. I will seek out the community café; maybe it is like Sam's Advice Bureau, and will ask for Ninia, as suggested by Rebel. I must find out as much as I can about the Prophet Corporation Medical Plant.

It is strange being in Manya's bedroom, and I deliberately don't pry, but I do notice that it is not set out for one person, but two, with two sets of pillows, and two bedside tables, both cluttered with personal items. Maybe I need to be alert for Manya having a partner? That wouldn't be permitted in the Central Area where such things are tightly controlled, although I know that much ex-marital subterfuge happens under the radar.

After freshening up in the small bathroom, surprising myself as I see my stylish short hair in the mirror, I greet Aldous the cat, tip the food into his dish, and rummage in the kitchen cupboards for some breakfast. Supplies of food are very different here compared with the Central Area. They must have to visit shops like in the old days. Manya seems to like to bake herself, which is very unusual. There are packets of flour, sugar and a drum of salt, and glass jars of herbs and spices, and varieties of dried beans. She has piles of long-store vacuum packets of meals, not made by the Prophet Corporation; soups, curries and something like powdered custard. I suppose she needs to be able to grab a meal quickly when she drops back home midweek. Behind the packets there are unlabelled bags of a white powder, and ground-up leaves, maybe a form of green tea, but nothing for breakfast. Then I see a small domestic cold storage unit where I find bread, various jars containing pastes and jams, and long-store milk. This will do fine. I sit at her small wooden table, feeling like a character from a fairy tale, and attempt to slice the bread with a knife which is too small and too blunt, but succeed, and enjoy the ragged hunk covered in jam.

I have never seen a tin kettle on an open methane stove in a real kitchen before, only in pictures. It is similar to Rebel's small coffee ring in the barn yesterday. I can see that I will have to light it if I am to have coffee. After an unsuccessful search for something to light the gas, I remember that I put a packet of Lyn's matches in my rucksack, and fetch them. I am not easily frightened, but the hiss of live gas when I turn on the burner, and the small explosion when I put my lighted match to it, set my heart racing. There must be some instant coffee somewhere; all I can see is coarsely ground beans. Eventually I find a half-empty jar of powdered coffee and pour the now boiling water on the spoonful. It smells of the free coffee at the Advice Bureau. I add milk, remembering an old fairy story about a cat drinking milk from a saucer, and call to Aldous. He trots up to me, and I pour milk on to a dish. He laps it up greedily while I drink my coffee. It is reassuring not to be totally alone here.

The only way to clean crockery seems to be by using water in a bowl, because there is no air-cleaning as in Central Area kitchens. I like feeling more in control. Life out in the Periphery is much more basic than I am used to. I don't remember it being so antiquated when I visited Lyn in Wales, but then I was the guest, and she took care of all the practicalities. Everyday tasks take so much longer here.

I tidy up and move into the lounge to peruse the map again, pack my shoulder bag, and conceal my scintillated eyes behind my dark glasses. Leaving the cottage for the day's expedition, I remember to double-lock the ancient mechanism with the fob given to me by Manya, and I stride off towards the centre of the village where I saw a bus stop by the village green.

The narrow streets are already busy with people idly wrapped in loose grey and brown coats. They look as if they have come from a film about times past. Families are hurrying to the bus stop, presumably for a school bus, and there is an old-style tractor pulling a large trailer, puffing fumes out into the air. They all turn their heads to look at me, and then look away and return to their tasks. I realise that although I view myself as rather downtrodden in the Central Area, here my clothing is uncharacteristically clean and modern.

I stand at a polite distance from the bus stop and ask a young girl of similar age to me, who is scuffing a stone as she slowly makes her way along the pavement, if I can get a bus to East Braunton. 'Yep,' she says, 'Take the bus with the little children, not my bus,' and hurries on, giving me a wide berth. I stand silently and watch. The younger children are not very well-behaved, but, I remember, there is no sherbet milk here. I mustn't view the Periphery as an outsider anymore. There are mothers and fathers fussing over the youngest children, talking loudly in a variety of unfamiliar accents. The pathos of my situation hits me; no one ever cared for me enough to take me to the bus stop. From a very early age I either walked to the Grammar Academy on my own, or hitched up with friends, and as I kept moving from one home to another, changing schools, I always felt solitary, an outsider. I turned the situation to my advantage, becoming fiercely independent, but moments like this remind me what I have missed, and how fragile I can be underneath.

Fortunately, an ancient electric bus soon draws up and the children pile on noisily. There is nowhere to wave a fob, nowhere to pay at all, and so I just sit down, hoping I will know when to get off. The vehicle slowly makes its way out of the village, stopping to pick up children all along the route. For me, it is bizarre seeing blank eyes everywhere, no scintillation at all. We are soon travelling through a shanty town, and then along a larger road for a short distance, when we turn again between more rows of cabins and towards the centre of East Braunton. I stare through the dirty bus windows, fascinated, as I see people going about their daily business unaware of how outdated they are, seemingly with no desire, or means, to live the dream of Future Success that is championed in the Central Area.

I don't like to draw attention to myself by getting my map out on this overcrowded bus, and so I work from memory. We stop by a school in the outskirts and about twenty children get off. Then at the next school the whole busload decamps, so I follow, still not having paid for my journey.

The reek of something brown and green like stale cabbage, so characteristic of the Periphery, hits me as I alight. The school gates are well-supervised, and the children run keenly in, laughing in groups. There are no orderly lines of grammar scholars here.

Gaggles of parents have accumulated around the school gates. Some wave at their children, and others are smoking! The smoking of cigarettes is forbidden in the Central Area, although I sometimes saw people smoking when they thought no one was looking, even in the underground. I shudder at the memory of sleeping communally, deep under the streets in the disused underground track-beds. I turn to an older lady carrying a small child, asking her the way into the centre of town. She points without speaking. I don't think people like my dark glasses; it looks as if I am hiding my eyes, which I am I suppose. I walk on in the direction she indicated and soon find myself walking past shops where people buy what they need. This is novel, and I walk slowly, taking in the scenes. It is as if I have travelled back fifty years in time. Now I can see a roughly painted board hanging on chains above a very small brick shop, with an open door. The bright yellow painted writing says, 'East Braunton Community Café,' so I enter.

Chapter 32

The Prophet Corporation Medical Plant, nearly an hour's journey from Aldness, was concealed from the road by long rows of tall, dark Cupressus trees that were some distance from the actual buildings. Behind the trees were high metal fences topped with razor wire, and then a series of old watch towers. To the seaward direction, less protection was necessary due to the steep rock face. At high tide the waves pummelled the foot of the towering cliffs, and at low tide there was only a small strip of stony beach, completely unapproachable by boat.

Over the last fifteen years the three-hundred-acre plant had been operating in the same way each weekday. The chief operatives had been lulled into the assumption that their work was routine, and the people of the nearby villages and shanty towns of the Periphery were not interested in the plant unless it provided them with work.

Lines of Prophet factories skirted the Periphery, providing for the needs of the Central Area residents, who didn't cook for themselves due to the fast pace of their lives. Many manual and factory workers had relocated to the Periphery before the education migrations, when jobs were plentiful. Prophet workers enjoyed benefits such as basic medical insurance, subsidised cafeterias and access to medications, so jobs in the factories were prized.

The commercial success of the Prophet Corporation, however, was down to the systematic removal of any competitors in the market over decades, and not due to the company being well-managed. In fact, standards were mediocre and practices were no better than satisfactory. Specific individual Prophet enterprises stood out as success stories. The chain of Prophet Cafés in the Central Area, for example, provided a welcome everyday service to many citizens who sought a cheap, cheerful meal or a safe place for a drink with friends, and they turned a hefty surplus each year. The food ordering and delivery service was also highly valued by millions of customers in the Central Area, and some in the North. Professionals liked to purchase one of the freshly baked items, which were universally applauded as quick and easy street snacks.

Maximillian Morgan had joined his profitable commercial activities with the education system back in the 2030s starting with his Academy Trust, which hoovered up floundering schools in the Central Area, and instilled a more commercially focused approach to their operation. He introduced a cheaper workforce and concentrated on both policing and instructing learners. He led a large outsourcing programme enabling school business managers to purchase all the services and materials needed at a fraction of the previous costs. He completely replaced educational books with digital content, setting up a charity to redistribute the redundant text books to needy schools in the Periphery.

In the 2030s, his invention of the Central Area pupil medication programme proved a huge success because it gave parents the benefit of more compliant children, the children loved the addictive taste of the sweet soda, marketed as kind to teeth and proven to build strong muscles, and it eased the workload of the staff in the grammar academies in the Central Area. A series of advertising slogans aimed at parents included "fizzier means busier", "calm in class" and "success with soda" were designed to reassure them about the new practice of compulsory daily medication in the academies.

By the late 2060s, Maximillian Morgan had introduced the scintillation programme, this time not visibly through the Prophet Corporation but through the High Council's Department for Wellbeing. The tender for the infant screening programme was put to the market and the Prophet Corporation won the contract. Scintillation was one small part of a wider health and wellbeing programme for new-born babies in the Central Area.

The Prophet Corporation Medical Plant was immense. It contained a dozen development cells where scientists perfected medicines, as well as over a hundred mini-plants, called laboratories, where production of large-scale batches of medication took place. Once a formula proved successful, production continued to roll out year after year. There was only minimal investment in research to further develop products while sales levels were maintained, and as there was a guaranteed continuing market for academy medication in the Central Area, both the school medication and the scintillation laboratories had remained unchanged for many years.

Chapter 33

The East Braunton Community Café is cramped and busy, with ramshackle noticeboards all around the walls, and a counter where you can buy drinks and small snacks, all only costing one-pound sterling. I am expecting Ninia to be young like Sam, but when I ask for him, he turns out to be a she, a swarthy middle-aged woman with black hair tied in a bun, her arms covered in tattoos and jewellery. Her ears are jangling with hoops and symbols, and her nose is pierced with a sparkling stud. She is wearing colourful woven clothes, and large strong boots; quite a contrast to my recent companions, Alexandra and Manya. I need to concentrate hard as she speaks very fast and with a melodious accent unfamiliar to me.

'Are you Zade?' she asks. Without stopping for a reply, she continues, 'I am Ninia; you see, I had eight big brothers and sisters, and I was the ninth to be born, the ninth!' She stretches her arms wide, inadvertently touching several customers in the crush. 'Rebel told me to look out for you, and that you would be wearing sunglasses, and here you are, at our community café!' She scoops the remains of someone's breakfast off one end a small table that is already occupied, dumping the plates and cups on the servery and calling over her young, pale assistant to cover her duties while she sits with me. We perch on wobbly wooden chairs at the corner of the table, surrounded by tall bearded men and stony-faced women, as well as several unscintillated teenagers. As Ninia announces my arrival so loudly to herself, they look across at us, and then return to their conversations.

She may be effusive, but she is practical, waving to her assistant for two coffees, and asking me for my phone. She places it in front of me on the greasy boards of the table, takes her phone and links them up, my phone buzzing with her contact details. Seeing my confusion, she says, 'It's an old system called Bluetooth. It still works well out here. You young Londoners will have seen nothing like this!' She waves her arm around the café smiling at the greatness of her bustling domain, saying, 'I was in London fifteen years ago, and I knew Mike Morgan; he was younger in those days!' I start to pay more attention to her. She rattles on, 'In London we helped the families to escape the tyranny.' When she says the word "tyranny", her eyes harden and her face looks both sad and angry. I ask,

'What tyranny Ninia?' and the words flow forth in a river of common sense;

'Mike Morgan, he took it too far, like Max, like his father. The poor children were all drugged up, and their parents were told that it is so good for them. And then he made designer eyes.' She raises her eyes towards the ceiling with despair.

'What about the ones with no designer eyes I said, but they didn't listen. They just brought in teachers trained by the army. We raised a stink. I went to the New Parliament and made a speech, but they sent me to the cells, thinking of those poor little children with no sparkle in their eyes, packing their bags, not wanted.' She slurps her coffee and gesticulating at my dark glasses asks, 'Zade, what do you think of all this, you with your double-sparklers?'

There is a pause, while we sink into the burble of background conversation, and then I respond, simply saying, 'Ninia, we have to somehow stop the scintillation programme.' She launches back into life.

'Ah, and even you say this Zade, sitting in East Braunton Community Café, with your beautifully scintillated eyes. Do show me your eyes, just once?' I am used to using my scintillated eyes (how does she know to call them "double-sparklers?") to gain advantage, but not like this, as a motivational spectacle. I remove my glasses and gaze at Ninia, and she exclaims, 'Yes, now I remember,' and I quickly cover them again, not wishing to cause a disturbance, as people are looking curiously in our direction. I ask Ninia how she can help me.

She adopts a much more serious tone, and lays out a proposal, speaking very quietly this time, 'I have a friend, Nazar. He can take you to see his wife Bonnie. Bonnie works in the Plant where there is scintlab2. You know of it?' I nod.

Drinking my coffee down in one-go I realise it is surprisingly good, and say so. 'Ah we are fortunate to be able to import directly from the ships that land round the coast…' While she tells me the story of her imported coffee, a rarity in the Periphery at this time, I think about my next steps. I take advantage of a short gap in her tale and insist,

'Ninia, I must see Nazar today; this morning.'

'Okay, I'll get him now,' she says, picking up her phone, calling a number, and putting it to her ear. She speaks in a language which I do not recognise, ends the call, and says to me, 'Nazar will come now, in five minutes.'

'Who is Nazar?' I ask nervously.

'Nazar arrived last month with his wife and two little boys. They didn't get scintillated and he is angry, proper angry. They live in the shanty over there.'

I thank Ninia profusely, mirroring her over-enthusiastic gestures, subconsciously trying to please her, and, grinning, she returns to her place behind the servery, to the relief of the pale girl, who is slow and by now has amassed a long queue of customers. I wait for Nazar. Will he be tattooed and be-jewelled too I wonder? He certainly takes longer than five minutes, but I am encouraged by periodic smiling glances in my direction from Ninia as she serves hundreds of morning drinks, taking the trouble to talk to each and every customer.

When Nazar arrives at the café, heads turn, and there is a momentary hush. He doesn't come in but stands blocking the doorway with his tall and imposing frame. He is not at all as I imagined, seeming to be very young to have a family. I can see immediately from his demeanour that he is, as Ninia says, angry. He makes it clear to anyone who cares to look, that he carries some sort of weapon under his body armour. He looks like a vigilante. I am unsure whether it is safe to leave with this man. My instincts tell me to be wary.

He scans the room. His deep black eyes eventually land on me and he beckons.

Chapter 34

'Prove to me you're Zade,' he demands, looking down at me. I glare at him and produce my passport, which I show him without letting go of it. He grunts and steers me out of the doorway towards a sporty driverless, ushering me towards the shiny seats. I stand firm on the pavement, and ask him,

'How can I be sure who you are, Mr Nazar?'

'Nazar,' he spits, 'Just Nazar; here, I still have this after we were forced to move out into this dead-beat hole for the kids' school.' He shows me his fob for the driverless, still bearing his Central Area photographic ID. It gives me his name, Nazar Lopez, his date of birth in 2054, making him 26 years old, and his previous address in outer London. Satisfied, to a degree, I get into the driverless, which he programmes, saying to me curtly, 'Ninia said to take you to Bonnie; you want to know about the Prophet Medical Plant?' I say yes, still weighing him up. He says he will take me there, a trip of about forty kilometres, and I can speak with her in her lunch break. He is becoming slightly less arrogant and more curious, continuing, 'Ninia says you are connected with people in high places. She says you can help us, but you are just a kid, and a scintillated kid at that. What are you doing? I don't want to be helping the other side.'

The driverless is fast, too fast, and swanky, not the sort I am used to. He resumes, 'As long as you don't work for that bitch Alexandra Essex.'

I reply, 'Mr Lopez, I may have scintillated eyes myself, but I am totally opposed to the scintillation programme, and indeed to the education system in the Central Area. In my view it is immoral that unscintillated children are sent to schools in the Periphery. It is not only immoral but it is totally unacceptable that families like yours are required to move to the Periphery. I am studying the history of education so I have sufficient evidence of exactly what is going on...'

Irritated by my righteous tone he interjects, 'I can tell you what is fucking going on,' continuing, 'Those bastards don't like the look of some of us and we are sent away'. He shifts his legs so they stretch uncomfortably close to mine, like a barricade, and we sit in an awkward silence throughout the seemingly endless journey until, after half an hour, the driverless eventually pulls into the plant. We have been travelling so fast, and the window glass is shaded, so I have no idea exactly where we are or how we got here, beyond the fact that he drove straight through the security checks on the access road to the plant.

The tension eases as he holds his black shiny Haptic-style device out towards me and my phone buzzes. 'Call me if you need transport back,' he offers in a calmer tone, adding, 'Ask for Bonnie Lopez at reception and go to the canteen.

She will have a lunch break around midday; I messaged her just now so she knows to look out for you. Say to the guards I brought you here.' I conclude his frustrations are not with me personally, and thank him for his help, leaving the driverless with relief, and watching him accelerate back down the access road, dust flying.

I am standing alone in a deserted forecourt beside a large sign announcing "The Prophet Corporation Medical Plant" with various directions and instructions listed below in smaller print. The sign is old and dappled with the translucent green and black pollution deposits of the Periphery. In the lower right-hand corner, something seems to have been overpainted with white in years gone by; perhaps it was graffiti once showing an "A" in a circle.

In the distance, a large Prophet Corporation water tanker turns silently into the carriageway, veering off on to a side access road. I can read a slogan on the body of the tanker, 'Purified by Prophet to save lives.'

In front of me is a grand entrance, with revolving glass doors, and I approach it with interest, now seeing shadowy guards inside the building. Safely behind my dark glasses, I enter through the revolving doors and smile at the two guards, who are armed with automatic rifles, and who bar my way. 'You came with Nazar?' one asks; they must have observed my arrival. I stick to the script,

'Hi, yes; I have come to see Bonnie Lopez; we are meeting in the canteen.' To my astonishment they wave me through, and I follow a sign directing me to the canteen, passing large notices on closed doors saying, 'No members of the public beyond this point.' It seems the canteen is a public area, in fact I am able to buy a coffee using loose change, and I sit at a small table where I can see who comes in and out.

Customers for the canteen are starting to build as it is now nearly lunchtime, and I sit and watch, unsure what to do next. The workers have cards which they swipe to obtain their lunch. As is the style of the Prophet Corporation, they are entitled to regulated portions of Prophet-branded foods, hot or cold. I imagine this is seen as a real advantage out here in the Periphery. Most of the workers are young and they all wear the same white overalls with gauze hats covering their hair. As they enter the canteen, they disappear into a cloakroom area and emerge in ordinary clothes, presumably having taken off their uniforms.

I see Bonnie before she sees me because she doesn't hide that she is looking for someone. She emerges from the cloakroom looking this way and that, her coiffured appearance reminiscent of Central Area fashion. I stand up, and she spots me across the rows of filling tables, naively giving me a thumbs-up as she collects her lunch tray. She joins me with a waft of cheap Central Area perfume, asking, 'Zade?'

I respond with, 'Yes; you are Bonnie?' She confirms that she is indeed Bonnie, Nazar's wife. She says she really misses the old ways of the Central Area, so she is pleased to see me. We exchange pleasantries and I start to realise she knows very little about scintillation except that her two sons didn't have it. She rattles on about the difficulties of living in such a small cabin in the shanty town, about the boys' school being overcrowded, and that Nazar is out of work and angry. She asks me about the latest films, fashions and fads in the Central Area, but I know I disappoint her, not having moved in those circles myself. I tell her of London, and the latest range of Chateau Privee cakes, having seen these advertised on the display boards, which pacifies her.

She laments rhetorically, 'Will we ever get back there?'

While she eats her regulation portion of Prophet beef substitute, sandwiched in a roll and smeared with relish, I ask her about working at the plant. She explains, between mouthfuls, that she was fortunate to get the job and it brings welcome wages into the household, despite the distance she has to travel each day. She tells me that Nazar resents her earning, and that her mother came with them to the Periphery, and looks after the boys, so she can work. She has little idea what the plant does beyond making medications for the Central Area, and shows no interest in this. However, I capture her attention when I momentarily lift my glasses, revealing my scintillated eyes, saying, 'It is not fair that some of us can stay in the Central Area and others are sent away.' She looks longingly at my eyes saying that she did so want her little darlings to scintillate, the sparkle looks so beautiful, and the academies are so excellent. I do not take the time to disagree, and am becoming weary of a conversation which is going nowhere, as she finishes her meal and looks as if she will go.

I make a final attempt, 'Bonnie, I am writing an essay about scintillation and I need to know more about the work that goes on here in the plant.' She looks blank.

'I work in the pain relief section,' she says, 'I don't know about scintillation,' adding, 'I wish I did.' At this point an older female worker files past our table looking for a space to sit, and Bonnie calls to her, 'Hi, you work in the scintlab, come and meet Zade.' The woman seems to know Bonnie, but looks warily at me. This may be my only chance to find out more and I turn on all my charm, removing my dark glasses, and luring the woman with my eyes. She cannot help smiling at the sparkle, and joins us at the table. I wish that Bonnie hadn't given her my name.

I explain to her that I am researching the history of education for my final assessments in my grammar academy in London, hoping she will not be able to check this out. I explain I am keen to know how the scintillation process works. She tells us that she has worked in the scintlab for five years, and in the plant for nearly ten years. She doesn't know how the process works but she has never seen scintillated eyes in the flesh before, and so this is wonderful, actually seeing my eyes; the results of their programme. At this point Bonnie chips in saying that there is a new boy at the local school in East Bridge, called Lucas, with scintillated eyes, the only one in the school. She sees him most days and has become friendly with his father at the school nursery.

Bonnie then gets up, waves her old Periphery phone across mine, presumably to share her number with me, and says it has been nice to meet me. She leaves me with the scintlab woman, who works through her meal, looking up at my eyes between mouthfuls. 'We are not meant to talk about the scintlab out of work,' she says. I reassure her that I am only a schoolgirl, and this is only for my schoolwork. She reluctantly starts to tell me about her role in the laboratory. 'There are usually only two of us in the scintlab, me and my colleague Martin, and we operate two product runs,' she begins, 'The A and the B.'

'Ah yes, I have read about this,' I reassure her, adding, 'it is the Cyclopentolate.'

'Yes!' she confirms, relieved I already know something about it. 'So, we simply monitor the medication runs; they are all automatic. Four days in the week, Monday to Thursday, we run the A cycle, and every Thursday night before we lock up, we close off the A valves ready for a B cycle on the Friday. It is the same week after week. Boring work actually. Martin and I just check the hygiene, make sure there are no leaks, check the monitors; things like that.' I gather my courage and ask,

'So, the scintillation fluid is pre-mixed then; you don't check the make-up of the chemicals?' She looks puzzled at my question and simply says,

'That's right; fluid A and fluid B are bottled in completely separate processes, but the Cyclopentolate feed is the same for both. It's been running like this for years.'

She finishes her meal and drinks her bright pink soda drink. 'It's good working here because they give us perks like the soda,' she says, smiling, and gazing at my eyes. I thank her for her time, say it has been nice meeting her and decide it is in my best interests to leave as soon as I can before any attention is drawn to my visit. I watch her disappear into the cloakroom; she is completely unaware that she may have given me the key which could unlock the biggest education scandal in the history of our troubled nation.

Chapter 35

At the same time as Zade walked back down the wide driveway from the Prophet Corporation Medical Plant, carrying in her head at least some of the information she had sought there, John Martine was teaching his afternoon English class at St Mary's High School. His mind was not on the lesson, and as the lively fourth form set B wrangled with characterisation and the theme of inequality in Orwell's "Animal Farm", there was more chattering noise than usual. Even when his star students came up with a re-enactment of the moment when the animals drove Mr Jones from his farm, focusing on something they called the "swinging of the inequality pendulum", he struggled to show the enthusiasm their innovative exercise deserved.

Eventually, a bell rang for the end of the period, he dismissed the students, and then put his head in his hands, closing his eyes for a moment, emerging to see the empty classroom before him. He collected two sets of exercise books from the trays by the door and spent the next forty minutes working through each book, marking, commenting, and occasionally smiling, as for a short while, he succeeded in taking his mind away from his worries, becoming absorbed in his student's valiant attempts in their books. He preferred to teach using pen and paper rather than digital methods, which were now widely available even in the Periphery, because he could tell exactly what each student needed to do to improve. He was seen by his colleagues as proudly old-school.

Despite his weariness, the students had worked well today. Always diligent and detailed, he finished marking the final exercise book. He then completed his preparation for the first lesson of the next day, selecting the texts, and checking his plans. Satisfied, he left the room, closing the classroom door and making his way along the now quiet corridor to the school office where several other teachers were leaving for the day.

'Hey John, are you off to the hospital now?' his colleague Kim asked kindly. The other teachers knew how ill his wife had been and despite his attempts to maintain some privacy, they cared about their quiet, bluff colleague. He welcomed Kim's enquiry and sighed, saying that he had been expecting a call from the hospital all day, as she had been extremely poorly yesterday when he visited. He said, as if to air the words,

'She is close to death, I know.' Kim felt tears prick her eyes at the pathos of the situation, and at his honesty in facing up to reality, not cloaking the word "death" in polite euphemisms. Just like him; direct, she thought.

'I have my car today and can drop you off at the hospital if you like?' He didn't usually accept lifts and never offered invitations for others to visit him at home, but today he knew her company would be welcome, and so this time he accepted gratefully.

She took him to the gates of the hospital in her small twenty-year-old electric car, which was unreliable and rattled terribly. Mercifully it behaved well; she was keen to offer her colleague a better option than the slow and very public bus, even if it meant her driving out of her way. Her car was a remnant from a past initiative to encourage teachers to become car-owners in the Central Area, before she moved to teach in the Periphery. Too many people were purchasing driverless options in the early 2060s and as the supply of the new vehicles was limited, cheap manual electric versions were churned out in batches. Many of them had now found their way to the Periphery and were limping on thanks to the initiative of vehicle engineers who remained fond of the old technologies.

He thanked her for the lift; it was kind of her and he really appreciated it. She watched the sad figure in his old brown suit, as he showed his identity card to the uniformed warder guarding the large iron gates of the mental hospital. A nice old guy, she thought to herself, not knowing anything of his past other than his wife had been ill as long as he had taught at the school.

His evening visits, after work, took the same pattern every day. He walked slowly up the pathway, through the gardens, today thinking sadly that he had not been able to drop into the second-hand bookshop to see if there was another message about Zade. He registered his arrival at the reception desk in the hallway of the large converted house, checking where he would find his wife. They shifted the patients regularly, as new ones arrived, and according to medical staff availability. He was told she had been moved to a small room off Ward 113, where intensive nursing and supervision was possible. Owen peered into the ward through the reinforced glass in the door before he entered, but could only see anonymous mounds in the six bays.

He pressed the buzzer for entry to the ward and no one came. This was usual. After a while, he pressed it again, but all was quiet. Eventually an unfamiliar nurse hurried to the door, apologising, saying they were short-staffed that evening. Looking at this new nurse, a young man not much older than the students who he taught, he asked for his wife Janie Martine, lying convincingly about her name, as he had done every day since she was placed here. The nurse directed him to a small, private room just off the ward, containing one bed, and an iron chair, bolted to the floor, saying softly, 'She is very weak, sir; we are monitoring her carefully, call me by pressing the button if you need me.' He left John Martine there beside the immobile figure. Unusually, she was attached to wires which were connected to a monitor on wheels, with small flashing lights. There was also an intravenous feeding tube attached to her arm, but he could see no surveillance camera or visual monitor in the small room.

She was breathing noisily, with effort, her fists still clenched. He approached slowly sitting on the chair, whispering as usual, 'Mathilde, I'm here; it's Owen.'

He took her clenched fists in his hands and stroked them gently. She gave no reaction; her fingers no longer uncurled to his touch.

He watched her tense face struggle for breath, and knew that even if he had received further news of their daughter Zade, his wife was now too ill to understand. While he stroked her taut fists, his thoughts were taken back to the events that led to their arrest over fifteen years ago. They had bonded early in the campaign, working tirelessly with their fellow conspirators, determined and effective, ruthless to a ridiculous degree. He could remember with clarity how that day he had told his wife to stay back at their safe house, which was in the hills just over the border into Wales, because she was so heavily pregnant. She had insisted, in her characteristic way, that she was needed as look-out on the border and that she was feeling fit and well. This was true, but with the benefit of hindsight, it had been the wrong call, and had totally determined the rest of their lives.

They had masterminded similar escapes many times, and used a well-oiled routine; perhaps too well-oiled as the border guards were getting wise to their methods. They had a massive following in those days, with teachers recognising them as heroic leaders. He hadn't felt heroic, but he simply knew they were standing up for what was right, speaking out against the dominance of Maximillian, and then Michael Morgan's Central Area Grammar Academy Trust, speaking out against the forced medication of pupils.

At first, they had campaigned openly, holding rallies and marches, but the powers of the Law Enforcement Officers were strengthened by the High Council. When arrests and imprisonments escalated, teachers feared for their livelihoods, for the safety of their families, indeed for their future place in society. So the protestors went underground. Owen systematically ensured that every teacher who had been arrested, detained, or who was on the Central Area watch list, was given the option to decamp to the Periphery where the teaching profession welcomed them with open arms. The schools in the Periphery were building momentum and were offering what he knew was a far better education than the false grammar academies in the Central Area. He and Mathilde were young and brimming with principled belief. They were iconic figures, he reflected, for a profession that was being dehumanised by a repressive regime, by people who did not understand the true nature of their work.

He pictured Mathilde that day, resplendent and determined; foolhardy it turned out. She was passionate about the children who she taught; she was a teacher who believed fervently in helping those children who found it most difficult to succeed. She gave them belief in themselves. When the pilot medication programme was introduced in the school where she taught at the time, she boycotted it, refusing to administer the sherbet-flavoured milk. In fact, that was the first time he saw her, speaking at a rather chaotic rally in London, urging headteachers to refuse to sign up to the deliveries of the Prophet Corporation's magic medication that controlled behaviour, dulled spirits and subdued inquisitive minds. Rallies were not illegal at the time, but were soon after, once legislation had been passed.

Continuing to gently stroke her fists, he recalled their wedding day, the autumn rain in the Welsh marches, their own diverse families, and the hundreds of teachers who attended, spilling out of the old church into the churchyard. His parents were still alive then, in fact, his father had organised the service himself, as he was a lay preacher. Mathilde was dressed simply in white, with wild flowers in her hair. She was truly stunning; her eyes shone with a natural beauty in those days. It was at the height of their success in the education underground, fellow conspirators played in a band and they danced deep into the early hours, before taking their places for another rescue exercise the next morning. The courageous campaigners thought they were invincible.

But on the day of their arrest, luck was not on their side. It was a small operation with just six teachers due to arrive separately. They were not using the tunnels, as the security forces had become aware of them. He could see that extra guards had been brought in as reinforcements at the railway station, and they looked mean, but he had no fear in those days. He successfully assembled all six people with their bags; there was too much luggage too he remembered. As planned, he drove the truck loaded with the escapees on a circuitous route. They passed through a small village on the border, and an unmarked van started following. He realised afterwards that his vehicle and its route must have been monitored and tracked. As he approached the small mountainous track where they had planned to cross the border unnoticed, he saw Mathilde high on the pass, at her allotted lookout post, signalling to him. She stood proudly above the road, and as he drove immediately beneath her, he knew something was wrong. It all happened so quickly, lights and sirens behind, and in front, armed security guards approaching from the Periphery and from the Central Area, in a ring. They were all trapped.

He winced at the memory, still deeply affected by both guilt and anger; the police guards had clinically removed the six teachers from the scene using tranquiliser darts, but not him, or Mathilde; they were the prize and were made to suffer. He had never imagined what it would be like if they were captured, and did not want to remember it now. He knew it would have been better for Mathilde if she had been killed outright then, while she was heroic and successful. He stroked her hand, thinking of her when she was young and fearless. Her lined face was still strikingly beautiful, but she was so ill; wild, possessed and desperate.

For a brief moment, as they were bundled into their different cells, he remembered how their arms brushed, and he saw the intense fear in her eyes, not for herself, he knew, but for their unborn child. They were separated from that moment. He later discovered she went into labour that night, and was rushed to the prison hospital, where Zade was born in the early hours of the morning. They had agreed on Zade as the name for the baby, while they were hiding out in the mountains, because they had once met an itinerant relative of Mathilde's, called Zade, who had struck them with his wisdom, resilience and creative thinking.

He knew Mathilde and her baby had been transferred in an armed ambulance back to London. He had been told that from the moment she was separated from her child, and confined to a small cell, Mathilde sank into deep depression and became violent. She never recovered from the harrowing experience, and he held himself responsible. He should have been stronger. He should have told her not to stand guard that day.

The only spark of hope during this disastrous time was the way the Sisters of Christ; he didn't to this day know exactly who, secretly took baby Zade from the prison hospital to St Thomas's. The Sisters volunteered there, supporting the young parents. His father had told him about this soon after the arrests. At the time he wondered if his father had made up the story to calm his guilt and her distraught anguish. He still wasn't sure, as they had heard no more. He didn't even know if their daughter was still called Zade.

He looked down at Mathilde, a tortured shadow of her former self, wishing again that she had died there, at the scene of the arrests, a martyr to their cause. Like the poor incarcerated teachers, they had been in the wrong place at the wrong time. His failure.

Nearly a year later, the Sisters of Christ had also assisted Mathilde's escape from the prison hospital, but by then little Zade had been placed in foster care in London and had disappeared into the system. The vigilantes of the education underground had stormed the jail where he was incarcerated, while he was on an exercise break in the small yard. More activists were captured, and lives were ruined then, too, in the jail and at the border. It had all happened so quickly, and without any warning. He had found himself bundled under a tarpaulin on a lorry, and in a rapid chase into the protection of the Periphery. He had been officially removed from all High Council records, due to their embarrassment at his successful escape. All records of him and Mathilde kept by the education underground were wiped, for their own safety. His friends and fellow conspirators had organised a completely new identity for him as John Martine, and their final act was to transfer him across the Bristol Channel in a fishing boat, delivering him with his new documents, money and a suitcase, to the far South West, where he had managed to remain undiscovered for nearly fifteen years.

The Sisters did not know what to do with Mathilde. Her behaviour had become unpredictable and she had lost all semblance of logic. So, when it was proposed she should be reunited with her husband, everyone involved had agreed, having run out of options for the illegal and troubled escaped convict. They eventually asked him to take her back in, under her new identity, and he had not hesitated to do so. She was his wife, and he knew that he was responsible for her desperate plight.

At first, living together with new identities in the far South West had been hard; her mental illness was un-medicated and unpredictable, and he had no knowledge of how to manage her violent outbursts. They had lived in the small cabin in the shanty town drawing state benefits; she, unable to work for mental health reasons, and he, as her permanent carer. He had learnt to read her moods and her vulnerabilities. He knew not to mention Zade, as this invariably sent Mathilde into a deep depression that lasted for days.

He recalled, as he held on to her weakly clenched fists and listened to her slow breathing, that by 2070, or 2071, he had reluctantly sought help from the Periphery Wellbeing Department. He had not been able to explain Mathilde's history to the medics, as their previous identities had to remain completely unknown, but the doctors had been very helpful and medications had been prescribed. After a series of violent incidents in public places, when she manged to slip his rudimentary security measures, it was finally agreed that, for her own protection, and that of the public, she would be sectioned, and admitted to the local secure unit.

His biggest fear was that, in the care of others, she would give them both away through loose talk, revealing their real identities, condemning them to the increasingly rigorous justice system in the Central Area. However, she seemed to know deep down in her core not to do this, and as the medics and carers often dismissed her rantings as hallucinations, she and her husband had remained safe over the years that ensued.

He regularly admitted to himself that he was guilty of causing her illness, but he was unable to share this with anyone. He also felt a deep sense of failure. So many times, he had longed to share his concerns, his thoughts and feelings with the one person with whom he could talk with complete honesty, but, of course, his wife was too ill to provide this listening ear for him, and, he reflected, it was wrong of him to even ask it of her. He had remained loyal to his wife through her illness because he loved her, and not through his guilt. He had always loved her, and that was why he was sitting there at her side now, willing her tired body to give up the fight, willing her to float quietly away from all her torment.

Although she spoke no words, it was as if she spoke to him, pleading with him. In the dim silence, he stood up, bent over her gently, kissing each of her pale cheeks, and put on a pair of medical gloves from the trolley. He scanned the ward outside, drew the curtain across the small window in the door, carefully and quickly disconnected the monitor, and picked up a pillow.

Part 3

Chapter 36

Reluctantly, I message Nazar, asking for a lift back to East Braunton. I know from Manya's old map that the town is about forty kilometres away so I need some form of transport. I set off down the access road on foot, not wishing to hang about near the plant. My mind is buzzing, trying to understand how the scintlab works, and wondering how I might attempt to use the small lighted fob which Danielle, the old lady, gave to me when we met at the Advice Bureau. The dilapidated road sign points right to East Braunton and left to Ipswich, so I turn right and pick my way along the verge. I like walking; I used to walk miles in London after Lyn and Kira left for the Periphery.

The roadside is open and dusty and the air smells of chemicals. This seems to be a regular route for old flatbed lorries and delivery vehicles. I continue to walk, instead of standing waiting for Nazar, and several more water tankers pass, bearing the slogan, 'Purified by Prophet to save lives.' They disgust me; so many lives have been wrecked by the Prophet Corporation's medication and scintillation programmes. More importantly, how am I going to switch off scintillation? One thing is certain, that this is the only plant where the scintillation fluid is manufactured and distributed. As to how this can be disrupted, I am still unsure, but I feel the answer is within my grasp.

Realising this is not a good route to be taking, after a rough-looking driver pulls over and tries to entice me into his van, I pick up my pace and hope Nazar responds soon. Unsurprisingly I hear nothing from him, and after twenty minutes of brisk walking along the edge of the weedy cornfield, hidden behind the hedge rather than visible on the verge, I think I have covered several kilometres. I check my Periphery phone every few minutes, but still do not hear from Nazar. Now I am approaching the edge of a shanty town; a pavement appears and I march onwards, feeling slightly safer with other people around.

Row after row of dilapidated cabins are painted in pastel colours, some blue, others pink or yellow, maybe in an attempt to cheer up the scene, but now faded and grimy. There are four or five residences in each joined row, like a terrace, and people have tried to create fences and boundaries so the small patches of dirt out the front can be used as gardens. Garden is a polite term for the squares of land, which are often filled with rubbish, or barking dogs. I am frightened of the dogs; there were no pets in the Central Area, only working animals, and these growling snapping creatures fill me with dread. Fortunately, they are usually tied up, or kept behind ramshackle metal gates. Occasionally, a garden has flowers growing in it, or children's play equipment.

Walking briskly through the dusty streets, I soon see a small queue of waiting figures on my side of the road. As I approach, I can see that it is indeed a bus stop, and mercifully a bus seems to be due. Once they get settled in the shanty towns, migrants rely on the buses, which offer a good service from what I can see. I reach the queue, join the end of it, and fortunately a bus soon appears, way in the distance. Heads turn and watch the old electric vehicle approach through the dusty haze. It pulls up and we get on. This time I am asked to pay, and when I ask hopefully for Aldness, the driver shakes his head and issues a ticket to East Braunton, in return for some of the cash given to me by Manya. Dutifully, I message Nazar saying no worries as I have caught a bus, not wishing to make an enemy by inconveniencing the short-tempered man. But he still doesn't reply.

The long bus journey is tediously uneventful, with stops in a string of rural villages and shanty towns, and after an interminable hour, we are passing through the outskirts of East Braunton, where the bus terminates.

My Periphery phone buzzes with a message, surprisingly from an unknown contact; someone called Patels. The message simply says, 'For Zade come to see us today 5pm 236 yellow East Bridge shanty. Pass food store on corner then turn left. Patels (friends of Bonnie).'

Chapter 37

So, I am invited to visit cabin 236 in the East Bridge shanty town near East Braunton at 5pm this afternoon, by friends of Bonnie. This might be a trap, and I am wary. It is already nearly 5pm and so I set off on foot, anxious to discover the identity of "Patels" and hoping they are genuine friends of Bonnie. The cabin seems to be near the food store, which I passed on my way to see Ninia so I think I can find my way.

The clouds are rolling in from the sea and the afternoon becomes grey and damp, so I pull my coat closely around me and walk hopefully in the direction of the East Bridge shanty town. On foot, I make good progress, soon passing the food store on the corner of the street, as Patels described. Just as it starts to rain, I arrive at the small yellow single-storey cabin number 236, interestingly with a smart Central Area driverless parked in front. I knock and hear voices inside.

A father opens the door with two small boys holding on to his leg, and they introduce themselves as Mr Patel, Lucas and Noah. So, this is Lucas, who Bonnie mentioned. He looks six or seven years old and has bright scintillated eyes. I remove my dark glasses, showing my eyes to him. We instantly have a connection. We are two refugees from the Central Area; two bright-eyed misfits. Mr Patel invites me in, saying that Bonnie messaged him suggesting we should meet. They have not been in the Periphery long and are keen to talk with me. They are anxious about their driverless, he says, out the front where everyone can see it, and they are going to trade it in for a more practical vehicle as soon as they can, hoping it isn't vandalised in the meantime.

I am told that Mrs Patel is due back from work soon. They explain that a colleague drops her home from the school where she teaches each day; meanwhile I sit in the small lounge and play with the boys. They have brought basketfuls of toys with them from the Central Area, and show me their favourites, wooden bricks, small painted figures and a set of miniature driverless vehicles, designed very realistically. Lucas keeps looking at my eyes, and eventually asks me whether, like him, my brother didn't get sparkling eyes too. I smile and say that I don't have a brother like him; I am visiting the Periphery and am staying with a friend. He tells me that they are not visiting, but are staying, and that he likes his new home and his school, but there is no sherbet milk. He seems worried that without it he will not grow strong; such is the indoctrination in the grammar academies, so I say he looks good and strong without it, and anyway, I didn't like the taste of it. He considers this and says that his new school is much better because they can play outside more. He rummages in a drawer and starts to show me the maps he has drawn of castles and islands, showing me cliffs and mountain paths, moats and drawbridges.

While Noah trundles the cars up and down the slope of the settee, and Mr Patel is busy in the tiny kitchen at the back of the cabin, Lucas says to me, 'Zade, I will tell you a secret. We went for an adventure along the sea, under the cliffs.' He searches for his map, pointing and saying, 'There is a big factory, here, where they make our eyes. We had to be very quiet but when the people came with guns we stood behind the rocks and when they went away, we came home. I love the sea, but not the guns.'

Mr Patel bustles through into the lounge carrying a tray of drinks for the boys and me, in safety cups. 'It's good to see you Zade,' he says cheerfully. 'Someone from civilisation. What do you make of it out here?' I tell him that, like Lucas, I love the sea, and the wild places, but find the shanty towns depressing.

He responds by telling me of the kindness of the people after they arrived. He says that although you have to be careful, there is a freedom which they never felt in the Central Area. He and his wife like the schools out here. As he is completely unaware of my life story, I volunteer, 'I am not a supporter of the grammar academies in the Central Area.'

'You should talk with my wife; she says that teaching classes out here is completely different to teaching back home. She is pleased to be staying here, and says it is much better for the boys. Maybe Noah not scintillating did us a favour, although at first it didn't seem like that.' I notice he still refers to the Central Area as "home".

He checks his watch, an expensive central-area jewellery item, which looks out of place in the cheap cabin. He glances out of the window seeking signs of his wife's return saying, 'We can't get used to the Periphery phones though, so unreliable compared with Haptic technology…' his voice tails off, as he stops himself making negative comparisons.

I begin to be fascinated by this welcoming family and wonder why they have contacted me.

The noise of a car door closing disturbs the street, and the boys leap up shouting, 'Mummy, Mummy.' As Mrs Patel hugs the boys, she asks cheerily,

'Who have we here?'

The boys chorus, 'It's Zade, Zade,' repeating my name over and over in their exuberant and playful chant. Mrs Patel deposits her briefcase in the narrow hallway and scoops the boys up in a great bear-hug. In the face of all their recent challenges, the Patels convey resilience and hope, and despite my nagging awareness that I never had the benefit of this kind of genuine family love, or a family to share my story, I quickly feel included in their small world. Mrs Patel shakes my hand warmly, and little Noah jumps up towards me, singing, 'Zade, Zade.' Lucas stands by my side and holds my hand, and we all laugh. I can't remember when I last laughed with pleasure.

The parents take me through to sit at their kitchen table, which is strewn with the debris of the day, and fetch a large Prophet Store notepad, which Mrs Patel opens to reveal their scribbled plans. They settle the boys in the lounge. Keeping the doors open, so they can see them playing, Mr Patel asks me, 'Zade, what do you know of scintillation?'

Initially I hesitate. This is not a subject for idle gossip. He helps me by explaining how they met with Alexandra Essex and obtained a resettlement agreement because Noah's eyes didn't scintillate, they are subject to a gagging clause and all manner of restrictions, but they are not prevented from holding private conversations like this. They are in contact with a Central Area lawyer who works for the education underground, who is advising them. Mrs Patel interjects, clarifying for me that they accept their personal situation, but want to play a part in changing the future for others.

Reassured, I now feel more confident. I say that, like them, I want to change the future for generations to come; I am determined to end the most discriminatory and I'll-conceived policy in our country's educational history. I say that it is not only scintillation, and the Four Plus, but also the compulsory medication programme which must end, adding that Michael Morgan's plans for the CenSA Grammar Academy Trust to expand into the North must somehow be halted. Mrs Patel explains that she knows several ex-colleagues in towns in the North who are leading the rebellion. 'They are making Michael Morgan's days very difficult at present,' she adds.

We have quickly established a common purpose, and I feel strangely relieved I am not carrying the heavy load of scintillation alone. I knew of the education underground, but until I met Rebel and now the Patels, I had no links into the movement. I ask them if they know Rebel, but they haven't heard of him. I decide I must not reveal who is kindly accommodating me; I am keen to protect Manya's identity. I am not entirely sure whether she is complicit with the education underground, and really don't want to risk upsetting her, given her kindness towards me.

We begin by comparing our knowledge of the scintillation process. I know more than they do about the history, and fill in gaps for them, without specifically mentioning yet that I have a copy of the S. Herbert pamphlet. They are very interested in the sharing of data between the Department for Future Success and the Department for Wellbeing, and in the categorisation of babies as A or B. They know more about the way babies are treated, having experienced this first-hand. Mr Patel, being a nursery teacher, has listened to the stories told by many young parents of both scintillated and unscintillated children, and as parents of young children, they have also experienced the process first-hand. He says that Wellbeing Officers visit all new parents in the Central Area shortly after babies are born. He has watched them complete their checks on new babies; hearing, sight, limbs, breathing and so on. He is confident that the Wellbeing Officers are completely unaware of the role they play in scintillation. They are provided with a post-birth examination pack for each new baby and simply use it. He describes the sealed pack which contains inoculation phials, and a sealed capsule of eye drops to dilate the pupil for inspection with an ophthalmoscope. Both the front of the pack and the capsule are stamped with a very small batch number. Some start with A, he says, and others with B…

The sky is turning a deep purple as pollution mixes with dust and rain in the darkening haze at the close of the day. Mrs Patel draws across the blinds. I am anxious about returning to Manya's cottage after dark, but do not want to leave just when we are pooling our fragmentary information and are potentially broaching new ground. Noah is nearly asleep on the settee and Lucas trots through to the kitchen, taking hold of my hand asking sweetly, 'Zade, are you coming again tomorrow?'

'Tomorrow is Tuesday,' Mrs Patel muses, 'Would you like to join us for supper? Perhaps you could come round to see the boys after school, and stay on to share a meal with us; on Tuesdays we eat late, together as a family?' We agree that I will meet Mr Patel in front of the East Bridge school gates at 5.30, after he has closed the day-care. They press me to accept a lift home but I decline, unwilling to expose Manya's address and wanting to be as independent as possible. Aware of the failing light, I hurriedly bid them all a warm goodbye, seeing Lucas' eyes shining after me as I walk out to the roadway.

In the deepening dusk, I march at speed, recalling the simple route accurately. There seem to be fewer buses after dark out here. Thankfully the roads are quiet and I can concentrate on making rapid progress in the half-light. As I leave the shanty town, trees tower above me on either side, creaking in the wind, birds of the twilight flitting across my path. I am not used to this, and feel both exhilarated and yet scared. I turn on to the main road just in time to see the weak disc of the sun dip below the horizon. The air becomes chill and the lengthening shadows disappear into a pool of blackness. I feel so conspicuous; surely, I will reach Aldness soon.

My periphery phone vibrates in my pocket, and I stop to reply to Manya, not wishing to alarm her. She asks if I am okay and I reply saying, 'All fine thanks, see you on Friday!' and then break into a jog along the pavement. I hadn't realised how far it was. Yellow lights flicker in the distance, gradually getting closer and closer, and I slow back to a walking pace, passing people with their dogs. Once I am in the shanty town near to Aldness I know I am nearly back, and relax a little. I pass rows and rows of homes, their windows lit up, some with curtains, many with blinds, and some showing their lives to the street. The drains reek and every time I hear barking dogs, I can feel my heart beating faster. I walk on, out the other side of the settlement and down the winding road to Aldness. There are no lights and I follow the white lines at the edge of the road. I am not used to night-time in the Periphery and realise I really should have accepted the Patel's offer of a lift back. I was foolish not to take a torch with me. Passing the village green, I see the red door illuminated by the light from the neighbour's window, and sigh with relief.

I realise that my heart is beating much faster than usual, and I am breathing in desperate gulps, as I fumble in my pocket to locate Manya's fob. With relief, I unlock and enter, putting lights on, and stumbling into the kitchen where I sit and catch my breath. Once myself again, I fill the kettle, lighting the hob. I check the door is double-locked before closing the curtains and sinking into a chair. At this moment my meowing companion arrives in the lounge, and I drag myself up again, to fill his food bowl. He gratefully rubs against my legs and tucks into the food.

I have been unable to reflect on the revelations of the day due to the tensions of finding my way home in the dark, but I now I begin to revive, I know that I need to do some serious planning. I get the old S. Herbert booklet out of my rucksack, and the small winking fob from Danielle. I unwrap the paper around the fob and notice for the first time that when unfolded, it reveals some faint, scrawled writing. Why on earth haven't I noticed this before? It is hard to see clearly and I focus through the magnifier on my phone, seeing a list and making out a sketched plan, as if of rooms, and a series of words in an unfamiliar hand, 'Cliff entrance, low tunnel to end, scintlab2 door 1, second left door 2, end.' This is significant indeed.

What does it mean? Who had given this to Danielle, why did she hand it secretly to me? What am I to do next? I weigh up one scenario after another, trying to grasp solutions that are just out of my reach.

The distant roar of the waves is the only sound now interrupting my thoughts, and as I drift in and out of sleep, I am at the foot of towering cliffs, looking up at the walls of the Medical Plant, with a brave little boy holding hopefully on to my hand.

Chapter 38

It is Tuesday afternoon and I am standing outside the closed metal gates at East Bridge School, feeling the chill of the autumn air. Earlier in the afternoon the street would no doubt have slowly filled with parents, grandparents and neighbours, all dressed in the characteristic faded clothes of the Periphery, with their babies, dogs and sweets in their pockets, collecting their primary school children. Now the street is empty, the school day-care has closed and I feel conspicuous, huddling against the fence, trying to blend into the scene despite my Central Area clothes and my large coat, which is completely not the fashion here. In my pocket I have brought both the S. Herbert pamphlet and Danielle's fob, carefully wrapped in the important scrap of paper.

After ten minutes I hear the sound of the Patel's driverless which slowly advances across the empty playground and triggers the automatic school gates. I get in and am suddenly sucked into a whirl of greetings. The enthusiastic boys clamber all over me singing my name. Lucas sparkles his eyes with pleasure. Mr Patel settles them back into their seats, laughing. He tells me that they have all three been at the school since very early this morning, as they do the breakfasts on a Tuesday, but he doesn't complain, in fact his pride in the school, and his new role, strikes me; it is so different from the detached mechanistic attitudes of staff in the grammar academies.

We quickly reach the once-yellow cabin and hurry inside, to be greeted by a wonderful smell of fragrant cooking. I realise how hungry I feel, when I am reminded, and ask what is for supper. 'Oh, I just put the slow cooker on for a casserole before we left this morning,' he explains, adding, 'There are much better vegetables out here; fresh and tasty.' They must have been manually chopping vegetables before the sun rose. My series of foster carers had either sent me to a Prophet Café, or simply provided the standard instant Prophet meals eaten by the vast population in the Central Area. Lyn was fond of the Meal Deals which were manufactured to taste of real meat and vegetables but which were knitted in the Prophet Food Plant, in the Periphery, and transported into the Central Area daily. I have never been bothered by meals, but this smell is different.

There is not long for me to play with Lucas and Noah, as Mrs Patel soon arrives, and we squeeze in around the small kitchen table where Mr Patel places the casserole, warning the boys that it is very hot. Then he shares out pieces of real crusty bread. He ladles the steaming stew into our bowls and there is a comfortable silence while we eat, dipping chunks of bread until they are so hot and soggy, they drop into our bowls and we have to eat them with a spoon. I ask whether they have cooked the amazing casserole because I am here or whether they eat like this regularly. Mr Patel is keen to put me at ease and tells me that they have slow cook casserole every Tuesday because it is such a long day for the boys. He is only on the late rota on Tuesdays.

Mrs Patel starts telling the family about her day. There was a fire practice and the whole school had to assemble in rows on the field. The school rule was that everyone must exit the building immediately. Two classes of boys were changing for sports lessons and had lined up for the fire drill in their underclothes, without shoes or socks on. Lucas and Noah laugh at the amusing picture. Mrs Patel tells us the headteacher is thinking of changing the routine so students must grab their bag of clothes before exiting the building, so they can continue dressing in the lines. Turning to me, she says that it was actually funny at the time but needs sorting out as there has been a spate of bomb hoaxes recently and you can never be too sure. Lucas announces that he doesn't like bombs or guns, and we all agree with him. There is not a morsel of supper left. The boys head off upstairs with their dad to prepare for bed and I attempt to wash the crockery, not being used to this practice. Mrs Patel sympathises, saying, 'It's such a shock having to do these things by hand.'

We settle in the lounge and read with the two boys, who are ready for bed in their Earlies pyjamas. We read, not from a Prexia, or even a tablet, but using real books. With supreme confidence, Lucas reads a really complicated story to me about a mysterious castle adventure. He nestles into me while he reads, smelling of soap, as we squeeze into the large armchair. Mr Patel reads a jolly story about exotic animals to Lucas. Two boys, both equally keen, even after such a long day, and yet one was designated for greatness with his scintillated eyes, and the other has been discarded by the system, and sent to the Periphery.

Despite wanting to play with me, they are both flagging. They say goodnight with much, yawning, and head upstairs to bed with their dad who settles them down and returns to the lounge. I check my phone for messages and see Manya's regular check on me, so reply saying, 'All fine thanks; Aldous is good company!'

At last I am sitting with Mr and Mrs Patel and we can plan. We start by summarising all we know about scintillation. I decide to show them the S. Herbert pamphlet, which they read avidly, cover to cover, exclaiming at the injustices and seething at the audacity. I nervously allow Mr Patel to scan and record each page using his personal Periphery phone. He eventually hands the battered pamphlet back to me expressing respect for me in sharing it, but with disdain for the contents.

They describe what they know of the Prophet Corporation Medical Plant. Mr Patel has quizzed Bonnie too. They know the scintlabs are right at the back of the plant, in the older laboratories, above the cliffs and that they are heavily protected on the landward side by a series of security doors and 24-hour armed guards, even though the production only runs during the day. The scintillation fluid is bottled in individual capsules in scintlab2 before the post birth packs are assembled in a different area of the plant. At this point I bring out Danielle's small package, dramatically laying it on the palm of my hand and unwrapping it. The small red light is still winking. I turn the fragment of paper over to reveal the recently discovered diagram and they gasp.

'This key fob should allow entrance to the scintlab?' I ask, unsure.

'Yes,' they confirm eagerly. Mr Patel studies the scrap of paper, adding,

'And we can access it via this tunnel through the cliffs; I was told that a series of large drainage pipes were included in the original design by Maximillian Morgan and his inner circle of scientists. They were intended to drain he cliff and to double as emergency escape routes. They were drilled out and lined when the plant was constructed in the 2060s. The sea level here was lower even twenty years ago.'

'But even if we can gain entry to the scintlab, what can we do?' I ask, still puzzled.

Mr Patel suggests coffee might help, and goes into the kitchen, returning with a jug of steaming coffee and three mugs. The coffee is good, and very welcome. I refocus my mind on the conundrum, thinking out loud, 'It would be easier to somehow replace the fluid in the B capsules, the pure Cyclopentolate, with the fluid contaminated for scintillation, due to the smaller volume. It is less likely to be detected.'

'I found out from my friend Martin, that, in the lab, they call that fluid the "human tapetum", not mentioning the word scintillation,' Mr Patel volunteers, adding, 'So fluid A is Cyclopentolate with Tapetum and fluid B is pure Cyclopentolate. You are saying we should contaminate all Cyclopentolate with the Tapetum. In other words, switch on scintillation for all babies to remove the discrimination?' I agree, thinking this would stand a better chance of success than trying to remove the Tapetum from 75% of the mixture.

'It depends how the chemical processes work,' interjects Mrs Patel.

'We really don't know,' I respond, and we lapse into silence, each of us deep in thought.

After a few minutes, Mr Patel makes a suggestion that we should talk with his friend Martin, who works in the scintlab with a colleague, Hanna, who I met in the canteen. Apparently, Martin is a parent of two children who attend East Bridge School. It was Martin who suggested that Bonnie went for the job at the plant. He thinks Martin might help. I am nervous as we may have already alerted workers at the plant to our interest in the scintlab. I say, 'We don't want to risk involving more people?'

While we are talking, Mr Patel is flicking his fingers on his old Central Area Haptic, and he makes us jump by announcing, 'Got it.' We crowd round the small screen to see a series of screen shots inside a laboratory.

'What are these?' I ask intrigued. He explains that the education underground keeps an online library of useful data and information and that he recalled seeing these images when he was researching scintillation. He wisely downloaded the series of ten images when still in the Central Area where the upgraded cyberspace works more readily. We study them in detail.

The images are not dated and could have been superseded by more recent developments, although we guess no changes have been made in the scintillation process since the 2060s. They show banks of computer monitors, large sealed vats for chemicals, and machines which automatically fill the small biodegradable individual phials with the designated liquid. We are not specialists but can soon see from the photographs that there is only one production line and that there are two thin pipelines feeding into the main dispensing machine. Mr Patel zooms into the image until it blurs, easing back, and we read "Scint A shut off" above a mechanism on one pipe and "Scint B shutoff" above the other. It seems to my untrained eye that the scint B pipe is the main feed in, and that scint A adds something later in the flow, presumably the Tapetum. 'Can we permanently disable scint A?' I ask, adding, 'So every phial is filled with scint B, the Cyclopentolate without the Tapetum. Could we do this without leaving any visible indication? Would the computers detect it?'

Then Mr Patel's eyes are drawn to the tiny scribbled notes that were made by the person who took, or obtained, the photographs; they are signed by someone called "Owen". He has added the following text: 'To permanently remove Tapetum from the mix, close valve A12 and remove safety catch.'

'Can we do this?' I ask urgently.

The three of us agree a plan. It seems a long shot to me, but we will lose nothing by trying, as long as we remain undetected. Mr and Mrs Patel consult their tide timetables. I have never seen such things before. They record when tides are high or low, and how far up the beach they come. There is a very limited tidal reach on the cliffs below the plant which means there is a very short window when the tunnel is dry. There are huge risks in this plan.

We agree that Mr Patel will collect me from the Aldness junction on the main road tomorrow at 8pm, and we will travel in their driverless to an obscure place beyond the security fences of the plant, where he can park up unnoticed. We will make our way down to the foot of the cliffs and at low tide will be able to walk along to the tunnel entrance. We believe the diameter of the pipes to be narrower in places so I will climb up them, with him keeping watch on the small beach; despite my height I am much more agile than Mr Patel. Tomorrow we will simply see how far I can get. If I can get to an entrance, I will attempt to use the winking fob to gain access, and will then attempt to permanently close off valve A12, if it still exists, removing the safety catch. I must then return to Mr Patel who will be looking out at the entrance to the passage.

We will carry minimal kit: a phone, a torch, and I will wear gloves. We are not aware of surveillance monitors in the scintlab, but they are sure to be there, and we will need to avoid stepping into range if possible. I am hopeful, pleased to be actually doing something about scintillation at last, but realistic enough to know our chances of success are small. We are risking being shot, injured or captured. We need to play on the complacency of the Prophet Corporation. Things have definitely slipped into a rather weary routine at the plant. Hopefully we can catch them off their guard.

Chapter 39

It is now Wednesday evening and I am waiting in the twilight at the agreed place on the road junction. I have already messaged Manya to reassure her that all is fine. The usual sorry queues of Periphery cars pass by; grey figures driving behind yellow headlights. After a short, anxious wait, the Patel's driverless purrs up, and again I find myself in its plush interior. We both wish we were in a less conspicuous vehicle, but it is fast and comfortable. Despite the poor quality of the coastal roads, we take a rural route, and yet still make good time. We are both nervous; both out of our comfort zone. Only a few months ago Mr Patel was a successful Central Area professional, abiding by the rules, and now, I suspect he is worried that he is risking too much with too small a chance of success, particularly with his family responsibilities.

It is a tedious and anxious forty kilometres to the remote coastal car park, once loved by tourists, but now hidden in the densely overgrown foliage. We sit in silence in the darkness for a good five minutes, checking our arrival has not disturbed any local security patrols. Mr Patel nods at me, and we creep out of the driverless, closing the doors slowly with a barely discernible click of the locks. I check, and recheck the pockets in my black jeans for my phone, the fob, my small powerful torch and an adjustable spanner, provided by Mr Patel, having studied the images in detail. We walk in silence, barely crunching the stones underfoot. I follow my fellow conspirator, trying to remember our route in case we are separated. Although it is pitch dark where we are walking, we can see the strident security lighting of the Medical Plant up on the cliffs. Bathed in a fluorescent glow in the distance, it is misleadingly welcoming.

He stops, a black statue, listening and peering into the dark bushes surrounding our path. I wait. He continues. We clamber carefully down on to the boulders which are just above the water line. Now we are protected by the incessant beating of the waves on the stones. Suddenly a screech sets my heart beating even faster. 'Just a seabird,' he whispers. I breathe slowly and deeply as we crunch along the narrow band of shingle following the line of the gradually retreating surf, until we are right under the cliffs upon which the plant sits.

He takes us straight to the mouth of the tunnel, having been there once before, when the family explored. It is less of a tunnel and more of a pipe, a large outlet pipe, protected by a loose grill, which we manage to slide slowly to one side. 'Good luck. I will be here waiting unless guards arrive, in which case I will attempt to retreat to the driverless. Take care Zade,' he reassures me. I climb over the grill and into the darkness of the pipe. The damp air smells vaguely of chemicals and the stale draughts cling to my throat. I illuminate my torch and crawl upwards in the tube, which is running with small rivulets. I note the time is 20.44. As the outgoing tide will turn in half an hour and will eventually wash up and into the passage, I need to maintain my grip on reality, especially on the time.

At first, the pipe is wet and steep, and as I crawl, my clothes soak up the water…is it water? This escapade feels foolhardy and unsafe. After five minutes I find I am able to stand as the pipe has widened into a chamber. I focus on making progress upwards, using my torch as little as I can, and trying to creep as silently possible. Another five minutes pass and I am in a drier passage with loose stones underfoot. My sense of direction is confused as the darkness is all-consuming. I try to focus, checking my pockets, feeling the fob, my phone, and breathing long and slow. I am moving beyond fear into a numb state, driven forward only by my overwhelming determination to end scintillation.

The terrain underfoot is becoming rough and uneven, slowing my pace. Shining my torch around I see rock falls, jumbles of jagged pieces of stone balanced precariously. Just as I am becoming concerned that the tunnel is narrowing due to the fallen boulders, I see a tiny red light in the distance. Petrified in case there is a guard, I pause and listen, but detect nothing.

With renewed resolve I press on, struggling over the jagged rocks. The light must be about ten metres away. It is winking u der some sort of security light. But the tunnel is becoming too narrow for me, with only a small aperture between the sides. I stop and listen again. Complete silence, no, a faint buzzing from the winking red light, that is all.

I check the time on my phone. It is just after nine o'clock. I know the tunnel is too narrow for me, but continue to try desperately to push my body through. I am so close. Bitterly disappointed, I admit to myself that I cannot proceed, so reluctantly decide to turn and retrace my steps as quickly as the conditions allow. First, I focus the camera on my phone on the gap in the rocks, and the winking light, and as I take the shot, the tunnel suddenly lights up with the flash, stunning me into shame. Idiot, I think. I pause, waiting in case I have alerted anything, or anyone, but there is a deep silence except for the faint continuous buzzing. I hurry back down the tunnel, through the chamber, over the rock debris and into the section of pipe near the entrance.

After what seems like interminable downhill stumbling, in the distance I see Mr Patel's anxious outline silhouetted against the faintly moonlit semi-circle of sky. Now he can hear my approach. I lurch through the final passage, nearly on all-fours. I burst out into fresher air, and he catches me, his finger to his lips. I shake my head to indicate my lack of success, and we move cautiously without speaking, back along the boulders which are already being nibbled by the waves. The sound of the water on the rocks camouflages the splashing of our feet as we hasten towards the driverless.

I am bowed with the frustration of failure as we hurry through the undergrowth. He remembers the route and we are soon on the edge of the derelict car park. He signals to me to wait while he creeps towards the driverless, checking each direction. Then he beckons, and unlocks the vehicle. We tumble in, he programmes the destination as East Bridge, and we purr off on to the country lanes. 'I am sorry,' I begin. 'I reached the top of the passage but there has been a rock fall and I simply couldn't get through.'

'The top!' he exclaims, 'Zade; that's great. I honestly didn't think you would get so far. It was pitch dark in there, and wet. Well done!' His praise is genuine, and I start to feel slightly better about our small achievement. He messages Mrs Patel, to reassure her we are both safe, and I realise how cold and wet I have become. As the adrenalin eases, I shiver.

Mr Patel is a true hero. He not only passes me a blanket, but produces a bag from under the seat which contains supplies; biscuits and a hot drink. 'It is called a vacuum flask, and is the best discovery of the Periphery to date,' he announces as he pours steaming coffee out of a flask. I have never seen such an ingenious drinks bottle before. I suppose there was no need in the Central Area where you could always find a café. Holding the cup warms my hands, I feel strangely close to this brave and kind father-figure who is explaining to me about the vacuum in the walls of the flask as a method to keep drinks hot, or cold.

I show him the bright blurred image on my phone, which displays clearly the small aperture in the tumbled rocks, the entrance to the scintlab, and the winking light which seems to be the security pad for Danielle's fob. Although he is impressed, I am embarrassed by forgetting to disable the flash. I will not make that error again.

'What next?' I ask. Our eyes meet and we know that we are both considering the same scenario. 'Do you think he could do it?' I ask anxiously.

'He could,' Mr Patel responds, adding, 'But I am not sure if he should.'

We sit in silence. I am desperate to achieve a step forwards, but I respect the Patel family, and am holding myself back from demanding too much of them. 'Maybe I could take a pickaxe and widen the passage?' I suggest, but we both agree it is not realistic and would be far too noisy. Both tired, we sink into an anxious silence until the driverless approaches the turning to Aldness, my drop-off point. Mr Patel says

'I will discuss it with my wife tonight. I am not promising anything, but I suggest we meet at the same place, same time, tomorrow and repeat the trip in the knowledge gained from today.'

He insists on driving me down to the village green in Aldness as it is late, and my clothes are damp. I do not reveal exactly where I am staying. As I get out of the driverless, he says, 'See you tomorrow at 8pm up on the main road; we are one step further ahead than we were!'

The next day is Thursday. The last evening before Manya returns to Aldness for the weekend.

Chapter 40

Mrs Patel was holding back the blind, peering anxiously into the street, when the driverless drew up. Her husband strode along the short path, she opened the door to him and they held each other tightly. She smelt the sea on his clothes and felt his body relax in the safety of their cabin.

They didn't talk properly until they were lying in bed, with everything ready for the next morning. He had already told her how Zade was just too big to make it through to the winking light, and she began the conversation, saying, 'You want to take Lucas with you tomorrow, don't you?' He turned over to face his wife and caressed her cheek.

'I told Zade I could promise nothing, and that we would discuss it. In fact, I actually said that although I was confident he could do it, I wasn't sure whether he should.' Mr Patel's professional training both helped and hindered. He knew from many years working with young children that their capabilities often exceeded expectations. He also knew his oldest son well. Lucas was resilient, confident, capable, kind, but he was still so innocent and trusting. It would be a huge risk involving him in this. He paused, asking his wife, 'What do you think, love?'

Mrs Patel thought long and hard. Like her husband, she did not think it was fair to expect Lucas to play a part, but with a touch of pragmatism she agreed he could easily crawl through the gap, hold the fob at the winking security pad, even enter the scintlab. Whether he could close valve A12 and remove the safety catch, she was not sure. He would, of course, also need to exit the laboratory safely, assuming he had not activated any security alarms. 'I would be as close as I could be,' Mr Patel volunteered, adding extravagantly, 'He would be able to come straight back to me in the tunnel. I promise you that I will make sure he comes to no harm.' They agreed to sleep on it.

The morning dawned with a cool blustery wind, and weak sunlight. The Patel family sat around the small kitchen table grabbing a quick breakfast before they departed for their busy Friday. The parents were tired, subdued and thoughtful, and Noah had caught a cold so was irritable and sniffly, refusing to eat or drink, with the resolve and determination of a two-year-old.

Lucas, however, was on form. He had picked up various snippets of conversation over the last few days, and was totally devoted to Zade, who he treated as his special big sister. He interrupted his mother's attempts at feeding Lucas by asking, 'Did Daddy go out with Zade last night?' Keen to be as open and honest as possible, his parents confirmed Lucas was correct, and that Mr

Patel and Zade were going out again tonight, just for a while, and would be back before the grown-up's bedtime. Mrs Patel looked at her precious, enthusiastic son. Then she thought of the injustice of the system in generating unscintillated children, like Noah, and she asked Lucas, without encouragement in her voice,

'Would you like to stay up late and to go on the adventure too?' Mr Patel looked up from his coffee, raised his eyebrows at his wife, and smiled, a worried and tense smile. Lucas, predictably, was very keen to join Zade and his dad, and so his parents made a preliminary, brave, or possibly irresponsible, commitment.

Mr Patel hauled Lucas up on to his knee, saying, 'You will be too big to fit on my knee much longer young man!' Lucas squirmed excitedly, listening to his father's serious voice, picking up on the grave nature of the conversation between his parents. 'We will draw a map together at teatime; showing where we will go for our night walk,' Mr Patel explained, 'And then we will collect Zade, and go on an adventure together. Mummy will stay with Noah.'

'Okay, Daddy,' Lucas said, with due seriousness, and they prepared to leave for school.

***

One of the advantages of the teaching profession is that there is no time to think about your home life from the start of the day until you leave at night. Once they were back at home, Mr and Mrs Patel began to consider the full import of the impetuous decision they had made over breakfast, and by then, it seemed to be too late for them to change their minds. Lucas was serious, keen, and could think of nothing other than his night adventure. He had drawn the map himself, sitting listening to his dad's description of the car park, the path, the cave, and the tunnel. He had coloured a little red dot to denote the access pad, and he had studied a few of the images of the laboratory. He understood what he had to do, and he sounded confident when he described it to his father.

They had decided to play down the importance of the trip. Lucas was bound to tell someone at school about it, and so the less secrecy, the less likely he was to behave suspiciously. It was just an evening adventure. Lucas often told stories about his amazing imaginary exploits, and so, with luck on their side, their son wouldn't draw attention to this specific quest. The Patels often took the boys out on long rambles and explorations. They had visited the municipal parks back near their old home, and now explored the locality to find out more about their new environment. They thought through the implications, and both confirmed that the evening trip could go ahead.

Armed with a fresh flask of coffee, a drink for Lucas, and some adventure chocolate biscuits purchased from the store on the corner of the street, along with spare clothes, blankets and towels, they were ready to depart. Lucas had opted to wear his winter tracksuit, a head-torch and his blue wellington boots. He would only carry two items; Zade's access fob in one hand and the spanner in the other. He had watched how to use the spanner and had practised on several household items including Noah's high chair and the bolts on his bed. Mrs Patel tried not to reveal her anxiety when she kissed them goodbye. They loaded the driverless, and left.

Chapter 41

It is really cold and dark tonight. After the rain, the ground is sodden, and smells dank. It will be slippery on the rocks. I haven't been able to concentrate on anything all day, so I tidied Manya's house, and walked out amongst the beached fishing boats by the ancient harbour. Ordinarily I would have revelled in the freedom, and in exploring the new location, but not today.

I don't know whether Lucas will be joining us. If not, I will have to work out how to get through the rock fall myself. I think I can do this, if Mr Patel brings tools, and I feel better prepared now I know what to expect. I have been waiting up on the main road since ten to eight, my eyes focused keenly on the lane from East Bridge. The wait seems interminable, but at eight o'clock I spot the Patel's driverless, and as it sweeps into the layby, I glimpse two sparkling eyes looking out for me.

Clambering in, I see Lucas is on his best behaviour, quiet and respectful in the darkness of the driverless. He is trying hard to curtail his enthusiasm. 'Hello Zade,' he whispers, telling me, 'Now, you mustn't make any loud noises. It is VERY important.' His naivety in the face of tonight's task is both touching and worrying. Mr Patel and I are aware we must not alarm or confuse the little fellow, and so we limit our conversation. Mr Patel explains the plan to me; he will carry Lucas down to the shore, and we will make our way to the mouth of the tunnel. Lucas is wearing his wellies, and so it doesn't matter if his feet get wet. Then I will stand guard while he leads the way up the pipes, until they reach the rock fall, when it is over to Lucas.

We talk Lucas through the route, and the actions needed, one final time. I am impressed at his memory, and hand him the small winking access fob, which he clutches proudly. Ever-practical Mr Patel takes out a length of twine, which he threads through the ring on the fob, securing it to Lucas' wrist. I confess that I feel disappointed not to be taking Lucas up the tunnel myself, but I know this is the right plan to maximise our chances of success. He needs his dad up there.

The drive is smooth but irritatingly long and we play quiet games with Lucas to keep him alert. We begin by thinking of animals starting with each letter of the alphabet, and when we eventually reach "zebra" Lucas teaches me to play 'When Granny Patel went shopping' and we end up laughing. As Granny Patel remembers the chocolate biscuits, Mr Patel digs into his bag and reveals the adventure biscuits, which keep us munching until the driverless pulls into the derelict car park and the lights are switched off.

As before, we sit in the pitch darkness, in silence, checking we are alone, and calming Lucas by holding his hand, as he is looking wary. After five minutes, we exit the driverless, closing the doors as quietly as we can, and quickly making our way to the path in the bushes. Mr Patel carries Lucas on his back. Everything is sodden, and I am soon wet through from brushing against the bushes. We reach the shoreline and Lucas hops down on to the rocks, obediently silent. We stop and listen, but only hear the beating of the retreating tide. Mr Patel is easily able to locate Lucas and I due to our scintillating eyes. I reflect that Maximillian Morgan would never have imagined scintillation would play such a strange part in the potential destruction of his programme. But I am ahead of myself. There is much to achieve before we can have such confidence.

I find that I am less nervous this time because I am focused on Lucas. Responsibility for him weighs heavily on me. We need him to succeed tonight, and to deliver him safely back to his mother. I think of Mrs Patel, who must be really worried back at their home. I reflect that no one has ever worried about me in that way. Mustering all the stubborn determination that I can, I march purposefully forwards, treading carefully, my eyes on my feet, and on Lucas who is tripping along more confidently than I am. Every so often we pause and listen.

I remember what Hanna told me in the canteen, 'Monday to Thursday, we run the A cycle, and every Thursday night before we lock up, we close off the A valves ready for a B cycle on the Friday.' I forgot to tell the Patels this; does it matter? Should it have been yesterday that we shut off valve A12? Have we missed our chance?

I breathe slowly to calm myself and follow Lucas who is treading in Mr Patel's footsteps. We make slower progress than we did yesterday, accompanied by someone with much shorter legs, but we eventually reach the opening to the tunnel. It seems to be exactly as we left it last night, only wetter due to the weather. As Lucas and his dad disappear up the pipe I begin to feel very alone in the darkness. It is imperative I remain vigilant. I scan each direction in constant surveillance, and I listen so hard that my ears hurt. Periodically I check the time on my phone. They left at 8.52, and it is now only nine o'clock. It is way past Lucas' bedtime. I hope he doesn't get too tired and lose concentration. I scan the dim horizon, to the right across the rocks, straight ahead across the lapping waves, and to the left where I can see the distant glow of the Medical Plant on the cliffs. I see nothing unexpected or alarming. The damp chill begins to penetrate my coat and I shiver, silently stretching, wiggling my toes and fingers to stay alert.

Five more minutes pass, and I continue to scan the surroundings, taking my watch seriously, never relaxing. Until now, the moon has been obscured by heavy clouds, but for a few minutes the cloud lifts and it emerges, clear and bright, suddenly illuminating the sea with alarming clarity. I huddle into the rock face, out of the pale beams. Then the clouds mass again and the moon disappears. The darkness is welcome tonight as we want to blend invisibly into our surroundings. You never know where there might be security cameras, or watching eyes. More time passes.

I am starting to worry now as I optimistically expected them to return down the pipe after forty minutes. Last night it took me about a quarter of an hour each way. Will Lucas be able to enter the scintlab? How long will it take him? Will he trigger the alarms? Will he manage to turn off the valve? Will it work? I cannot hear anything up on the cliffs. All continues to be quiet and still. More alarming is the progress of the tide, now creeping back up over the rocks and towards the mouth of the tunnel. There will come a point when I will have to relocate higher on the wall of rock and our exit route along the narrow band of shingle will become compromised. Manya's words resonate in my mind, 'The water can come in really quickly and you need to be able to reach dry land.'

By now I am very stiff with the damp and the cold. I shift my feet, aware that the strongest waves are already lapping at my toes. I check my phone and the time is now quarter to ten. Alarmingly, the tide has risen over my feet. I peer up the pipe; Mr Patel and Lucas could credibly stay in the tunnel overnight and wait for the tide to recede, but the driverless would become visible in the dawn. I know I could programme it if needed. In the Central Area illegal occupation of a driverless is punishable with a long prison sentence, but I am not sure of the law out here.

I think that I hear the faint noise of footfall. Holding my breath, I strain my ears, and hear it again. Is it coming from the tunnel, or from the cliff? Or is the tide playing tricks on me? I am now standing in pools of water, and the waves are washing up into the opening of the pipe, but I do not panic. I just think of Lucas, young and bold, with the whole of his life before him. I must remain strong for him.

Suddenly, the rhythm of the waves is broken by the crashing of feet, and the glare of a torch blinds me.

Chapter 42

While Zade was poised on the incoming tide, Alexandra was working late. She was attending the Department for Future Success annual awards night, celebrating the highest-achieving students in the Central Area. The event had been sponsored by the Prophet Corporation each year for at least ten years, and Michael Morgan was officiating, dressed impeccably, bronzed and beaming as he handed out the certificates, cups and trophies.

Gold balloons and swirling confetti pumped out across the audience as the successful students, dressed in their high-society gowns and suits, strutted up to receive their awards. The loud music and continuous applause were giving Alexandra a headache, but she was enjoying the glitz and the pageantry. She swallowed two stamina pills with her alcoholic soda and then resumed clapping.

Michael looked across at her and swelled with pride. The event was running smoothly. The Prophet Corporation had these programmes honed to perfection. Proud parents were filming and cheering. By nine-thirty they had completed the presentations, and had listened to short contributions from headteachers and inspirational speakers from the Prophet Corporation Board.

The conference venue, used daily for motivational Prophet Corporation staff training and events, was state of the art. Guests had been treated to a six-course tasting menu, and the many themed bars had been open to parents and officials, with extra soda and non-alcoholic spirits for the students. The auditorium had been decorated with no expense spared, and students were taking photographs in front of the lasers, light shows and mirror walls.

Newsfeed journalists had been treated to the extravaganza too, and had committed to write extensive features in their weekend publications.

The event closed with a spectacular indoor firework medley which accompanied a series of short motivational films made by several of the newly constituted student commercial companies, organised through the Budding-Prophet initiative in partnership with the biblios. The event, and the films, focused on a scintillated generation producing a scintillating economy. The final applause was overwhelming, and the guests donated generously as they left the auditorium, spilling out into the roads with a collective glow of success.

Alexandra congratulated Michael on the best-ever celebration event, and he puffed up with pride, congratulating her in return for the part which she had played, and encouraging her to share a nightcap with him at his club nearby. They walked down the beautifully lit avenue and into the historic building, through the classical columns and across the sparkling mosaic into a private lounge. Over their brandy, they talked of the success of the scintillation programme, of improvements in the North and of his hopes for the future. He took a packet of expensive cigarettes from his inner pocket and offered one to her. She was genuinely shocked and started to say, 'But –'

He reassured her,

'It's okay in here; beyond the law,' he drooled. She declined his offer.

His face started to take on a vaguely demonic air as he took pleasure in her company, the brandy and the cigarette. She watched his expression and imagined he was starting to look like Maximillian. Relieved she had kept her counsel in recent months and resisted the temptation to broach contentious subjects with him, she was rewarded. He spoke slowly and deliberately, 'I am thinking of retiring,' he said, 'Perhaps at the end of the year. Can we put some dates in our diaries to talk through the implications?' Graciously, she agreed.

She wondered where Zade was, and what she was doing.

Chapter 43

The security alarms are blasting through the night air. The Medical Plant is not only illuminated on the cliff, but blue flashing lights are summoning the emergency services. Mr Patel stumbles out of the mouth of the tunnel, carrying Lucas under his left arm, above the swelling tide, and balancing his torch in his right hand. 'Quick; to the driverless; the tide is too high. We must leave,' he instructs me, with alarm in his voice. The boulders are covered with lapping black seawater. We skirt the very foot of the cliff where there is a slightly raised platform of rock. In places we have to cross deep pools of swirling water. There is no time for fear; I focus all my energy on controlling my feet and on staying upright. The power of the waves is formidable, but we are just in time, traversing the route before the water reaches its highest point. The roar of water on rock drowns the sound of our struggling feet. As we clear the deepest part, Mr Patel stops on a dry platform, placing Lucas down gently. The three of us stand wide-eyed and panting, Lucas' eyes glittering brightly, as the plant on the cliff flashes urgently in the moonless night.

'We will talk in the driverless,' Mr Patel pants, and we pick up our pace, Lucas now on his father's back. Traversing the overgrown path, over the brow and beyond the shoreline, we suddenly become aware of silence. Have the alarms turned off? We proceed half-running, wet clothes flapping, our legs swishing against the foliage.

On reaching the edge of the disused car park, Mr Patel signals to me to wait. He drops Lucas down beside me and I clasp his free hand while his father checks the driverless. My mind is generating scenarios and solutions. What if they have found the driverless and we are trapped? What if armed guards burst out of the dark bushes? I am pulled back to reality by a barely audible voice at my side, and I stoop to listen. 'Zade,' Lucas whispers, 'I did close the valve. It did say A12, but when I took off the handle, the alarms started up. I ran to Dad. I found these in the lab.' He hands me a small packet. At that instant, Mr Patel signals a thumbs up and we run together to the parked driverless. As soon as we are inside, it purrs into life and accelerates away from the car park, on to the narrow lane and towards East Bridge.

I turn to Lucas, and say it really doesn't matter that he triggered the alarms; it was bound to happen, but his eyes are already firmly closed in sleep. It must be nearly midnight. Mr Patel is phoning his wife, saying cryptically and calmly, 'All okay dear, we are on our way back. Due in East Bridge in less than an hour.' He has programmed the driverless to take us along a circuitous route to reduce the risk of being stopped by the emergency services, security patrols or even bandits, and we sit back in our comfortable Central Area seats, not worried that we are soaking wet, just keen to get back safely.

'Do you think he managed it?' I ask anxiously.

'He says he did, and I believe him. He even managed to remove the safety catch. I am sure of this because he brought it back to me. I posted it down a deep crack in the rock halfway down the tunnels. But they will find out and will turn it back on again, I am certain.' He rubs his sore back, and I show him the packet which Lucas handed to me. It is labelled "test" with a series of numbers and contains two small phials of liquid. One is labelled "A: cyclopentolate-tapetum" and the other "B; cyclopentolate".

'Good lad,' Mr Patel whispers, 'This is useful evidence.' I place the package in my wet coat pocket, along with the winking fob from Lucas' wrist.

We huddle under the blanket and drink the coffee, but my eyes keep closing and I know I cannot stay awake any longer. When I wake, Lucas has rested his sleeping head on my damp lap, and Mr Patel, alert and in control, is waking me, asking, 'Zade, I need to know when you are safely home. Do you have your door fob? Will you message me once you are inside safely?'

'Yes, of course,' I reply, quickly regaining my control. I lift Lucas' sleeping head, placing it gently on the seat, and rise awkwardly as the driverless pulls up by the Aldness village green, my clothes wet and my limbs sore. Mr Patel takes my hand, shakes it in an old-fashioned way, and says,

'All the best Zade, keep in touch; come to supper again. Now we must wait and see what happens. Back to normal life for a while.' I don't know how to leave this brave fellow-conspirator, so I shake his hand and thank him, smile at Lucas, and climb out of the driverless, watching it speed off into the distance as I unlock Manya's homely red door and stagger into comfort again, remembering to message Mr Patel to confirm I am safely inside. There is plenty of time tomorrow to dry my clothes, but I smell of seawater, so I use Manya's shower, and once clean, fall into bed.

The morning is an anti-climax. I wake refreshed, with my adrenalin still high, but all I face is domestic tasks, Manya's return, and the end of my freedom. I feel heavy and disinterested in the day. I desperately want to know what is happening at the Medical Plant, if anything. Given that we set the alarms off, I doubt we will have changed anything. We will just have alerted them to our presence.

Today, Manya's beautiful, simple home seems small and drab. The frustrations of being in the Periphery; the intermittent cyberspace and the antiquated way of life start to irritate me. I even find myself longing for the pace and "success" of the Central Area. I am dissatisfied and fear that despite my small recent actions, scintillation and discrimination will continue indefinitely.

I treasure my memories of last night. Despite our naivety, we were brave, especially Lucas who excelled. He remained quiet and calm, and completed his task. I inhale the salty smell in my clothes, before plunging them into a bowl of hot water, wringing them, and hanging them out on Manya's outdoor washing line, in the late autumn sunshine.

Manya messaged me late last night; she is expecting to be back around seven o'clock tonight. She issued detailed instructions for me to prepare supper, which I will do later. Meanwhile I will walk down to the harbour and explore my surroundings, to pass the hours.

Sitting on an upturned rowing boat, I gaze out towards the blurred horizon where the grey-blue of the sea meets the heavy sky. While I have been busy and focused on my quest against scintillation, time has passed so quickly. I realise that in only ten weeks I will reach my sixteenth birthday, and technically be independent at last. I know that I have missed out on nearly two years of my education. I should be working towards my final examinations in a Central Area grammar academy, and I do have regrets. I wonder whether attending school out in the Periphery will be the answer for me or not. I am a misfit; have I forfeited my chance of a professional career? What do I really want out of my life?

I decide to take counsel from Manya when she returns, and I saunter on round the sea wall.

Manya Gray is a kind and insightful woman. She arrives home after a demanding working week, her precious hidden gem of a home having been invaded by me, a lone unconventional teenager, and she gives me exactly what I need.

We sit over supper, a wholesome stew made of vegetables and real meat from her freezer, which I have prepared according to her instructions, and which tastes good. She says to me, 'Well Zade, I won't even ask what you have been getting up to this week, but you have kept my home well, and Aldous is happy, so let's talk about next steps shall we?' I tell her nothing about the Patels, nothing about Lucas, the scintlab, or Bonnie or Ninia, and certainly not about Nazar.

She surprizes me by suggesting that I might travel to the far South West next. I seem to have been born to move, a lone itinerant. I smile, saying that I have been to Wales, and to the East, so now the South West; a tourist of the Periphery! 'I thought that I was destined to attend school out here?' I ask her.

'You are destined to go back to school, because you want to learn, and your real potential is completely untapped, but not here, and not now,' she summarises. I realise that I am, after all, very attached to her coastal refuge, and I was not expecting to leave so soon. I tell her this, thanking her again for trusting me.

'So why the far South West?' I ask.

Manya's response is totally unexpected and I sit, unable to move or speak for a while, holding back tears, controlling my feelings. She has been in communication with Rebel, from the education underground. He has provided some completely confidential information about my parents. Manya says she is sorry; we are too late; if only we had made contact with Rebel a few weeks earlier, but actually perhaps it is for the best. She gently explains that last week my mother, my brave and beautiful mother, died. She died in hospital, of heart-failure. Manya recalls Rebel's words that Mathilde had been ill for many years, and her death is seen by those who know her as a relief; as an end to her suffering.

There is to be a very small funeral next week, on Tuesday, in the chapel of the hospital. Manya explains to me that my mother and father have lived under changed identities, answering to the names John and Janie Martine for the last fifteen years, not Owen and Mathilde Beaufort. Both being escaped convicted criminals from the Central Area, they have led quiet lives in the South West, living incognito. 'Rebel says your father wants to see you very much, but only if you want to see him. That is the message which he asked me to pass on to you.'

I do not hesitate to say I will go, and I will go alone. That is how I like to travel.

Chapter 44

It has taken me a whole day to reach Penzance. At the crack of dawn this morning, Manya took me swiftly out of the East through the gate on the Isle of Ely. I bid her farewell at Ely station, catching a high-speed hydrogen train, and crossing the diagonal of the Central Area, avoiding London. There are several gates to the Periphery in the South West, and I crossed at Tiverton Parkway railway station. Passengers had to leave the train, pass through security checks on platform 1a, before re-embarking on the same train which had shunted forwards, up the far end of the platform, called 1b. Then I spent five-hours on the train travelling through Devon and Cornwall, worrying about how I should behave when I see my father for the first time in my life.

I also thought of Lucas; will he tell his friends, or his teachers, about our adventure? Will this prompt an investigation. Will the Patels and I get caught, and deported to prison in the Central Area? Time on the train allowed me to reflect on many questions which I had conveniently ignored in the heat of the moment, while with the Patels.

Coming out of Exeter, we skirted the coast at dusk, and I saw a seagull catching a crab in the estuary. I had no idea the country was so big, and the terrain so diverse. Everywhere that I have travelled in the Periphery, from the East this morning, and out in the South West this afternoon, I have seen the same collections of worried people, bowed and serious, and I have felt their desire to live outside the repressed menace of the Central Area. These are not healthy times. If scintillation stopped, and if medication stopped, we might stand a chance of getting society back on track. I doze for the remainder of the journey, waking each time the train stops. At St Erth I force myself to stay alert as I knew my destination is next.

Weary, but alert with anticipation, I finally hear the in-train computer announcing our imminent arrival in Penzance. We are cruising into the brightly lit stone edifice, coming to a halt under the domed glass roof and I am feeling more nervous than I have throughout all of my recent travels. Something deeper than I understand is urging me to run; to be somewhere else, but I resist.

I realise my whole identity has been built on being proudly independent and remaining rootless. I have survived for nearly sixteen years by my own ingenuity and resilience. I don't want to be tied down, and am reluctant to accept there is a parent waiting for me to arrive, but I am curious. I desperately want to know what happened when I was born, who I really am, and to enhance my already strong self-image with the new knowledge of my origins.

My mother seems to have been iconic; beautiful; striking. I can picture her face from the blurred news-cutting which Alexandra passed to me, but I don't know what to expect when I see my father. I follow the queue of evening travellers out of the train door and on to the platform, planting my rucksack by my feet as I scan the station concourse, hoping to see him. This arrangement has been made in such a hurried and covert manner that I don't know where we are to meet. I find myself hoping he doesn't turn up at all, and I can travel back to Manya's cottage tomorrow.

I see an older man waiting, but another traveller greets him and they walk off together. I see a tramp picking through the debris of the day, turning over packets on the dirty ground, looking for stumps of cigarettes. I see a parade of grey humanity passing through Penzance station, but no one looking for me.

Then, a hand lightly touches my shoulder, and a soft, quiet voice asks, 'Zade?' I swing round, and look straight into his piercing blue eyes. We are suspended, both knowing that this is a moment we have always secretly craved, but thought would never happen. He asks again, 'Zade?' and his gentle tone is heavy with emotion. I stand tall, on a level with him.

I just say, 'Yes,' letting him embrace me, leaning my head on his shoulder, breathing his musty air, and sharing his space.

After several minutes, he steps back, touches my hands, and my face with his strong fingers, asking himself, 'Is this real?' He does not take the lead. He does not assert his parental authority; instead he is respectful, giving us the time we both need.

The platform is now completely empty except for our two uncertain figures. The train is idling, the gentle whirring of its engine protecting us from complete silence. Once we begin to speak, we realise there is so much of such importance for us to say. There are no pleasantries, no awkward silences, and he falls into an unexpectedly comfortable rhythm. 'I have waited sixteen years for this moment,' he begins, 'I had no expectations; I just imagined there might possibly be such a moment. I thought it would never happen.' I respond awkwardly by saying that until very recently, I didn't know he, or my mother, existed. I say that this has all come suddenly to me, at a time when I am really taken up with other matters, which sounds callous. He smiles, telling me I glare just like my mother did in her younger days, with determination.

He looks directly into my heavily scintillated eyes, asking rhetorically, 'They called you Zade; they didn't change your name?' I tell him that Zade is the only name I have ever answered to. I suddenly realise that the small silver cross has not been the only link I have held to my parents, perhaps even more precious was my name.

'And your surname?' he asks anxiously.

'They gave me the names of my foster parents. It was very unusual being fostered in the Central Area. The names changed over the years.'

'But when he contacted me to arrange this meeting, Rebel mentioned...' he whispers, '...Beaufort?'

'Yes, only a few weeks ago Alexandra Essex, the Central Area School Commissioner, unearthed information for me…'

'Good grief; what on earth were you doing with her?' he asks, wide-eyed. I reflect on the extraordinary nature of my recent weeks, saying,

'It's a long story; shall we go somewhere more private?' He apologises, saying that it is only ten-minutes on foot to his home, and we walk.

The station café is closing, and we pass an old-style public house, lights ablaze, dirty, busy and slightly intimidating. He can see I am well-used to carrying my rucksack, and strides alongside me, protectively. We walk along small urban streets and into a shanty area. The cabins are completely different here, older, more dilapidated, interspersed with trees and bushes. He leads me up to his modest home, a cabin on its own, slightly obscured by a row of old brick houses and a derelict garage, with pieces of vehicles heaped by the weedy pavement.

There is no double-locking fob here. He takes a real metal key out of his pocket and fits it into the lock, turning a handle, and opening the door on to a chaotic hallway, cluttered with boxes and papers. 'I'm not very tidy,' he apologises, adding, 'Sorry, it's been a busy week at school, and what with Mathilde…your mother…I haven't tidied up.' As he turns on the bare old-style light bulb, I see he looks down-at-heel, his hair unruly, his clothes poorly fitting, and his house a mess. We move into the small front room, which is packed with books and paper maps. They are heaped on shelves, on a desk, and in wooden boxes. I see poetry, novels, authors who I haven't heard of. Resting my rucksack on the only spare patch of floor, I open the zipped pocket, and spontaneously draw out S. Herbert's pamphlet. I present it to him, with a flourish, saying,

'Here is an interesting book for you to add to your collection.' He reads the title on the crumbling cover, looks at me, and looks again at the book.

'How on earth…' he begins, taking the small packet from me with great care. Then I show him the two phials of liquid which Lucas took from the scintlab.

***

We didn't sleep at all last night, which was, on reflection, unwise as we now need to travel to the funeral, which seems to be a short bus-ride away. Our eyes are heavy with tiredness, but we are brimming with the new knowledge we have gained of each other, and of our strongly held beliefs. I told him my story, with pride, and in detail, and he wanted to hear. I showed him the small, winking access fob that Lucas had held on to so tightly, still attached to the twine, and he held it in his hand, turning it over and over. He spent the night touching the Herbert pamphlet as if it was a rare jewel, and gazing at the two phials of liquid. His knowledge of the Central Area is way out of date. He asked me so many questions.

Then he told me about his early life, his face lighting up as he spoke of Mathilde, my mother. He related the details of their successes when working with the education underground, and the fateful day when they were arrested. He looked tired and old when he talked me through the days that he spent in prison, not knowing where I had been taken. It seems that I owe a great debt to the Sisters of Christ, who intervened both at my birth, and when my mother and I were moved to London. He didn't understand why or how I had become scintillated in both places.

He then explained how he was helped to escape by his friends and devotees in the education underground, and told me about the most recent decade, when he had cared for Mathilde. He finds it hard to talk about her death. It seems she became ill as soon as she lost me, and never really recovered. It is dreadfully sad, and I keep thinking I am just too late. If only we had known of each other earlier, she might not have become so gravely ill.

I am concerned about the funeral because we are both very tired and, although neither of us would admit it, emotionally vulnerable. He tells me that the short ceremony is scheduled for ten o'clock, in the small chapel of rest at the hospital. He has the morning off work, but had intended to return to school to teach his afternoon classes, before he knew of my arrival.

Domestic arrangements do not appear to be his forte, and I offer him one of my emergency oat bars as there seems to be no breakfast. There is also no coffee, and he drinks whisky.

As neither of us owns the expected funeral clothes, we decide to go as we are, believing Mathilde would have wanted that.

Chapter 45

I am sitting on the damp sand, looking out across Penzance harbour towards the sea. A string of industrial buildings skirts the coast here, but the air is much fresher than in London. I pull my coat around me for warmth, and reflect on the morning. We attended the funeral together, the only guests at a routine cremation ceremony conducted by a disinterested priest. I was strangely unmoved by the event. I had never known my mother, and she will still live as an icon in my mind. More disturbing for me was the hospital, where the old mansion housed hundreds of people for whom the challenges of surviving in society had proved too much. My father was obviously used to the smells, the alarms, the sporadic shouting, and the distressed moans of the residents, but they haunted me. I have not been in such a place before. It reminded me of the nights I spent sleeping in the underground.

I was also alert to my father's suffering. He had plainly been desperately in love with my mother, and was finding this extremely difficult. The alcohol, and the lack of sleep meant he was uncommunicative and clearly deeply troubled. He seems to hold himself responsible for my mother's illness, and her death, and looked as though he was bearing a very heavy burden. I am not sure he should have gone back to his school this afternoon, but he said that the normality of the routine might help him.

After the funeral, we returned to his cabin, he left for work, and I have walked out here for some space to think.

I feel very disconnected down here in the South West, a long way from all that has been familiar to me. It is like a foreign country. Lyn's flat will probably now be inhabited by a new tenant, Sam will still be cheering people up at the Advice Bureau, and Alexandra will still be dashing into the Chateau Privee for a coffee and a frangipane. Manya will be commuting between her Central Area office and Aldness, making her contacts, living a double life pleasing her boss Michael Morgan, but also enabling the education underground to succeed in the Periphery. The Patels will have sat round their kitchen table for breakfast this morning, returning with relief to normality. Noah's cold will be better and Lucas will be asking, 'When will we see Zade again?'

I have reconciled myself to the certainty that Mr Patel, Lucas and I have not affected the national supply of eye drops, and that the Human Tapetum is still being pumped into the Cyclopentolate. We were very fortunate not to be caught in our attempted act of sabotage during our dramatic night under the cliffs. I take the packet containing the two phials, so cleverly stolen by Lucas from the scintlab, out of my pocket. Holding the tiny phial "A" up against the sky I marvel that such an apparently innocent watery solution could be responsible for wreaking so much havoc. Suddenly anxious someone might be watching, I return the packet containing the phials to the safety of my pocket, and return to my thoughts.

And the medication programme continues, as does indoctrination in the Central Area grammar academies. I decide there are two ways to try to change this, firstly directly through Alexandra, and Manya, and secondly through the education underground, and my father. I am not sure who or which to commit to, and I know that I cannot bind myself to both simultaneously while retaining my integrity. Do I stay out in the Periphery and go underground, or do I try to return to the Central Area, and try to influence those who run the system?

I know Alexandra's power will be limited as long as Michael Morgan presides as High Commissioner for Future Success. Perhaps that factor alone points me towards the education underground for support in my quest.

As soon as I reach my sixteenth birthday, I will enter a new phase in my life, no longer technically dependent on adults, and my foster allowance, so cleverly re-routed to me by Manya, will end, but my stubbornly scintillated eyes create real issues because no other young adults have eyes like mine. I am a freak, a direct casualty of Maximillian and Michael Morgan's brutal experimentation, and having been dosed with human tapetum twice, in two different places.

A small ship appears on the horizon, visible between the wind turbines and the armed security towers, and as I look into the far distance, I realise that I must not lose my long-term direction. What sort of an adult do I want to become? What do I want to be able to say I have achieved when I am as old as my father, or even as old as Danielle? My father can say that if he hadn't been alive, five thousand teachers would not have been able to develop their careers in the educationally enlightened Periphery, and millions of children would not have benefitted from their teaching. He can say that he has inspired others in the education underground to speak up honestly for what they believe, and to change things for the better. He has been a true leader, despite his current modesty and weary guilt. No doubt he would also say that innocent people have lost their lives because of him, and that Mathilde's life was blighted by mental illness as a direct result of his decisions.

Last night, as I related my recent experiences to him, describing how I crawled up the pipe in the darkness, how I waited at the mouth of the tunnel, having masterminded the operation with Mr and Mrs Patel, I could see he felt a deep pride in my bravery. It is quite extraordinary that despite not knowing my parents, I have ended up attempting to fight similar battles.

He remembered, years ago, saving the images of the interior of the scintlab on the education underground database, and signing them "Owen". He has continued to work on archiving and recording despite living out here under a new identity. Maybe there are possibilities for me to work more closely with him?

Focusing on my own future, I recall Manya's recent words to me, 'You are destined to go back to school, because you want to learn, and your real potential is completely untapped,' and I reflect on my father's absolute commitment to his students, his undeniable love for me, and the fact that there is now a large hole in his life, following Mathilde's death. Maybe I would be better to lie low for a while, tidy up his cabin for him, read his books, ask him to prepare me for my exams, and just focus 100% on getting the right qualifications to then return to the Central Area. This plan starts to feel right.

To be honest, my head is all over the place. What with the night guarding the pipe, the unexpected journey out to Penzance, the emotional meeting with my father, and the realisation that despite our morally driven intentions, scintillation continues, I am all in.

I lie back on the sand in the late autumn sunshine and close my eyes, desperately tired, and drift comfortably in and out of sleep. The weak sun shines through my closed eyes and sends the scintillation inwards so I see an alluring sparkle on the dark red insides of my eyelids. I hate scintillation, but paradoxically it is such a familiar part of me that I am not sure how I would feel without it.

Chapter 46

I walked back to my father's cabin, used the metal key which he had hidden under a large stone by the door, and busied myself by tidying up until he returned from work in the early evening. Now we are sitting together over a cup of tea, and I am offering to re-organise his domestic arrangements. His small kitchen is a disgrace. I did eventually find some coffee, and tea, but no milk, so we are drinking it black, with sugar. In one way he is easy-going, pleased to accept my help, saying that anything I can do to spruce up the cabin is welcome. On the other hand, he is very set in his ways, keen to continue with his daily routine, and his teaching, which seems to give meaning to his life.

Used to my independence, and forgetting I am his guest, I find myself becoming easily frustrated, but I underestimate him. He puts down his mug and leans across to me, stroking my cheek, as if to reassure himself that I am not a hallucination. His fingers are coarse but gentle, his voice is deep yet hesitant. I listen as he talks to me again, of the education underground. 'You see,' he says, 'they are well-organised, but they lack the latest information. They are largely excluded from the Central Area, and like me, they have to lie low even in the Periphery. They rely on agents; teachers who secretly feed information to them, but they have little insight into the world of the High Council these days. And you do, or have done.'

'What are you suggesting,' I ask. He glances at the window, checks outside the only door, closing it securely, and resumes,

'If we pass your information to Rebel, the pamphlet, the phials of Cyclopentolate and Tapetum, the access fob, and the scrap of paper, as well as your observations on the secret back way into the plant, you could pass the responsibility over to them. They would…they could eliminate the scintlab completely.'

It has never occurred to me to completely pass the responsibility over to the education underground. I start to feel uncomfortable about a violent and illegal resolution. I have never supported terrorism or the anti-social actions of gangs and have never carried a weapon, despite my precarious life. My father has become inured by years of action, but I am wrangling with a powerful tension between my moral purpose and my ethical beliefs. I am totally convinced that scintillation needs to end but I am not at all sure that direct violence is the answer. If we could have ended scintillation by simply decontaminating the cyclopentolate, that night on the cliffs, I could have justified my action. No one would have been injured or directly harmed, and future generations could have been released from the tyranny. But I was naïve. Occasionally I understand how young I am, how inexperienced, and how vulnerable. I know that I must put this doubt to one side and continue on my resolute course.

My father is intuitive, and puts his arm around my shoulder. He tries to reassure me by talking about his early days, how he slipped into a life of protest, and tried to retain his determination to behave ethically. When people died as a result of his actions, he felt diminished as a person. He is not a typical hero, and he provides me with an interesting role model. 'The education underground exists Zade,' he says, continuing, 'they will be fighting scintillation whatever we do. You now have a chance to provide them with the information they seek, and to step back; let them do what they do well.' I am not entirely convinced, but agree we should contact Rebel.

He is interested that I have met Rebel and we agree that he is the person to target. I, of course, have Rebel's direct contact number, but we are not sure whether I will be able to reach him from a different part of the Periphery, or whether the call would be monitored. We conclude this is a risk worth taking. I retrieve both my phones, and he turns the Central Area phone over in his hands, marvelling at the technology, although I know it is way out of date compared with Haptics, which have been heavily marketed in the last few years. That phone is, of course, dead. My Periphery phone lights up, but doesn't seem to work either. I should have asked Manya whether it would operate out here. 'How do you communicate with Rebel?' I ask, and he explains the arrangement they have with the bookshop proprietor.

'I would never use the phone, unless in an emergency,' he says.

'But you do have a phone?' I check. He shows me a strange out-dated mobile phone, which he keeps near his rudimentary power ring, to keep the power topped up. I type Rebel's number into my father's phone, and try to call, but the signal is too weak.

'I have managed to get a signal in higher places; how about a walk,' he suggests, 'I can always get a signal up at Lescudjack Castle.'

It is suppertime, and as we exit the cabin, an appetising smell of cooking mingles with the dank fishy odour of the Periphery. He leads me uphill through the shanty town. We take a rough track which skirts a large hill, passing small plots of land which are being cultivated, I assume for vegetables. 'I kept an allotment years ago,' he says, breaking the silence, 'to try to get Mathilde interested in digging and growing. The peace and quiet up here was good.' I have never heard of "allotments" before.

We reach a rough summit between the plots, where worn paths lead to a patch of faded grass, strewn with litter. The place feels derelict, and despite its promising name, there is no castle; it is just the name of the mound. We look out over the bay, at the clouds massing on the horizon. He asks me to keep alert in case we are being watched as we don't want to be overheard.

Holding his phone high, he walks round, trying to secure a signal. In the Central Area this was never necessary, and it seems an absurdly antiquated practice. He gives me a thumbs up and tries to call, once, twice. On the third attempt, he seems to connect. I move closer to hear what he is saying, but his conversation is unintelligible as he speaks in cryptic whispers. 'Well?' I ask as he disconnects.

'He's interested,' he replies, and we walk back down to the cabin in thoughtful silence. Once back indoors he systematically destroys his phone, and then leaves again, to discreetly dispose of the broken parts across the town. Watching him take such care makes me feel like a clumsy amateur. I now understand that beneath his benign exterior is a highly experienced criminal. Having him onside is reassuring, but worrying. It places me in a dilemma regarding my liaison with Alexandra and Manya. My loyalties are confused.

He is gone for some time, and returns smelling of alcohol, carrying two paper parcels, which he lays on the kitchen table. 'I hope you like fish and chips?' he asks me.

'What is fish and chips?' I reply, unaware of this historical coastal delicacy. We unwrap the steaming parcels and eat with our fingers, every last crumb.

'We must wait to hear from Rebel. He will work it out. Meanwhile I suggest we focus on your exam preparation. I used to go to see Mathilde every evening, so now there is time for me to teach you.' We agree there is no way I could attend school out here without attracting unwanted attention, due to my scintillated eyes. He is knowledgeable about the syllabus for each examination and would be able to enter me for the core assessments legitimately, as a privately tutored student. If I could pass just the minimum required for college entry, that would be my ticket to the next stage of my education, either in the Periphery, or conceivably in the Central Area. Keen to keep busy, to learn, and to be purposeful, I agree.

Tidying the books and papers, we turn the small front room of the cabin into a temporary student den. We organise a sleeping bag on a mat on the floor, which rolls up during the daytime to allow space for a folding table for my studying. With none of the digital tools of the Central Area available to me out here, and without the distractions of a Prexia, cyberspace, messages, I read, write and quickly start to make progress. Manya, in her efficient and helpful way, re-routes my sterling allowance to my father, and my life settles into an easier rhythm.

Every weekend, my father visits the bookshop, but there have been no messages for six weeks. On the seventh Saturday our patience is rewarded and he returns through the rain bearing a small piece of paper, which he unfolds on my table. Written carefully in black pen, it says, 'Ready – bring all – TBs – Sunday.' Our hearts are beating quickly; we both know this announces the next step. 'They are ready then,' he says, unnecessarily, 'I thought they might send someone out to us, but, "TBs" means nothing to me?' We puzzle over "TBs" until I realise, bursting out exultantly,

'It's The Barns; I have been there; it is where I met Rebel with Manya.' I have no idea how to find the place again.'

Closing the blind, for privacy, my father demonstrates his skills in quickly locating a completely unknown place, and I am impressed. He finds a paper map of the Eastern Periphery amongst his papers, homes in on the gate on the Isle of

Ely, asks me how long it took Manya and I to reach The Barns, what the terrain looked like, and within ten minutes he has located a small building on the map, which we are both confident is the place. 'I'm a bit rusty, but it is good to be using my skills,' he says, with pride.

This time I am professionally prepared for my journey. My goal is to pass the access fob to Rebel in person, only to him. If I achieve nothing else, that is sufficient. Ideally, I will also hand to him the phials of cyclopentolate and tapetum, a separate package of papers, including the S. Herbert pamphlet, the scrap of paper from Danielle, and a copy, which we have made, of the ten pages of notes I provided for Alexandra. These have been secreted in separate pages of my textbooks, as if part of my study, ready for the security checks on route. We do, of course, have digital copies of these papers as a backup, but it is the fob, which should still allow access to the scintlab via the hidden cliff tunnels, which is the most important item, along with my knowledge of the scintlab.

My father plans the itinerary with me to the smallest detail. He not only provides me with an innocent-looking student rucksack which contains all I should need for self-defence and survival, including a small brass compass, and pepper spray disguised as deodorant, but also plentiful cash, which will easily cover the train fare and an overnight stay. We agree I will not travel armed, although he can provide a weapon if needed, from a range of hand guns he shows me, hidden under the floor of the airing cupboard. I am entering this underground world unwillingly, but am determined to do whatever it takes to end scintillation.

***

I expected to feel sad when the moment came to leave him at the station early on Saturday morning, my constant companion for the last few weeks, but we are both brimming with anticipation, and this overlays any sentimentality. To be honest, I am keen to be on the move by myself again. We could not have prepared more carefully, and I am confident. I can genuinely play the part of the student travelling back to the Central Area after attending a funeral, and have plenty of reading to complete on the long journey.

'Take care Zade,' he says, as he kisses my cheek. I am touched; no one has ever cared for me like this before. I leave him standing on the station platform and find a seat on the train, which is waiting to depart. The journey is tedious and uneventful until we reach Tiverton Parkway station when the heavy security of the Central Area suddenly becomes apparent. The train is relatively empty. Far more people travel into the Periphery than back out. All passengers are therefore under scrutiny. We disembark on platform 4b and are funnelled through bag scanners and security checks, first a bank of android robots that scan our bags and our bodies systematically, and then uniformed guards. They open my bag and sift through the books and papers. They check my pockets. They study my passport. They do not see the phials of liquid which are carefully sewn into the lining of my rucksack. A severe female security guard asks me why I am returning from the Periphery, and I look at her long and hard, through my scintillated eyes, saying that I have attended the funeral of my mother and am returning home. She waves me through.

I walk nonchalantly along the platform, through a series of gates and scanners, and on to platform 4a where the same train has drawn up. Doors are open, welcoming us back into the carriage, where a recorded message is playing, 'You are now entering the Central Area. If you enter this area without the correct authorisation you will be arrested. No dogs, no animals...' I find the same seat that I occupied from Penzance and settle down, opening my book. After the standard twenty-minute wait while border guards process all the security information provided by passengers, the train pulls out on its way to Reading. In the megalopolis of Reading I change trains for Oxford, and then in Oxford I take the Cambridge train. Compared with the Periphery, the trains are slick, the stations are efficient, and the air does not smell so rank. My eyes are an advantage rather than an embarrassment, there is plentiful coffee, and I feel at home.

Once in Cambridge, as planned, and donning my dark glasses once more, I walk to a large hostel near the railway station, where I secure a bunk for the night and try to get some sleep.

After a restless night, disturbed by the steady flow of giggling female students staggering in and out of the hostel dormitory, I pack up my compact kit, checking the precious items in their hiding places one by one, ready to travel back out of the Central Area into the East.

Unfortunately, the rain is beating down when I emerge on to the pavement. I march briskly back to the station, shaking the drips off my hair as I show my passport and purchase a return ticket to Brandon, a small station, the next stop after Ely and The Gate. After a short wait, I board the single-carriage train, having to stand in the corridor for the twenty minutes to Ely, where most fellow passengers depart. A few of us remain, disembarking for routine security checks as we exit the Central Area. After a tense wait on the covered platform, gazing out at the rain, I am able to re-join the train, and we proceed into the Eastern Periphery.

My father planned the journey forensically with me. Although not familiar with Brandon station, not far from Ely, I know exactly what to expect. Mercifully a few other travellers also leave the train here, and I try not to draw attention to myself. The familiar reek of the Eastern Periphery welcomes me as, on foot, I take the road to the small town. The rain is easing, but I am damp and nervous as I make my way to the bus stop, and stand, in a small queue, and wait. Eventually the bus draws in, and conveys me to a small rural village where I start my walk to The Barns.

This is the riskiest part of my journey to find Rebel because the landscape is open, and there is nowhere to hide. Military aircraft pass overhead and I have no choice but to continue, exposed on the long straight road. Agricultural traffic passes periodically, tractors and lorries, as well as migrant cars, and I walk on to the verge to avoid being sprayed with standing rainwater as they pass. I am totally focused on reaching The Barns, and am hoping I can find Rebel.

With relief, in the distance I think I recognise the rough lay-by where Manya once parked her driverless. Picking up my pace, I am sure of the place, and I am soon on the footpath, smelling the dank undergrowth, and remembering the map I studied with my father. I don't need the compass as I am confident in my memory, and soon find myself in the familiar clearing, facing the brick barn buildings.

Without warning, four armed men suddenly emerge from the buildings, and surround me. They snatch my rucksack and twist my arm up my back. One holds his hand roughly across my mouth while they march me into the building. I was not expecting this sort of welcome.

Chapter 47

His hand smells unpleasantly acrid as I close my teeth on his fingers and struggle to free my hands, enraged by this treatment. Their faces loom over me in the dim light of the barn, their rotten teeth bared and their suspicious eyes glaring. The ringleader removes his hand roughly from my mouth, and demands, 'Who are you?'

'And who do you think you are?' I retort angrily, not waiting for an answer. 'I am Zade, and I am here at Rebel's invitation; he said to come on Sunday,' I protest, indignantly. They mutter together in a huddle, and one of them says,

'I saw her before. She came with Manya Gray.' This swings their opinion of me considerably, and they ease their grasp on my arms, returning my rucksack. The ringleader introduces himself as Mikal, and apologises, explaining they cannot be too careful, and that they weren't expecting me. Apparently very few people approach The Barns on foot, especially unannounced.

The misunderstanding behind us, I ask for Rebel, but am told that he is not here today, and that Mikal is in charge. Once I get over the shock of having his disturbing face glaring so aggressively into mine, we strike up a reasonable conversation which results in him disappearing into an inner room to contact Rebel.

While he is away, I ask the three remaining men who they are, and why they are here. They remain silent, wary and uncommunicative, their hands sullenly in their pockets. I stand up and shine my scintillated eyes at each of them in turn, asking forcefully, 'Do you really know why you are here? It seems to me that this education underground is just an excuse to dress rough, hide out and terrorise people.' I add disparagingly, 'I don't think you are here because you want to change things at all.'

This prompts them into talking. The scrawny one, who said that he had seen me before, starts by saying, 'You are not right about that. It's just we have to be careful. I grew up in the Midlands. We ran a good school until that slut Sutton started interfering. They closed our school and re-opened it as a grammar academy. Same school, same kids, same teachers, but new name; all Xs and Vs. Then they forced the school to use the medication, the soda, and low and behold, they start filling us up from the bottom with scintillated kids like you. Me and my missus were sent away 'cos we said we didn't like what they were doing. You should see the first-rate school our kids go to now, the Periphery school. They helped us when we were at rock bottom. I've got friends back there, in the

Central Area, who are banking on us changing things. Rebel's the right guy. You listen to him talk and it all starts to make sense.'

The other two nod. The second man, long-haired with a ponytail, starts to tell me how he took his children out of school in the Central Area, and was hounded out by the Enforcement Officers who destroyed his home, his livelihood and his dogs. When he mentions his dogs, his eyes fill with tears. He wipes his nose on his hand and lowers his head.

Mikal returns and says that Rebel is busy addressing a meeting and he has left a message for him. He offers me coffee, but although I would love a coffee, I remember the thick muddy drink that I was offered on my previous visit, and decline.

I turn to the two men who have started to share their stories with me and ask if they think they can end scintillation, end the medication and the grammar academies. 'Fuck you,' Mikal interrupts, 'That's why we are here.'

'Do you know how to do it?' I ask.

'You tell us how, miss smarty pants,' the silent man speaks for the first time, with a snarl.

We are sitting on a low bench in the darkness of the barn, me on one side of the rough wooden table, and the four of them on the other. The smell is rank, and the floor filthy. They are tense, irritated. I take a deep breath, and start to tell them the story. I begin with Maximillian Morgan and the Prophet Corporation's medical programme, moving on to the start of scintillation. I explain how the data passes from the Department for Future Success to the Department for Wellbeing, and the Wellbeing Officers effectively inject the good babies with scintillation, leaving the potentially bad babies without. I explain how the Four Plus is used to drive the migrations to the Periphery, and end by mentioning that I know how scintillation can be stopped. I explain that have stood inside the Prophet Corporation Medical Plant, and been within touching distance of the scintlab. I carefully say nothing of Alexandra or Manya, nothing of the Patels or Lucas, but I tell them the truth about scintillation.

They look at each other, and at me, and Mikal says, 'You must see Rebel. If this is true…'

His phone buzzes, and he answers; it is Rebel. Mikal just says, 'Yes, okay,' and ends the call, turning to me and saying, 'Zade, I am mightily sorry we scared you earlier. We didn't know. I will take you to Rebel now, right now.'

The three men each shake my hand, one speaking for them all, 'If we are needed, we are here for you.'

Mikal nods at the men, says he will take me, and leads me into the back room of the barn. I am learning more about these education underground people and don't expect great conversation from Mikal. They are, rightly, guarded and reticent. We exit at the back of The Barns where two Periphery vehicles are parked. Getting into one, he gently places a small black sack over my head, so I cannot see. He apologises, saying, 'I am taking you to Rebel. He is leading a large meeting of the education underground in a secret location. It will take us twenty minutes to get there.' The sack is itchy and smells of smoke, or maybe

Mikal is smoking. I am disorientated and anxious. From the moment we set off I start counting, instinctively, slow and regular, both to calm my nerves and to estimate the distance we are travelling. If I tip my head back slightly, I can see shapes through the weave of the bag. Mikal says nothing until we arrive. I have counted steadily to 2450.

Without warning, he removes the sack and the brightness of the day floods back into my eyes. We are in a yard which is doubling as a car park. He leads me past a guard, through a battered fire door and down a dark passage. I can hear voices in the distance, and the sound of sporadic clapping, and cheering. We pass another guard and enter a foyer, with a bar, tables and chairs. Mikal settles me on a chair and goes to the bar, returning with a coffee for me, which he hands over saying, 'I'm off now. If you wait here, Rebel will be out in a minute,' and he leaves.

I drink the coffee, and get up to walk around, taking in all the details of the place. I can recognise Rebel through a window in one of a set of several doors which lead into a grand auditorium. He is on a stage and is addressing a large crowd, his voice rising and falling, playing for applause. His speech reaches a crescendo and the audience explodes into a tumultuous standing ovation. They are on their feet, stamping, bellowing with pride as Rebel makes his way down the aisle and out of the doors into the foyer. The people start to flood out after him, but he sees me, shakes my hand and takes me quickly into a small room so we avoid being engulfed by the buoyant crowd. We sit at a small table. He is sweating.

'They seem well-pleased with your speech,' I observe politely. He smiles, not with pride or with pleasure, but with a deep-rooted anger.

'They are ready for some action,' he responds, 'which is where you come in Zade...' We get straight to the point, and I extract the parcel of papers from my small rucksack, retrieving the access fob and the packet containing the phials. The fob is still winking. I hand them all over to him, and he studies the fob carefully before putting it into his pocket. He takes the phials of liquid and holds them up to the light, saying, 'So this is the cause of it all. We can use this...' He opens the package of papers and lays them out on the table, asking me to explain exactly what they are. He asks me many questions, and I calmly provide all the information that I can. He wants to know about the tunnels into the secret back entrance to the scintlab, about the scintlab staff, all that they told me. He also asks about Maximilian and Michael Morgan, about Danielle and S. Herbert. It seems he knows a lot already, but I am providing him with clarity, and new information about the scintlab. When he asks about Alexandra, I share very little.

'Okay,' he says, after half an hour, the foyer outside the door now quiet. 'I have all I need. Thank you. You are a credit to your parents, Zade; you are brave and principled. Now, you can forget the fight for a while, focus on getting those examinations, and trust us; leave it with us. You will not hear from us, but keep an eye on the newsfeed. Is there anything else you need now?'

I am surprised at the immense relief flooding over me as I pass responsibility to Rebel. Do I need anything else I ask myself? 'I want to go home,' I say, curiously, 'I want to be back in Penzance, with my father, and my books. You are right; I could do with a bit of a break from the battle against scintillation. The journey out of the Periphery is going to be tricky though. I need help getting through The Gate at the Isle of Ely.'

'Ah yes, we can help with that,' he reassures me, asking me to wait while he organises transport.

There are no windows here; it is rather like an interview room. Rebel has taken all my evidence with him. I feel weary, and welcome a few minutes' peace while I wait to see what magic transport he can conjure up for me. My father prepared me meticulously for the trip to The Barns, but not for the return journey. I only remember him saying, 'If you return to Penzance...' which seemed odd at the time.

Rebel comes back with a smart young executive, a man in his twenties wearing an expensive suit and carrying a briefcase, saying, 'After what you have done, you deserve to travel in style. Goodbye Zade; we will, no doubt meet again.'

The young man introduces himself as Ace. He takes me out of the front doors of the venue where a very smart Department driverless is standing. With a flick of the fob he opens the doors, settles me inside, sits beside me and programmes the driverless to go at speed to Cambridge railway station via Ely. There is no bag over my head this time. I feel light, with nothing of importance in my pockets or my rucksack. The seats are comfortable, and the vehicle travels very fast once on the expressway. We drive straight through The Gate on the Isle of Ely. Ace shows his ID and is waved through without any reference to me at all. I ask him who he is. He tells me that he works for Manya Gray as her chief liaison officer with the education underground, but doesn't volunteer any more information.

He drops me off at the station, where I buy a take-away coffee from a cheerful neutral vendor on the platform. The coffee stall is called "Choice", and I reflect on the triumph of genetic engineering, wondering what I would have opted for, had I been faced with gender options. I feel comfortable in the bustle of the Central Area with the sweet, clean smells and the convenience associated with success. Do I really want to endure the seven-hour journey out into the back of beyond? I have money in my pocket, and the gift of scintillated eyes will open doors for me here. For a moment I hesitate, doubting whether returning to the South West is best for me.

It is lunchtime and I board the next train for Oxford, activating my Central Area phone to check whether I can reach Penzance by early evening. The easy access to cyberspace is a welcome relief after the inefficient systems in the Periphery. I check the timetables and decide I will go back, for now.

The trip runs smoothly, and I deliberately don't contact my father, but plan to surprise him by knocking on his cabin door. I think that he half-expects me to remain in the Central Area, lured by the draw of affluence and success. He underestimates me.

My train draws in after dark, and the down-at-heel station feels pleasantly familiar. I walk the route to his cabin with a light step, relieved to see the light in the window. I knock on the front door. His anxious face peers out between the blinds in the front window, and he is unable to disguise his surprise and delight as he sees me. Opening the door wide to me, he says, 'I didn't think you would come back. Did you manage it?'

'Yes; job done,' I say, smiling, 'Now let's get back to studying!'

It is my sixteenth birthday in two weeks' time, but I am in no hurry to leave, yet.

Chapter 48

Encouraged by his confidence in Alexandra Essex, Michael Morgan had decided to retire on his 65th birthday, which was December 10th 2080. He had been invited to spend Christmas with an old friend on a particularly expensive Prophet Corporation cruise from the Caribbean. Few permits for cruises were issued these days, and having been offered the option of travelling out in early December, he wanted to benefit fully from the experience, and so departed from his influential role three weeks earlier than anticipated.

Alexandra had already been approved by the High Council as the new High Commissioner for Future Success, and started in the role on December 11th. Her first act was to recruit a formal deputy. She interviewed a broad field of candidates, appointing Manya Gray, officially handing her responsibility for education standards across the Periphery. She parted company with Sue Sutton immediately, asking Manya to get the headteachers in the North back on side.

Ten days into the new job, Alexandra knew that major changes were needed. Every evening, after completing the routine tasks for the day, she spent time working on her plan for the future of education, revelling in the potential of her new powers. She knew deep down that scintillation was unethical, but she was realistically aware that everything under her direction depended upon its continuation. Now she no longer had to play Michael's game, her intention was to phase out scintillation over a number of years.

Sitting in her lounge, she was hunched over her Prexia, working late and typing furiously, when she noticed the date and the time. It was 21 minutes past nine on 21st December; 21.21 on 21.12. She remembered there was something important about 21st December, as well as it being the shortest day of the year, and wracked her brain to recall what it might be, realising it was Zade's birthday. She recalled the date from the birth certificate she had seen back in the late summer. Zade had completely disappeared off her radar, and she wondered what the girl was doing; she must ask Manya if she had received any news of her.

At that moment her phone started buzzing as message after message flew in, which was unusual at this time of night. She glanced at a message tagged urgent from Manya saying, 'See newsfeed.'

Alexandra swiped through to the live newsfeed updates on her Prexia to be confronted by a scene of utter devastation; an enormous burning building, illuminated by the floodlights, surrounded by fire engines and enforcement vehicles. 'Breaking News,' it said. Her heart started racing when she realised where the disaster had occurred, 'Prophet Corporation Medical Plant, targeted by terrorists.'

***

I was celebrating my sixteenth birthday quietly with my father, eating fish and chips, when an unexpected message buzzed on my Periphery phone. I opened it cautiously, and read, 'Happy Birthday Zade.' Then there was a link to a newsfeed item…

***

On his holiday island in the Caribbean, Michael Morgan climbed the steps out of the swimming pool and headed for the sunbed on the terrace for an afternoon drink. He glimpsed the newsfeed screen as he passed the open patio doors into the lounge, and stopped in his tracks. Trembling, he retrieved the Haptic from his jacket pocket. Anxiously, he located the newsfeed headlines and grimaced, congratulating himself on the wisdom of relocating outside the legal jurisdiction of the Central Area Enforcement System. There would be questions to answer now.

***

Mr and Mrs Patel had settled the boys down for the night, eaten their supper, and were about to sit down together. Mr Patel was clearing toy fire engines and police cars off the sofa when his wife called to him from the kitchen, 'Darling, check the newsfeed. Something has happened at the Medical Plant…'

Chapter 49

The morning after the winter solstice dawned cold and dark. Alexandra had not slept, having felt compelled to keep up with newsfeed coverage of the burning plant on the Suffolk cliffs, issuing several diplomatically worded updates for the Communications Manager through the night. Manya had taken matters in hand in the Periphery. She had even managed to travel to the site, appearing on the newsfeed, windblown, and calming the waters, 'The Department for Future Success will issue a full statement tomorrow; allegations by terrorists that the Prophet Corporation Medical Plant has been dealing in illegal scintillation products have not been confirmed.'

By six thirty in the morning, Alexandra was sitting behind Michael's old desk on the top floor of the Department for Future Success buildings in Great Smith Street. Yesterday she had stretched her legs under the desk, and leaned back in the chair, smiling at the trappings of power and comfort around her, but this morning, her face looked grim as she realised the full import of this unprecedented situation. It was not just the total annihilation of the Medical Plant, but also the damaging statements which were appearing on the newsfeed from the education underground. As soon as the High Council Communications Department took down the content, it reappeared in even more graphic detail. Someone who was astute and well-informed was behind this.

The following statement alarmed her particularly. It kept re-appearing on all channels, 'Following destruction of the Prophet Corporation Medical Plant, the scintillation programme in the Central Area is exposed as a conspiracy. Senior High Council officials have allowed the Prophet Corporation to continue to engineer the intake of pupils to grammar academies through the Four Plus. Unethical drugs have not only been used to enable babies from advantaged families to develop scintillated eyes, but have been used to exclude babies from disadvantaged families from the programme. Scintillation is discrimination.' Many of the communications were accompanied by a photograph of two phials of liquid, labelled "A" and "B". The education underground was claiming to have ended scintillation by destroying the Medical Plant, and was sending anonymous messages in mass mail through all available channels. Responses from thousands of furious parents were already appearing on many platforms.

Alexandra convened a joint emergency management meeting of her commissioners and senior managers in the Department for Wellbeing, for eleven in the morning, to allow Manya, Sean and Peter time to travel into London, by which time she would have a fuller picture of the situation.

Manya arrived at half past ten saying, 'I don't know what they used but they have totally annihilated the place. The only blessing is that no one was in the building at the time.' Alexandra ushered her trusted colleague into her office, closing the door and the blinds.

'Manya, we knew, and we did nothing…they are right; you know they are right.'

Manya calmed the air; she had guessed who in the underground was behind the attack. She now realised there had been warning signs. 'Alex, how far advanced is your plan? And do you know where Michael is?'

'The plan could be ready to go, with a few tweaks in the light of this unexpected development. As for Michael, he is in the Caribbean, taking some time out before his cruise He is in a luxury villa owned by the Prophet Corporation.'

Manya was decisive, saying, 'Okay, between you and me, Michael has to be the fall-guy. We must present ourselves as the Phoenix rising from the ashes. I am well-in with the education underground. They will not want you and I to fall, if we present your plan quickly and convincingly. They want justice but most of all they want the system to be seen for what it is, and for it to end. We can deliver that.'

'Manya, I have to ask; did you know the destruction of the Medical Plant was on the cards?'

'No, not at all. It was as much of a surprise for me as it was for you last night. If Ace knew, I would be very surprised.'

'Who is Ace?'

'My chief liaison officer with the education underground; he met with their leaders only last week. He will be useful to us in the next few months.'

'Yesterday was Zade's sixteenth birthday,' Alexandra observed.

'Possibly not a coincidence,' Manya responded, adding, 'But let's not be drawn down that road; whether she betrayed us or not, we must re-establish some order. First things first; are you ready for the board meeting?' Alexandra was ready. She knew what she must do.

The senior officials filed into the High Council board room, their heads down. Ed Sergeant, the Chief Lawyer was followed by Robert Hall, the Communications Manager. Sean Price and Peter Edwards had hurried to London from the Periphery in the West and the South West, and the senior officers from the Department of Wellbeing arrived in a silent group. Manya placed herself beside Alexandra at the head of the table. Lance Richardson, Alexandra's Executive Assistant, arrived last, ready to take a record of the meeting, sending supportive glances in the direction of his new boss.

'Thank you for your attendance in person today; much appreciated in the circumstances,' Alexandra began, asking Lance to record action points only, not the discussion, which was, she reminded everyone, highly confidential.

She stood up, and looked round the room, engaging each person in brief eye contact before she began, 'Let's be honest, within these four walls; we all knew what was happening, even if we didn't know how, and we let it continue. But I am certainly not intending to resign, and I sincerely hope that each of you will stay too. It is in the best interests of the country that we see this through. I will spell it out; Maximillian Morgan, and Michael after him, engineered the scintillation programme, the medication programme and the grammar academies. They justified the programme through a series of lies, and it became entrenched. Although we were all complicit, we were not in full knowledge of the facts.' Ed nodded reassuringly.

'I need not tell you that this is big; very big. We must respond with a united front, and with a clear plan. Firstly, no one is to respond to any questions from the newsfeed journalists, from politicians, or from members of the public other than to draw attention to the official line in Robert's latest press release. Currently we are saying that The Department for Future Success has issued a full statement and allegations by terrorists that the Prophet Corporation Medical Plant has been dealing in illegal scintillation products have not been confirmed. Do not mention Michael Morgan. Leave that to the lawyers.'

The assembled senior managers were nodding in agreement with her, but were also looking confused. Sean asked Alexandra to explain to them, from the beginning, what was going on. He knew about scintillation, but he didn't understand what the Medical Plant did, or why there was such a rumpus. Sean added that he would support her 100%, but he didn't understand the facts.

Alexandra began, 'For many years we have presided over a sophisticated education system which has enabled the Central Area to succeed. As we all know, education in the Periphery has been dominated by the need to accommodate the fall-out from the Four Plus, the migrations… The education underground is correct in its allegation that scintillation is a social engineering programme. Maximillian Morgan set up a secret scintillation laboratory in the Prophet Corporation Medical Plant. There, two distinct batches of eye drops were manufactured for the Wellbeing Officers to administer to all new-born babies. Routine eye drops simply contain Cyclopentolate, to dilate the pupils during eye examination.' The Wellbeing officials nodded. 'Scintillation involves secretly adding a substance called Human Tapetum to the Cyclopentolate. This is designated as batch "A" and when dropped into the eyes leads to scintillation.' At this point the Wellbeing officials started to look concerned. Alexandra continued, 'A secret and sophisticated automatic digital download passes from the Department for Future Success to the Department for Wellbeing. Only Michael Morgan and a few close colleagues to him knew of this. Babies are designated as either "A"; suitable for scintillation, or "B" unsuitable. Wellbeing officers administer either eye drops A or B according to the designation. This has resulted in children being born to families meeting the Morgan's criteria for undesirable, not being scintillated, and ending up in the Periphery.'

Apart from Alexandra and Manya, the assembled senior officials had no idea that the process had been carefully engineered in this way. To say they were appalled would be an understatement. They each immediately expressed their disgust, and embarrassment and asked many questions which Alexandra tried to answer openly and clearly.

After allowing them time to process the information, Alexandra summarised, 'As I said earlier; we were not in full knowledge of the facts. Now that we are, we can ensure changes are made.' The faces round the table each turned to Alexandra wanting an answer. She continued, 'So we are faced with an opportunity to reflect, and to reform. This will inevitably involve evaluation of our practices in recent years, and an investigation into the impact of past policies. I will be initiating a formal independent investigation into scintillation today. I will also invoke the break clause in our indefinite contract with the Prophet Corporation for scintillation. With the plant destroyed, they cannot continue to meet their contractual obligations.' Alexandra was adamant; there would be no more scintillation. She told them that a concise, high-level Bill would be presented for approval to the High Council and then to the New Parliament. Existing legislation could be revoked and replaced in time for next September's school intake. That was the easy part, she reflected.

She explained how she would be asking for legislation to be drafted to remove the Four Plus from the Central Area assessment schedule, and it was her expectation that next September, a mixed cohort would be admitted to all grammar academies. The officials sitting round the boardroom table issued an audible collective gasp.

Alexandra asked Ed to explain the procedures for each of them to produce a signed affidavit for use in the investigation. 'It is about what you did not know. We need this protection,' she reassured them.

She scanned the faces of her close colleagues sitting around the table. Manya displaying her loyalty, had no hesitation in committing immediately, saying, 'Count me in Alex; we need to look forwards rather than backwards, and I am with you. I know that I have an important role to play in representing the Periphery. This is big, bigger than we might imagine, but I am confident we can achieve the reforms you are presenting to us today.'

Sean Price looked more relaxed than he had for years. He told the meeting that he was "in" and that these reforms were long-overdue. He was immensely proud of the education system in Wales and it would be an honour to contribute to the future direction. The group continued talking informally together for some time, and then dispersed. As Manya left Alexandra's office, she said, 'That was tough; you were great; it is good to be open. It will not be easy, but we both know it has to happen.'

In contrast to the regime under Maximillian, and then Michael, Alexandra's bottom line was openness, but many people were not ready for this. She had totally underestimated the opposition to her plans from many directions. Following the initial newsfeed article, parents were confused and student groups started to protest. Even the education underground was jittery.

Over the ensuing few months, she persisted, working closely with Robert, pushing out reassuring communications in sound-bites on the newsfeed, and attempting to enlighten the change-resistant populace. She facilitated a series of consultative forums; one in each of the areas of the Periphery, chaired by impartial experts, she opened formal negotiations with the new leaders of the education underground, following the conviction of those proved to be behind the destruction of the Medical Plant. She also opened fresh dialogue with the headteacher organisations, starting with the North, where there had been the strongest opposition to Michael's programme.

She had underestimated the bureaucratic confusion that would result. Even so, she stuck firm to her proposals, taking advice from the experts in her teams on how to deliver the reforms down to the finest detail.

The Department sent millions of e-messages saying, 'It is time to update the education system for the twenty-second century. The High Council will be considering submissions from interested parties before the detail of the reforms is finalised for legislation.' Gossip on the streets and in the staffrooms was that, with the old Boss out of the way, Alexandra, who had worked as a headteacher for years, was starting to assert herself. She would get their support, if she remained open and took change at a sensible pace, acknowledging the issues which were being thrown up as the long-established system crumbled, kick-started by the momentous destruction of the Medical Plant.

Taking advice from Ed Sergeant, and the Chief Finance Officer, she recouped a proportion of the financial resource committed to the Prophet Corporation scintillation contract, using the emergency a break clause. She allocated the funds to appoint of a bank of temporary staff who would manage the public consultation phase. These "Education Change Officers" organised a series of externally commissioned reviews, facilitated the public consultation and set up and serviced the new regional consultative forums. Controversially, she approved the hiring of practising teachers from the Periphery, rather than the Central Area, in these new, temporary roles. At interview they demonstrated fervour, commitment and the required knowledge.

In March, the Education Inclusivity Bill, legally ending the practice of scintillation, passed smoothly through the High Council and then the New Parliament. It was followed by a detailed manifesto for educational change, which resulted from the extensive consultation exercise. This blueprint for the future started with a significant increase in funding for the fully inclusive pre-school system. By focusing on providing the highest quality educators for the youngest children, and by working more closely with parents, as had been the practice in the Periphery for many years, it was intended that the universal medication programme could, in time, be phased out. Alexandra was overwhelmed by the strength of feeling from students who did not want to be dependent upon the soda. Senior managers in the Department for Wellbeing were divided however, with some remaining convinced of the efficacy of the well-established medication programme. Others displayed a new-found commitment to developing future drug-free generations. Alexandra persisted, with professionalism, and achieved agreement at the High Council for the gradual phasing out of universal pupil medication.

By the summer, the education underground had formally re-named their movement the Education Overground, and fought their battles in the open. Their leaders, led by those in the North, argued fervently for a reformed curriculum in the Central Area, and influenced the High Council to take bold steps towards establishing this. The Chief Executive of the largest education trust in the North, a charismatic leader with considerable experience and a large following, had come to see Alexandra in person, bearing a signed commitment from the trusts and unions in the North, determined to support her reforms.

Small but significant changes were made. Following the Education Inclusivity Act of 2081, the next Act of the New Parliament, was a single page of legislation repealing all previous laws preventing home education. Sean Price took great pride in taking this through the various statutory stages for Alexandra. The newsfeed pictured him triumphant on the day when the Bill became law. He was shown beaming, surrounded by cheering parents from the Home Education movement in Wales, who had developed the new guidance document. Home Education in the Central Area would be regulated and checked, but would no longer be a criminal offence.

As the Director of the CenSA Grammar Academy Trust, Alexandra encountered much opposition from Board members to her proposed policy to break up the Trust entirely, and she had to negotiate compromises. She accepted more time would be needed to completely reform the grammar academies. She knew that, without scintillation, or the Four Plus, "grammar academy" would become a historical label rather than an elitist ethos.

She launched a student competition, seeking a new designation to apply to all schools, so they could unite under a common identity. The word would be applied to all educational establishments across the Periphery and the Central Area. Parents in the Central Area generally favoured retaining the words "grammar academy" and extending this to the Periphery, while parents from the Periphery were passionately in favour of using the word "school" across the whole country. Through the competition, the High Council sought a fresh label that would cut across the old boundaries. The winning suggestions were "Conservatoire", "Learning Community", "e-COLL" and "Brainery". A public vote was undertaken, administered as fairly as possible through all grammar academies and schools. After a massive publicity campaign in the Periphery, with a significant young people's vote, and with the support of all teaching associations, the winning designation was "e-COLL". The acronym referred to Communities of Lifelong Learning. With the "e" simply as a reminder that the communities could be virtual. It was quickly adopted, and networks of e-COLLs were rapidly established in local areas. The terms "grammar academy" and even "school" were quickly replaced by e-COLL in the public vernacular.

In 2083, the Department for Future Success was rebranded as the Department for Community Lifelong Learning.

Postscript

The ethical fabric of society changed after the lengthy and damaging scintillation experiment. Despite unremitting technological advances, there emerged a collective and heart-felt public commitment to preserving the integrity of childhood, starting with increased investment in the youngest children.

On the streets, passers-by made excuses for not challenging the practice of scintillation. In cafés, others vowed that they would never, in their lifetime, allow such practices to happen again. They couldn't believe that scintillation had so smoothly become the norm.

The Prophet Corporation, forced to upgrade their standards, launched a fresh range of products. Parents could now purchase a "Prophet Moralometer" to assess the efficacy of their child's education, both at home and at school. Personal educational "EcoProphs" became best-sellers for students, replacing haptic technology, and deliberately using the unscintillated eye as their marketing logo.

The teaching profession slowly recovered and started to gain renewed respect from politicians and officials, who eased their fervour to control matters, delegating more decisions to the experts. The education underground, rebranded as the Education Overground, having been legalised, won a large national contract to coordinate the work of Periphery schools and grammar academies in the Central Area and the North.

Significant financial compensation for the scintillation experiment, provided by the Prophet Corporation to all schools, enabled much-needed investment in both education infrastructure, and to train teachers in the new curriculum. Slowly, a genuinely world-class system began to emerge.

Sixteen legacy cohorts of children with scintillated eyes moved through the grammar academies, and then their eyes faded as teenagers. Several parental lawsuits to claim individual settlements were unsuccessful, which was helpful for the system as a whole as it would have bankrupted the Department. By the turn of the new century, scintillation was reduced to a bizarre memory, and the word was no longer used.

Human Tapetum was added to the banned medications list, in response to the small residual parental desire for their children to boast designer-eyes. However, the positive legacy of the illusory S. Herbert was a prescribed sherbet soda, which, in the hands of parents seeking to support their children to cope in an increasingly demanding techno-social environment, could be used sparingly and effectively, in a targeted way. The daily dose of sherbet soda and sherbet milk eagerly consumed by generations of children on a daily basis was gradually replaced with healthier non-sedative versions of the products. These tasted good, and were reinforced with vitamins but did not control behaviour. So, all children benefitted from the vitamins, and those who genuinely found school-life challenging could access the sedative soda for fixed periods only, to help ease them back into positive participation.

With restrictions lifted, and the opening up of markets in the Periphery, many of the families who had migrated in recent years preferred to stay there. Some returned to their old haunts in the Central Area. The right to free movement within the country was re-instated and the gates to the Periphery were dismantled, standing as crumbling reminders of the Age of Scintillation. Roads crossing the borders were re-opened, and one unified cyberspace was re-established, with systematic upgrades in even the furthest reaches of the Periphery.

It was fortunate that the eye of the High Council was no longer focused on managing Future Success through the manipulative control of the education system because far more pressing priorities were emerging at the close of the twenty first century. Despite preventative measures over decades, resources were rapidly becoming outstripped by the population; not only was water in short supply, but so were essential medications and staple foods. Even more alarming was the quality of the air, which was becoming thinner and dirtier, resulting in a plethora of lung-related diseases. Education Enforcement Officers were re-trained as generic Enforcement Officers with a remit for controlling anti-eco-social behaviour.

***

As the bells tolled to celebrate the turn of the century, virtual pyrotechnics exploded across the land. Then the sun rose weakly, muddied by the swathes of semi-permanent layers of pollution. A young professor of geophysics had not joined the revelling taking place in the streets of Oxford, below his study windows. He had worked through the night, putting the finishing touches to the report which he would present to the High Council next month, 'The Art and Science of the Survival of the Species in the year 2100, Professor Lucas Patel.' He turned to his PrexiaPlus, checking-in with Noah, smiling at the proud new dad cradling his precious bundle. Then Lucas blinked his eyes, saying, 'Happy New Century Zade.'

And in Westminster, on the top floor of the Advice Bureau, in the room once occupied by a second-hand bookshop, now a high-tech office, sits Zade. As midnight turns, and the revellers on the Thames are transfixed by the light shows, she is hunched over her e-papers, working late. The golden plaque outside her door says, "Zade Beaufort KC; Pro Bono" and signs projected in blue light from miniscule projectors advertise "Walk-in Justice Advice Clinics every Thursday 8am-5p", "Specialising in education law; know your rights as a parent" and, "What are your rights if you are evicted?"

The sky is ablaze with the celebrations of the new century. Zade looks up from her work as the message from Lucas flashes on her screen, 'Happy New Century Zade.' She smiles and replies with a blink. Her resolute face is starting to show faint signs of age, and if you look very carefully, you can still see tiny residual grains of scintillation in her eyes.

CPSIA information can be obtained
at www.ICGtesting.com
Printed in the USA
LVHW082123180520
655952LV00007B/403